Vermin

Jonathan Wheatley

First Paperback edition May 2020
ISBN: 9798637729906

Cover design by Katrina Scott. Formatting by Jonathan Wheatley.

Published by Flesh and Bone Publishing

DEDICATION

This book is dedicated to my children, Sonny and Harlan, who are my muses, my reason for writing and the answer to all of life's hidden questions. This book was released during Lockdown in the UK and I haven't been able to give them a cuddle since the 10th of April, but it is because of these little boys that I keep on going. I will cuddle you again and smother you with kisses!!!

I would also like to dedicate it to my other half, Angela, who has put up with me during the Lockdown period and has shown me what true love really looks like and always pushes me to keep on going…

As always, I would like to thank my mum and dad for always letting me choose my own way and for all the support they have given me throughout my life.

ACKNOWLEDGMENTS

Writing a novel is more than a one man job. In this case I would like to thank Katrina Scott for the graphic design work including cover design and promotional material and Andrew Ormiston for the cracking editing job he has provided to get this book reader-ready. I would also like to thank everyone who follows me on Facebook and Instagram and everyone who has ever shared my posts, left me a review or helped me in anyway.

Vermin

PART ONE – CHAPTER ONE – JACOB

Far above, something crashed like a sonic boom. But when Jacob looked, the sky was pale blue with a splattering of white clouds – it didn't look like stormy weather.

Sam, his four-year-old son, was a little ahead of him on the yellow and orange leaf-strewn path. Jacob watched his eldest son as he bent down and picked a shiny conker from the grass verge under the big chestnut tree, the last leaves of summer clinging to it as a light breeze blew. His youngest clung to his leg, clawing to be picked up, his big blue eyes staring at him. At the corner of the boy's eyes were little tears. Not of sadness, but from the cold autumn air.

"Okay, buddy," he said and bent and picked him up. "Shoulders?"

Jack shook his head and wrapped his arms around Jacob's neck.

"Sam," Jacob said. "Wait for daddy, baby, okay?"

"Okay, daddy," Sam answered, rolling the conker in his gloved hands.

Once Jacob had Jack secure, he walked to Sam and knelt next to him. "What have you got? Is it a conker?" Sam showed it to him proudly. "Wowzers, baby, that's a big one."

The thunder crashed again. All three boys looked to the sky and saw something tracing a chemline-like trail across the blue. The roar grew as it stretched across the sky. A white truck with the name of the cement company Jacob worked for steamed past on the road next to the path and he jumped back in surprise. Jack screamed in his arms and tried to cover his little pink ears and Sam put his gloved hands over his.

Jacob watched as the object's speed increased and it broke into bright yellow flame with another loud crash. It would land close by. The wind increased and a cloud blocked out the low sun, making it seem later than it was. The three boys watched, like a slow-motion game of tennis with no returner, as the fire fizzled out and the object crashed into the woods near the quarry.

He scooped Sam into his arms, so he had Jack one side and Sam the other, and jogged to the opening in the hedgerow through the brambles and blackberries into the field leading to the quarry. He stopped and peered through the gap.

Just above the treeline of the woods, some 100 yards away, he saw the evaporating trail of the object and a thin line of black smoke coming from the middle of the trees. A plane crash? Jacob thought about taking the boys to explore, but the glow of the fire stopped him in his tracks – if it was just him he wouldn't have even thought about it, he'd be halfway across the muddy field running to the orange, yellow and red leaves of the treeline. But it was his weekend with the boys, and he didn't want to be responsible for the boys getting injured. Julie, his ex, would have a field day playing the irresponsible parent card.

"What is it, daddy?" Sam asked.

"I don't know, buddy, but I'm sure the police will be along soon."

They turned from the opening and carried on walking the mulchy path. Jacob lowered Sam to the floor, but Jack refused to let go. The smoke had drifted on the breeze, and Lucas smelled wood burning. Nothing to do with you, he thought, get the boys home to the warmth and put on a spooky Halloween family film.

Sam had stopped walking and Jacob bumped into him. "Sorry, Sam. What's the matter?"

His son in his oversized grey coat, blue wool hat with googly alien eyes and bright red gloves pointed to the bushes ahead of them.

"I saw something, daddy, something in the bush."

"What was it?" Jacob replied, switching Jack to his other arm. The bushes rattled ahead. "Get behind me, Sam." He moved in front of him thinking it could be a badger, and the boy cuddled up to his leg. Whatever was in the bushes was scuttling and moving, causing the last remaining little orange leaves to fall and flutter to the floor to join their comrades from the summer.

"I want to go home, daddy."

Jack cried in his arms, while Sam hugged his leg tighter. A creature the size of an RC car covered in wet-looking, spiked black fur ran from the bushes and through the long grass, its tall tail sticking up like a shark's fin. The tail disappeared into the long grass of the green and brown leaf-stricken verge. Jacob thought he could hear the flickering of the flames from far away as they stood motionless, watching the verge. He knew a lot of the wildlife in the area, but he didn't know what he'd just seen. The tall grass parted as the creature made its way towards them. It was 20 feet away.

"It's just a rat," he said, trying to convince himself, as much as the boys, he hadn't seen the glowing yellow eyes and extra spiny pink legs that sprouted from the thing's stomach. The creature moved fast with a sideway gait like a crab. Jacob picked Sam up from the path. Both boys were crying now.

"I don't like it, I don't like it, I don't like it…" Sam cried. Jacob turned from the verge. "Okay, baby, we're going, we're going." He went to step down the curb to cross the road when another truck flashed past so fast that his hat blew from his head. Another truck from his work. When he got back to the office on Monday he'd have words.

"Shit."

The boys were really crying now. He had one in each arm, both with big fat tears running down their red cheeks.

He checked both ways and ran across the road. When he reached the other side, he turned back to see if the thing was still coming. The long grass was still. Behind the bramble bushes he saw the black smoke was getting thicker. He squinted at the trees. The trunks looked like they were moving.

"What the fu—" he started, when the creature launched itself from the verge on the other side of the road. He glanced glowing yellow eyes and six thin black legs, just before it got hit by yet another thundering truck with his company's name on and turned into red mist. Jacob let out a breath, rebalanced the boys in his arms and jogged onto the estate towards home.

The sky turned heavy with full grey clouds hanging low in the sky. The only colours were the vivid red, fire orange and banana yellow of the leaves on the floor and those still clinging to life on the trees.

Jacob ran along the freshly-laid black tarmac paths with both boys held tight in his arms. His breath steamed in front of him. He rounded a corner and down a dark alleyway with blackberries growing among the wired-off, diamond fencing and rotting apples on the floor. The world was silent except for his sharp breaths and the snuffles of Sam and Jack.

"I can't... run... any... further," he said between breaths to the boys, stopping and putting them down. He leaned over with his hands on his knees. The boys clung to his sides as he waited for the heat in his chest to cool. He saw brown and mouldy insides of apples and the black stains of blackberries on the path, like blood splatters in the dark. They were only five-minutes from home. Once he'd caught his breath, he scooped up the boys again and carried on.

He put them down as he rounded the corner and arrived at his gravelled drive. Tall ferns rose on both sides, casting the red front door in shadow. Yellow gravel lay on the black tarmac path, like stars in the night sky. Jacob reached into his denim jacket pocket and pulled out his keys. He had them in the lock when he heard a squark from above. Fuck this, what now?

He opened the door and pushed the boys into the small porch that smelled of feet as he turned his head to the sky. Black silhouettes of birds, some large like kites, others small like robins, flew in ragged lines blocking out the grey sky behind. Something warm fell onto his face and he touched it with the tip of his finger. When he pulled it away, he saw blood. The squawking increased as the birds became more frenzied. He jumped into the porch and shut the door as a bird thumped into it with a bang. Another fell onto the roof of the car beyond with a dull metallic thud.

"What's going on?" he said to himself.

He helped Sam and Jack take off their coats and then entered the dimly lit living room. Scattered toys, colourful plastic dinosaurs and green toy army men, littered the floor. Both boys ran inside and jumped onto the soft brown sofa. Jacob went to the front window and pulled back the curtains. Dark drops fell from the sky, grey light reflecting from the red.

It was raining blood.

It soaked into the gravel on his drive. He saw a thick red puddle form on the road with pink froth and feathers floating on top as lifeless bodies of birds fell from the sky, hitting with soft whumps, muted by the double-glazed glass. He ran to the back of the room and opened the sliding patio doors. He heard the pitter-patter of blood hitting the plastic conservatory roof. Leaving the door open, even though the cold air from inside was already making the living room chilly, he sat down between Sam and Jack. They nuzzled into him and he wrapped his arms around them while he stared out the window at the birds falling from the sky and the soft tap, tap, tap of the red rain on the conservatory roof.

Both boys were snoring on the sofa next to him. The rain had stopped, and he had seen no birds fall from the sky for 10 minutes. He picked up his Samsung Galaxy and unlocked it with his fingerprint. No Wi-Fi or 4G. What was going on out there? He thought about calling Julie, but then thought: Fuck it, she wouldn't call me.

There had been no traffic down his cul-de-sac, which was strange. It had gone five, and the light was fading fast. Would the streetlights turn on? Jacob stood and looked out the window. There were no lights on in the neighbouring houses, and most driveways stood empty. Dark puddles, like oil, sat on the paths and the road. He went into the porch and hesitantly opened the front door. The air had a metallic taste mixed with the burning smell of wood. He peered around the corner up the street and saw an orange glow from the quarry. The fire had grown.

Jacob turned to his sleeping boys. He grabbed a cow-print blanket from the other sofa and covered them with it. They could sleep down here with him tonight. Julie wouldn't be home till tomorrow. God, he hoped this cohabiting would be over soon. Not just because the sofa was uncomfortable, but because he was excited. A fresh start. A new life. His own time with the boys where he wouldn't have someone nagging or telling him what he already knew or what to do like a fucking primary school teacher. The initial shock had given way to the excitement of starting afresh. He was free – he was ready to move on.

He sat down on the opposite sofa, watching the boys softly snoring. They'd be awake soon and wouldn't want to go to bed, but that didn't matter. How it looked outside, he thought it might be better if they were awake and alert. He tried the TV again, but without Wi-Fi he just got static. Picking up his phone, he relented and called 999. He hadn't wanted to waste their time but felt there was now no choice.

Beep. Beep. Beep. Shit, he thought. That's never a good sign.

Bang!… Bang!… Bang!… The front door. The boys stirred but didn't wake.

"Jacob, Jacob? It's me, Mike. I saw your lights on, let me in…" Mike, his next-door neighbour. The streetlights came on with a warm orange glow that cast Mike in an eerie light when Jacob opened the front door. Mike brushed past Jacob and straight into the living room. Jacob glanced past him out onto the estate. The orange lights reflected in the dark puddles.

"Come on in," Jacob said and shut the door.

Mike paced in the centre of the living room. His dirty brown boots leaving red bloody stains on the cream carpet, which Jacob tried to ignore. Fuck it, wouldn't be his problem soon. He looked at the state of the house behind the sleeping boys on the sofa and where Mike stood. The sliding doors into the conservatory were smeared with dirty little handprints which shone
ghost-like in the reflections from the lamp above. Crumbs littered the carpet, as did trampled in stains of Play-Doh and slime.

She'd stopped cleaning when it looked like he was keeping the house. Then when he changed his mind and decided to move (even though the separation was her idea) he'd expected her to start again. She hadn't. When it was her weekend away, he spent most of his time not playing with the boys but clearing up the mess in a house he would – not by choice – no longer be living in while she went out.

"Mike, what's going on? Have you heard anything?"

"The TV, the radio, they both went down about an hour ago, just before the fireball. The internet was already down," Mike looked at Jacob. "I'm scared, man," he looked at the sleeping boys. "How are they holding up?"

"We were outside when that thing crashed – something chased us, but they're okay – we're okay."

"That's good, that's good," he said, taking in the house's mess.

"Housekeeper on holiday?"

Jacob smiled. "Well since the separation, it's been kinda like me vs the volcano."

"Separation going smoothly, then? I saw her yesterday – she didn't say Hi. Can't say it surprised me, she always was – no offense – a bit of a strange one."

"None taken, ha ha! They say you don't truly know someone until you separate from them."

"Quite, quite, I'll tell you my story one day, but not today – slightly more pressing matters at hand, wouldn't you agree?"

Jacob nodded and went to the window. Mike joined him and together they stared out into the artificial orange light of the autumn evening. The cul-de-sac was quiet. Eight of the 11 brick driveways were empty, and Jacob saw yellow lights in only two of the houses.

"Where is everyone?" he asked.

"I don't know, I've been home all day."

"What do you think is going on, Mike?"

"I'm a bit older than you, Jacob, but I can honestly say I have experienced nothing like this before – it almost reminds me of that radio broadcast of 'War of the Worlds' back in the 1930s."

"What should we do?"

"Wait it out. Your boys are asleep – let them sleep. We can take it in turns to watch them, and then in the morning… we'll take whatever it brings."

Jacob reached a hand to Mike, who took it. "Thanks, Mike, I really appreciate it."

"Don't be silly – I'm all alone, my family left me, the best thing I can do is help you and yours."

"Still, it's appreciated, Mike. You can sleep first. I'll go get blankets."

"Deal."

The four boys hunkered down together in the messy living room, unaware of what was happening outside their safe four walls.

CHAPTER TWO – NANCY

Nancy slept through the fireball and the birds falling from the sky. She'd been partying through the weekend: from Friday evening, through Saturday day and night before passing out on her bed around midday on Sunday.

She reached and searched for a glass of water when she woke on her bed. Her mouth felt dry and furry, and tasted like an old ashtray left out in the rain. Her breath was hot. Nancy touched the glass on the side and, unconcerned about how long it had been there, downed it in one glug. Her stomach growled and then settled. She rolled over and stared at the ceiling. It moved and danced, zooming in and out. She closed her eyes. A thwump, thwump, thwump banged in her head, throbbing stronger in her left ear.

Nancy brought one hand up to her temple and rubbed in circular motions. It didn't help. Blurred images of the weekend flashed in her mind: her standing on top of a table in a noisy pub with men grabbing for her; being on her knees in a dirty toilet cubicle with a tall, ugly man; an argument with a bouncer at the nightclub. Shit. She covered her face with her arm. The memories made her cringe. She reached past the water to a silver packet of pills on her bedside cabinet. She popped one out of the tin foil and put it in her mouth. Nancy had drunk all the water, so she dry-swallowed it, her mouth tensing at the bitter taste.

The curtains were open, allowing the bright and low autumn sunshine into her room. One of her legs was burning, and she flopped herself over to avoid the sun, pulling the duvet around herself. Her left ear felt hot, too. Her movements in her bedding sounded muted and one-dimensional.

"Hello…" Must have stood too close to a speaker. Nancy cupped her palm and put it over her ear, creating a suction before pulling it away. A sharp pain erupted inside it as she did, and something tickled deep inside the canal. "Ahh," she hissed. I've done it this time – fucked myself up properly. Why do I do this every weekend?

She groped for her mobile. It wasn't on the side. Maybe it's in my handbag? She lifted her head and looked around the room. Glass daggers shot through her eyeballs and into the base of her skull. You'll need more than paracetamol today. Then she heard something. A sniff followed by a scuttle. Nancy jumped to the middle of the bed and sat hugging herself.

"Who's there?"

The room was silent. Then the sniff again. Did that come from inside me? She climbed off the bed and wobbled before making her way to the bathroom, using the peach-coloured wall for balance. The black and white lino floor of the bathroom made her squint. She looked in the mirror above the sink. Fuck, she looked rougher than she'd ever looked. Nancy took a sheet of toilet roll and attempted to blow her blocked nose, which had been making a whistling noise as she tried to breathe. Clumps of dry white, red and yellow powder stuck to the toilet paper. Never again.

With her hands on each side of the sink, she looked deep into the mirror at her bloodshot eyes with the black circles underneath. Are you dead? You look dead. She felt the scuttle this time inside her head. A tickle-like sensation similar to just before a sneeze. There was no release though; no sneeze, no orgasm. Something was inside her head – and not in a metaphorical way.

She tilted her head to the side, and like a cartoon character, she hit the side of it with her palm, trying to knock it out. Nothing. A high-pitched screech came from within, and she would later swear she heard it escape from her nose in a blocked whistle. Something scratched deep inside her ear.

Nancy ran out the bathroom to her bedroom. She chucked her bedsheets off, looking for her bag and her iPhone. She found the phone underneath the stained blue blouse she'd been wearing over the weekend and unlocked it. Scrolling through her contacts, she found the one she wanted and pressed dial. The line beeped at her, and she stared at the screen. She had no signal, Wi-Fi or 4G. The beeping made whatever was inside her ear dance a little skit which threw off her equilibrium. She had to grab the wall again to stop from falling.

With her arms held in front of her, like a man in the dark, she made her way to the kitchen. Dirty plates with rock-hard bread and half-empty glasses with cigarette butts littered the sides. She opened the top drawer and flicked through the odds and sods next to the grey plastic cutlery tray. Beneath a burned and lopsided plastic spatula she found what she was wanted.

Nancy stumbled back to the bathroom and looked into the mirror. She looked worse than before. Her skin was yellow-white and her usually full lips were pale and thin. She raised her hand towards her ear. She couldn't remember how long the chopstick had been in the cutlery drawer, but she was sure it had followed her from house to house with every move. It wasn't wooden, it was wood-effect plastic with red Chinese writing at the base. Its sibling had long since disappeared. Her hand shook as she moved the tip closer to her left ear.

She closed her eyes as she felt the warm tip of the chopstick enter her ear and then probe deeper, using the thick cartilage like a snooker player uses the flesh between the thumb and forefinger. Pressure built inside her head, and she had a sudden urge to sneeze. Something moved, scurried inside her head. It brushed against the chopstick and she felt the reverberations down the plastic and in her fingers. She pushed deeper, twisting and spinning the chopstick between her fingers.

Nancy opened her eyes. Something pushed the chopstick out of her ear and it dropped onto the floor. She watched with wide eyes as a furry, knuckled leg escaped her ear, followed by another and another. She counted eight in total and with a soft plop and a moment of pressure release, a fat black body the size of a penny plopped out of her ear and scurried down her face, through the opening at the top of her white tee-shirt and down her naked body. It tickled her skin, and she hit herself to get it out. A single drop of blood ran down her cheek from her ear canal.

Nancy jumped on the spot, shrieking as the thing fell out the bottom of her tee-shirt and scuttled along the black and white laminate floor to the door. She stamped after it in big, clumsy steps as tears fell from her face. It escaped the bathroom and sped down the hall towards the white plastic grille at the bottom of the wall near the patio door. It slunk through and disappeared into the day.

She ran to the patio door and peered out. The antennae at the top of the tall square building that was the local college stared down at her like the eyes of a praying mantis. Tips of yellow and orange trees were bright against the heavy grey sky. She saw movement among the fallen leaves and thought she saw the thing slink under the timber garden gate. She turned away from the patio door and slid down the wall, landing softly on her bum where she stayed, trying to regain control of her nerves as the tears flowed down her face.

CHAPTER THREE – MR NEIL

"I don't care."

"What do you mean you don't care?"

"Exactly as it sounds… I don't give a fuck anymore." Mr Neil looked out the office window over the cobbled streets and the old townhouses. "None of it matters in the grand scheme of things. We're all dead, anyway."

"Stop it, you're scaring me."

"I don't mean to, but I can't hide it anymore. Fuck it, from now on I will say what I want, do what I want when I want," he turned back to her at her desk. "It's enlightening, if only you could see what I now see."

"I don't want to – haven't you even noticed were the only ones in the office today?" she whispered.

"So we are," he answered with a cursory glance around and carried on. "That is your biggest problem, not just you, but everyone on this blue dot – you don't want to see, so you never do." He pulled at his paisley blue tie, loosening it under his collar and undid his top button. "Starting from now, this very moment, I am free. I let you in."

"Free from what? Let who in? I don't understand."

He swiped his hand around the small office like a dancer, did a spin on the stained red carpet and then pushed his computer off the desk. It landed with a plastic crash. He knelt next to it and pulled out the wires.

"What are you doing?" she asked, ducking down behind her screen.

"Whatever I want," he said, and smiled a big toothy grin while wrapping the grey computer leads around his fists. He pulled them apart and the remaining lead went taut. She pushed back in her chair, the wheels squeaking as she did. He jumped over her desk, pushing her computer to the floor and grabbed for her. She jerked back, but he grabbed a handful of her shiny brown hair. "It doesn't matter, Mary, none of it matters," he breathed, as he pulled her face towards his. He kissed her on her bright red lips and then slipped the lead around her neck.

As the life left her body, and her grip on his arms decreased, he sat down next to her and said: "I'm free, the world will burn." A shudder ran through his body. He closed his eyes, and then a moment later opened them again. Mr Neil looked around the office as if seeing it for the first time before his eyes settled on the lifeless body in the chair. He leaned over the desk, kissed her pale, lifeless cheek and exited the office into the reception area. The pretty receptionist smiled at him with her bright pink lipstick grin.

"Everything all right, Mr Neil? I thought I heard a crash…"

"Everything's fine," he said, then went blank for a microsecond before carrying on, "… Cynthia, we were just moving around the computers. If anyone calls for me, can you take a message, please, I'm going out for the afternoon."

"Of course, Mr Neil. Be careful out there, I'm not sure what's going on today, but the streets are empty. Have a nice afternoon."

"Oh, I will," he said. "I will."

Mr Neil – once Steven to his friends, but now an alien called Aatami – walked past the tall church, through the deserted Square and along the quiet High Street before turning down one of the stained-brick, low-ceilinged alleyways. He spat on the floor when he was out of sight of the people on the High Street, leaving behind a bubbling, yellow-green thick loogie-looking thing on the cobbles. Disgusting creatures, he thought. How did these animals end up the dominant life form on this rock?

Back at the office, that had been Mr Neil – the last part of Mr Neil anyway before he'd let *him* in. The final part that allowed him to take full control of this body. There would be three more bodies found murdered in Westford today, on top of the ones that were ripped to shreds.

Now he was whole, he could feel his Comrades working their way into this community. It was by chance that he'd landed where he had, and he hoped the others were as lucky – chance was a good thing where he came from. Chance gave them – him – the opportunity to test himself. And if there was one thing he loved it was the chance to prove himself. An added benefit of this chance location was the dark undercurrent that ran through the roots of this town. Something had happened here – he could still sense the power of something strong and ancient, which is why he knew they had chosen this town.

The bars and restaurants down the alleyway were closed. Their windows dark, casting his reflection back at him. He stopped and stood in front of one tall window and toyed with the face staring back at him – pulling down his eyelids with the tips of his fingers and fish hooking the corners of his mouth. What strange creatures.

He sensed something at the corner of his vision. A black shape scuttling sideways across the opening at the bottom of the alleyway. Damn. He hoped they hadn't made it into the town centre yet. Maybe it was one of those other creatures from this planet, he searched the memory of this Steven-creature. A rat, that's what they called it. He found another word for them: Vermin.

Vermin. That was a good word. A good word that applied to many things. Things like those he was here to hunt. Vermin. Yes, he liked it a lot.

He and his Comrades had arrived shortly after the Vermin, making less of an impression on the locals. In fact, he doubted if anyone had even noticed their arrival – until now, anyway. This town didn't have a clue what was about to happen.

CHAPTER FOUR – JACOB

Jacob didn't feel like he'd sleep, but when Mike woke at 4am to swap shifts, he climbed onto the sofa and snuggled up to his boys and was snoring five minutes later, only waking when Jack started screaming for a bottle. Sam stayed asleep while he carried Jack to the kitchen and heated some milk in a Tommee Tippee bottle in the microwave, raising his hand to Mike as he passed.

The microwave pinged, and Jack snatched the bottle from Jacob's hands. Jacob walked through the house and sat on the end of the sofa. Sam's feet found him and started pressing into him.

"Any news?" Jacob asked Mike.

"No 4G, but my phone keeps trying to connect to your Wi-Fi."

Jacob wiggled his hand under the weight of Jack, who was in a state of milky bliss and had turned into a dead weight on his lap. He found his Samsung Galaxy and turned it over in his hand. In the top right corner, the screen showed a full Wi-Fi signal. Jacob clicked on the blue Facebook app and it opened. The feed loaded. He scrolled through, reading posts from friends about the power cut and saw a news story about the thing that fell from the sky.

"It's working," he said to Mike. "The router's behind the TV, if you want to log-on to it too?"

Mike stood gingerly, rubbing his back, and made his way over to where the large flat-screen TV stood on an off-white sideboard. He reached around to the side and found the flimsy, black plastic router and turned it over in his hands looking confused.

Jacob made a flip gesture with his hand. "It's on the back."

"Gotya," he said, placing the router on the sideboard and touching the screen of his phone. "Sorted – now let's see what they're saying."

Jacob scrolled through his own phone, closing Facebook and opening

BBC News. Nothing. Whatever happened wasn't big enough news to make the major broadcasters it seemed. He looked at Mike, who was frowning at the screen, his bushy eyebrows furrowed. "I don't get it. There's nothing?"

"Open the curtains."

Mike turned around and pulled one side of the grey curtains to the edge of the window. Bright white light flooded the room, making Sam stir on the sofa.

"The driveways are still empty," he shook his head. "What's going on?"

"I don't know – but I don't like it."

"It looks normal out there, but nothing's moving."

Jacob looked at the phone in his hands. He clicked the Chrome symbol and typed Westford Meteor. The screen took a second to load, and when it did, it returned page upon page of useless results. How is this not news somewhere? He felt like he'd been deleted, like he didn't exist. He opened Facebook and wrote a post. Once written, he clicked the blue 'Post' bar underneath. It clicked. He waited five-seconds and then refreshed. Nothing. He refreshed his screen again. Nothing changed. There was no new post by him, and no new posts at all. He scrolled through and saw the most recent post was from yesterday afternoon; around the time the thing fell from the sky. Fuck this. He closed all the apps and dialled 999. The line beeped back at him.

"Mike, something's not right."

"Yes, I get that impression too."

When Sam woke, he was sad and wanted cuddles. Jack bounded around the living room playing with a red balloon on a white stick leftover from his birthday party a week ago. Mike smiled, watching Jacob's youngest and his boundless energy.

"He's a brute, that one," Jacob said to Mike, smiling.

"Yes, he is rather rambunctious isn't he."

"Future England Rugby captain," Jacob said, and then ruffled Sam's hair sitting on his lap. "This one is a storyteller and a bit sensitive."

"Bless him. What do you think then, Jacob? What's going on?"

"Did you ever watch the X-Files? It's like something straight from that. We were out there when whatever it was fell from the sky. Something chased us. Something's going on, and someone is covering it up."

"I agree. I'm not sure about the X-Files stuff, but something or someone seems to be covering this up."

"We should head towards town," Jacob said. "try to get to the town centre, maybe the police station…"

14

"I think you're right. We can take my car – I've got no car seats, however, I think we will be okay this once."

"Let's do it. I just need to grab some warmer clothes for the boys. Are you going to go home before we go?"

"Nothing I need from there," Mike replied, neither of them thinking about bringing anything that resembled a weapon.

Jacob found a warm, green jumper with the Gruffalo on the front for Sam and a fleecy, blue hoodie for Jack and got them on each boy after the initial fight from both died down. He found warm socks and searched under the sofa in the living room for the wellies they wore yesterday. Sam giggled as he made Jacob chase him around the house to get the last wellie on, while Jack sat on the floor removing the wellies and socks he'd got on him only minutes ago. Where was Julie? He needed to tell her the boys were okay. Regardless of how they'd split, he had to find her and let her know they were safe. He would find her for the boys sake. They needed their mum.

Mike watched the children running Jacob ragged. His children had long since grown up and moved away. He hadn't heard from them for three-months; they rarely spoke to him after the divorce. Self-pity was as bad as alcohol and he had to admit that everyone in a while he gave both their fair share of time in his home. But today he felt invigorated. A spark, long extinguished, had spluttered to life again. Someone counted on him. He hadn't realised how much he had missed the feeling of being depended on for something – anything. He didn't know what was going on; wasn't sure he really cared about anything anymore, but he cared about helping Jacob and his children. Today he could help. And if tomorrow he was no longer needed, at least he had that feeling one last time.

"You ready?" Jacob asked him. He was sitting on the sofa with both boys crawling and climbing over him.

"Damn straight I am," Mike said and smiled. "Troops, let's go."

The children felt it first. As soon as they walked out the front door and onto the driveway, they broke into tears. Jacob felt it, too. The air felt solid, heavy – as if all the anxiety and sadness in the world sat over the town in a blanket of grey. He looked at the sky. There wasn't a break to be seen in the clouds. Not a sliver of blue or gold.

"Do you feel that?" he asked Mike.

Mike nodded. A troubled look crossed over his face. "It feels like all the joy has been sucked out of the world."

"Back inside!" Sam shouted, pointing towards home.

The warmth of the inside of their home was tempting, but if they stayed there, they would never find out what was going on. Jacob held Sam's hand, soothing him as they walked, while holding Jack in his other arm. They crossed the grass to Mike's driveway and the silver Nissan X-Trail that sat there.

"It's open," Mike said.

Jacob grabbed the handle of the door and opened it. It smelled like a new car, not bad considering it was a 2011 model. He hoisted Jack into the seat and buckled him in, his thick grey coat holding him in place. He rounded the car and did the same for Sam, whose tears had slowed to little snuffles. Jacob used the back of his sleeve to first wipe the tears from the boy's face and then the snot from his top lip. He kissed him on his forehead and then closed the door.

He climbed into the front seat next to Mike, who started the engine with a push of a button and reversed off the drive.

They drove in silence. Mike tried the radio, but all that came through was static. The roads were quiet; they passed two cars on the way into Westford, and the usual smalltown congestion had disappeared. Jacob glanced out the window into the yellow and orange leaves that littered the grass verges, waiting to spot any movement. No one walked the paths. They whizzed down Scotgate and past the Red Lion. The traffic lights were green and Mike took a left, up the hill towards the recreation ground and the police station. Jacob watched the buildings on his right pass by. The old tattooist with exposed beams and faded white walls with blue graffiti stood derelict as it had for the past five years since he'd worked part time there.

Even this close to the centre of town, it was eerily quiet. The boys were silent in the back, staring out the windows, watching Westford flying by. They turned a corner, and Mike slammed on the brakes.

"What the fuck…"

It looked as though half the town was at the police station. People dressed in warm autumnal clothing filled the car park. A line of cars led up the road towards the entrance. People crammed together up to the entrance of the building, which was shut. There were no lights inside. One police car stood alone, surrounded by people.

"Turn around," Jacob said to Mike.

He reversed, but as he did, another car came up behind them, blocking them in. Mike undid his window and poked his head out into the cold grey day and then came back inside.

"It's the same the other way."

Jacob turned to Sam and Jack in the back seat. "Don't worry, boys, not much longer now, okay?"

Jack playfully kicked out at him and Sam nodded his head. Jacob turned to look at the police station and as he did, he saw a commotion as a wave of people backed away from the building and then scattered in different directions. He watched an old man run into one of the low wooden fences and slip on his ass while a woman with a small boy fell to the dark concrete and got trampled. He reached for his door handle and Mike stopped him.

"Don't…" Mike said, without taking his eyes off the building.

"Bu–" Jacob replied and then his eyes grew wide as they saw what Mike was looking at. On top of the police station he saw black shapes. He couldn't make out exactly what they were, but he already knew.

"Lock the doors, quick."

Mike flicked a button and they heard the mechanical dunk as the doors locked. They stared out into the grey, watching people run in all directions – some up the hill towards the recreation ground, others across the road and down an alley into the centre of town. A free-flowing stream of chaos.

The roof of the police station was moving. He saw the creatures climb down the walls like spiders. Only these weren't spiders. They were the size of dogs. Black with thick, wiry fur. They were bigger now. Quicker, too. He saw one leap from the side of the building onto a woman in a red coat pushing a silver pushchair. She tried to bat it away with flailing arms, and as she did, he watched another creature slinking low along the ground. He watched as it popped its head into the carrycot of the pushchair. Jacob turned away.

"We need to get out of here," said Mike, checking his mirrors. "Fuck it, sorry mate…" he said as he put the car into reverse and backed into a white Fiesta behind him. Jacob saw the man in the car behind raise a hand in fright. He had been watching the horror at the police station, and the jolt had made him jump. Mike drove forward hitting the car in front and then reversed again bumping into the Fiesta. He created enough space to get the front end out and he did a full turn in the road and headed back towards Scotgate and the traffic lights. Jacob watched behind as he saw other cars moving behind them. Two collided and blocked the road. The black creatures flooded over the vehicles and he shouted, "Fuck the lights, go, go, go now…"

The tyres screeched and with a quick prayer Mike hammered the X-Trail forward into the crossroads back the way they had come. They got to the Red Lion pub when they saw another car crash blocking the route. Mike slowed and took the left road instead. As Jacob looked out the window, he saw more of those things climbing over the roofs of the houses of Westford.

CHAPTER FIVE – NANCY

Her tears had stopped and the thing hadn't tried to get back in. She peered out into the grey sky and watched for movement on the green and yellow leaf-strewn lawn. Nothing. What the hell was that thing, and why was it in her ear? Her phone had gone weird on her too. Perhaps she had dropped it? Another drunken accident – pretty much like her whole life. She doubted her father would replace the phone again.

Nancy sat down on the stained, cream-fabric sofa and leaned forward with her head in her hands. She looked at the useless iPhone on the sofa next to her. The screen showed no 4G or Wi-Fi, but the signal bars had returned. She picked it up and unlocked it, dialled 999 and waited. Beep, beep, beep. Nancy threw the phone back down on the sofa. It bounced once and then landed on the wood-effect floor next to an empty baggy with the remnants of some white powder.

A high-pitched scream pierced the silence. Nancy froze. Her eyes finding their way to the window again. Nothing moved. The sky was one continuous cloud of ominous grey. She could see the house opposite, the green and yellow moss on its dark brown roof. The curtains were closed. A nearly-naked tree with a dozen yellow-red leaves danced lazily in the breeze.

What's going on out there? Nancy stood and walked to the window. She stared into the gloom, arching her neck and pressing her cheek against the cold window to glance down the road. The street was empty. She thought she saw movement on the roof of one of the houses. But when she looked again, she saw nothing. Nancy didn't want to go outside, but what other choice did she have? Her hangover hadn't appeared, which was a blessing, but it was the only one she could find so far today. The college opposite stood silent.

From outside she heard the screech of wheels, followed by a car speeding down the road. Then silence again. Where could she go? The

Police station? It was only a 10 minute walk... Her father's office in the centre of town? It was Monday morning, most of the people she partied with would be at work? Were there more of those things? She paced around her small living room and then went down the hallway to the kitchen. Were other people waking up with bugs in their brains? She flipped the switch on the kettle and waited for it to boil. Nancy bent one of the silver metal blinds, hearing the chink of thin metal, and looked out the front of her apartment. In the middle of the tarmac road was a dead black cat, its guts laying by its side. She couldn't take her eyes off it. The front street was silent and still. A red motorbike, half taken-apart as someone's project, stood on a grass verge in front of a house opposite.

She removed her hand and the blind snapped back into place with a metallic crash. The kettle clicked and she poured the steaming water into a mug with instant coffee. The mug was hot in her hands as she walked back through to the living room and sat down on the sofa. She had to go out – it was as simple as that. There wasn't enough food in her cupboards for her to last longer than a day cooped up inside here. While she waited for her coffee to cool, she got dressed in her bedroom, pulling on thick tights with a pair of jeans over and putting on a white vest with a thick moss-green wooly jumper.

The coffee was good and strong. It lifted some of the fog of her mind and she started to formulate a plan. Not a very good plan, but a plan. She found her hiking boots – a gift from another dead-end relationship that ended a long time ago – grabbed her phone, a thick maroon jacket from her cupboard and opened her front door.

The stillness of the day hit her straight away. She glanced at the dead cat in the middle of the road. Then she glanced up the street. The houses stood grey, cold and ominous. She didn't see any lights in any of the houses. The air felt heavy and foreboding, like walking through thick gravy. Littered on the paths and the road further up were bodies of birds.

Nancy took a step outside, turned and closed the door.

It wasn't just her street that was quiet. She walked past the empty park on her right. The children's swings were still on the black ground. No birdsong. A pink liquid had left snail-like stains down the metal slide. Nancy followed the path to the main road. She sidestepped a puddle that was a strange shade of red. There were no cars. No pedestrians. The tall, five-storey college stood silent, its antennas reaching into the sky. The windows were dark. The usually busy car park was empty. Where is everyone? It's Monday morning. She carried on walking up the tree-lined road, towards the Recreation ground and the police station.

She thought she saw a pair of curtains twitch in one of the large detached houses on her left. She stopped and waited for them to move again. They didn't. The sky had an eerie yellow tint.

On the path, 20 feet ahead, she saw a dark shape. It was the size of a dog. As she approached it unfurled itself like a hedgehog from a ball and stood with an odd sideways gait. Two large yellow eyes looked at her. It had thick brown-black fur, spikes like a porcupine coming from its spine and it stood silently studying her. Someone had a worse weekend than me, she smiled to herself.

It moved. Its pink limbs spread from its body like an elongated crab and it side-waddled towards her faster than she expected. Her legs were stuck in place. The creature never took its yellow eyes off hers. 10 feet now. She saw exposed, serrated teeth jutting from its pink slash of a mouth. Nancy didn't hear or see the car as it pulled up beside her.

"Get in," a man yelled. She turned in a daze. A silver Nissan X-Trail with two men in the front sat next to her on the road, its engine purring. "Get in," the younger of the two men shouted again.

She moved, keeping one eye on the creature that was sprinting towards her. Nancy could hear the clicks of its claws on the path. *Tick-a-tick-a-tick-a-tick-a-tick.* She flung open the back door, was momentarily shocked to see two children in the back seat, and then jumped in, shutting the door behind her just as the thing launched itself at the window. It hit with a dull thud and bounced backwards onto the pavement.

"GO, GO, GO…" the younger man shouted to the older man. Nancy squeezed through to the middle seat and sat, her arms resting uncomfortably on the kids' car seats in the back with her. The older boy was asleep, while the younger boy looked at her and smiled a goofy grin.

"What's going on?" she asked.

"We don't know, but it's not safe outside," the younger man answered. "My name's Jacob, this is Mike and next to you are my two kids, Sam and Jack. Sam's the one asleep."

"Right, well thanks," Nancy said, she caught herself in the mirror and realised how much of a mess she looked. Jacob was quite good looking in a younger-dad-kind-of way. "My name's Nancy." she pushed a bang of light brown hair away from her forehead. Lines of mascara ran down her cheeks from the tears she'd cried earlier.

"Where were you going?"

"Into town, either to the police station or to my dad's office, why?"

"The fireball from the sky…"

"What fireball from the sky?"

"It crashed towards Little Beckton, near the Shell garage yesterday afternoon."

Nancy stared blankly at the man. Fireball? What the fuck was he talking about? "A fireball?" she asked, raising one eyebrow.

"I know it sounds crazy, but I was there – I saw it crash…" Jacob took a breath, "and then we were chased by something, something very similar to what just tried to attack you."

"What are you talking about? That thing? That was a scabby dog or something."

"I don't think it was," the older man said. Nancy leaned back in her seat watching the quiet world pass them by as they drove up the main road away from her home and the college. "My phone…" she started.

The younger man nodded and turned in his seat to look at her. "All the phones are down, same for internet and social media."

"Look, guys, I'm going to level with you. I have the hangover from hell and I just want to go back to bed, but that doesn't seem like an option. So, where are you going?"

The two men looked at each other. "All the roads are blocked. We went to the police station but…" Jacob looked at Mike who shook his head. "We were trying to get back home, but we couldn't get there either."

Mike braked hard as one of the creatures ran in front of the car. It stopped and watched them, sitting motionless in the road as if daring them to drive on. Nancy looked past the creature and saw more dark shapes crawling over the walls of the red-brick houses. She looked out the side window and saw one stalking across the rooftops.

"Uh, guys…"

Jacob turned around and seeing the look on Nancy's face, followed her eyes towards the roofs. He saw the creatures slinking around in the grey day. It had started to rain; a thin mist that made the pavements and paths shine like dull moonlight with a hint of pink.

"Don't panic," Jacob said to Nancy, holding up his hand. "Mike, we need to get out of here… now."

Mike turned, and saw the creatures on the brown rooftops and further down the road. The creature in the middle of the road still sat watching them, blocking off their exit to the front. Mike turned in his seat looking out the rear window. Jacob reached through and let Jack take his little finger and squeeze. The two-year old gurgled and giggled. Sam was still fast asleep on the other side of Nancy. To all three, Jacob said: "It'll be okay." He stroked Sam's blond hair and the little boy stirred and then closed his eyes again.

"Ready?" Mike asked.

"Go," Jacob replied.

Mike put the pedal to the floor and with a screech they shot backwards.

He spun the wheel and they turned. Nancy's stomach lurched. Jack giggled again. Mike jerked the gears and with a clunk, he spun the wheel again and they shot forward and away from the creature in the middle of the road. Nancy looked behind them and saw it still sat there. Not moving. Behind it, first two, then four, then a dozen of those creatures joined it and sat watching as they sped off.

"Where are we going?"

"I don't know – any ideas are very welcome though…" said Mike.

They were heading away from the college, which was a shame, thought Nancy. That fifth floor looked really appealing right now. "We need somewhere high and not surrounded by houses…"

"Like where?"

"Westford Academy?" Nancy replied, but then tilted her head. "But, I'm not sure how I feel about open fields…"

"No open fields," Jacob agreed.

"What about the town centre?" asked Mike.

"Will you be able to get through? Do we really want to go into the town centre if we're avoiding crowded places?" Jacob asked.

"Plenty of places to hide in the town centre and it's a Monday morning – it'll be quiet. And the buildings on the High Street are tall and interconnected," said Nancy.

"Interconnected?" asked Mike. They approached the top of the road and a T-junction. Left would take them into town, right would take them to the estate. Mike put the car in neutral and looked both ways. "Well?"

"Locke's hospital on Almshouse Street…" Nancy started. "I used to be a cleaner there and we were told stories about how beneath it there are tunnels; one goes to the Corn Exchange Theatre across the road – I've used it."

"Come on, everyone in Westford has heard those stories – they're a myth, a legend. They're not real, and didn't we just say we wanted to be up high?" Mike replied.

"They are real," Nancy said, her voice petulant. "And I don't know about you, but wherever we go, I'd like to have an emergency exit."

"Okay, both of you," Jacob said, he couldn't argue with her logic. "We have two choices. We go into town and take our chances, or we go onto the housing estate… and take our chances." He looked at Jack and Sam who was still snoring softly. "I vote for the town centre – if anything happens, there are plenty more buildings to run to, and the buildings are tall with plenty of old hidey-holes."

Nancy smiled. "I vote town centre too."

"Okay, fine," Mike said and he pulled out and turned left onto a road of old Victorian houses. On the right was a long row of red-brick, terraced houses, with small courtyard areas surrounded by low brick walls. In the window of one, Nancy thought she saw a young girl looking out. On the left, the houses were larger; a selection of individual semi-detached and detached Victorian houses with mock-Tudor, black and white striped turrets and bay windows. Cars were parked bumper-to-bumper down both sides of the road meaning it was one-way traffic only. They were the only car on the road.

"Where is everyone?" Nancy asked.

"We don't know," Jacob said. "Hiding would be my guess."

"Where are the Police, the Army, anyone?"

"Well now, little girl, that's part of the problem you see," Mike began. "Me and my amigo here believe they are in on it – they are the ones who've blocked your phone from working."

"But why?"

"The oldest reason in the book... a good old-fashioned cover-up," Mike turned back to look at her, and she saw not a kind old man but a weird conspiracy theorist. "Something landed in that field and we saw those things attacking people at the Police Station. Believe me, this shit is real..."

Nancy leaned back in her chair. She glanced at both boys, happily oblivious to the mess they were in. Fuck. She needed to talk to her father, he would know what was going on.

At the end of the road, with the private school adjacent, they turned right onto one of the (usually) busiest roads in Westford. The car park they passed sat empty, naked. The Pelican crossing lights stayed on green with no-one to press the button. Nancy could see beyond the car park to the Recreation ground. The multi-coloured playpark stood empty. One of the blue swings looked like it was moving, swaying in the breeze maybe, she couldn't be sure, but she thought she saw a dark shape the size of a dog sitting on its black plastic seat. Did all these things come out of people's ears, like the one that came from hers? If she hadn't got it out of the house, or her ear, for that matter, would it have killed her? Did these guys know about where the creatures came from? What was that term they used in *Saving Private Ryan*? *FUBAR*? *'Fucked up beyond all recognition.'* Yeah, that seemed like the right word for today. She pondered on the strange choice of memory her mind had just thrown at her. She'd watched a thousand war movies with Jesse, but that one always stuck in her head – maybe because it was after that one that he'd nearly killed her?

She shook the memory away and joined Jacob looking out the windows at the silent and still town. They approached the Police station. It stood lonely, ransacked. The queue of cars Jacob and Mike had escaped earlier sat in deadlock with no drivers. The floor of the car park was wet and Nancy saw tints of bright red liquid dripping down the curb to the drain. The remains of a black iCandy pushchair sat in a heap on the stairs that led to the front door. The cloth was ripped from the carrycot and the metal wheels and frame buckled.

"They left nothing," stated Mike.

"Come on, get us past these cars and onto Almshouse Street."

Mike used the bumper of the X-Trail to move a black Ford Focus out of their way. His X-Trail had plenty of power and didn't struggle with the job. Eventually, they got to the bottom of the road. Nancy couldn't believe they hadn't seen a single soul all this time. They were at the crossroads where the sinkhole had been last year. Nancy saw Jacob point to the right, but that was away from the town centre. He turned to her. "Look… can you see it?" She followed his finger and saw a pack of the creatures blocking the route out of town. The road split into two and two groups of about 50 creatures – one for each road – sat waiting for anyone trying to get past.

As if reading her thoughts, Jacob said: "They're smart – that's how they stopped us last time."

"How can they be smart?"

"I don't know, all I know is they're dangerous and we need to get inside somewhere safe. Mike, take it slowly – try not to alert them."

Mike inched forward, careful to avoid any glass on the road from previous accidents. "Come on, baby," he said. They entered a narrow road with tall, limestone buildings looming high above them on either side. The X-Trail moved slowly, careful to avoid the few deserted cars that blocked both sides of the road intermittently. They passed a small, bright-orange Fiat, and barely squeezed past without touching it. A break in the buildings to their left, allowed a brick wall with black iron railings to guide their way. Nancy couldn't see past the shrubs and bushes that stood tall, blocking the view into the garden of the huge house beyond.

The car entered Broadleaf Square. The usually busy main square of the town sat silent and unloved. No-one walked on the cobbles. No lights shone from inside the butchers, newsagents or the coffee shop. The lights of the Pelican crossing switched from red to green automatically. But when the green man appeared, there was no beep. St Michan's church stared down at them, and the silent square. Nancy wanted to wind down her window and listen; to check if it really was as quiet as it seemed in the car.

Mike stopped and they all looked at the ghost town. The rain still fell in a fine mist. The window wipers squeaked. The road leading to Locke's hospital was blocked by a dirty, white delivery truck which had collided with a black BMW.

"We could drive up the High Street, and then up Ironmonger Street?" Nancy suggested. "It's not like there's any police around."

"I don't know – I don't like it. Those things could be waiting in the shops or down an alleyway," said Mike.

"We run," said Jacob. "We carry the boys and we run – it's not that far – 100 metres, if that…"

"What ab… "

"We're going to have to get out of the car at some point," Nancy said, interrupting Mike. "I agree with Jacob, we run."

Mike's shoulders slumped. "Okay, we do it your way," he said. "How do we get in when we get there?"

"If it's not already open; there's a keycode – it hasn't been changed forever."

Jacob took a breath and gently nudged Sam's feet. "Wake up baby-boy, it's time to go."

Sam stirred. His big brown eyes looked into his dad's. "Daddy, where we go?" he asked, mid-yawn.

"We're going on adventure – are you ready?"

"An adventure! Yay! Yay! I ready daddy."

"Nancy," Jacob said, "do you mind undoing Jack's seatbelt, while I get Sam's?"

Nancy looked at the contraption that held the drooling child locked into place. Jacob must have seen something in her eyes as he said, "Between his legs, there's a button – click that and it'll undo."

"Thanks." Behind her she heard Sam's belt unclick followed by the boy jumping from his seat onto the floor. She struggled with Jack's belt, trying to avoid his grubby little hands that pawed at her and his snotty nose.

"Let's go, daddy, let's go."

"We will baby, just let me get Jack. Now listen to me, Sam, this is very important – are you listening?"

Nancy watched Sam nod at Jacob. His brown eyes never left his daddy's. They obviously took adventures very seriously, she thought. She finally heard the click as Jack's seat belt came undone. He reached out to her and she tried to ignore him, but he carried on reaching to her to be let out of the seat.

"When we get out there, Sam, we can't make any noise. Do you understand?"

"Yes, daddy," answered the boy.

"Now, one of us is going to carry you, and the other will carry Jack – who do you want to carry you?"

Without hesitation, the little-boy's arm shot up and he pointed a pale white finger at Jacob. That was a no-brainer, thought Nancy.

"Okay, Mike. Will you be able to carry Jack, please?"

"Yes, of course."

Jacob turned to the front and looked out the window. He took a deep breath. Mike moved his hand to the plastic door handle. Nancy held Jack back with an arm across his chest to stop him from throwing himself out of his seat. His grunts of annoyance were the only noise inside or outside the car. "Ready?" Jacob said quietly. "Go."

CHAPTER SIX – MR NEIL

Mr Neil waited in the shadows. The situation had turned faster than he'd expected. The Vermin were working their way through this town quicker than he'd ever seen them work their way through anywhere. He didn't want to announce his arrival… yet. Mr Neil watched and waited.

He'd found an empty apartment above a clothes shop on the High Street. It had large sash windows with white paint flaking off onto the cigarette-stained blue carpet. He sat on a graffitied chair with a black leather seat and stared down at the empty street. Mr Neil was waiting for his comrades.

They had the orders drilled into them by their superiors from an early age. He knew they would find their way to the centre of Westford; which in Westford's case was one-third of the way up the High Street from Broadleaf Square – below where he now sat. Staring out over the cobbled street, he saw a pack of the Vermin hiding in the shadows in a dark stone-walled alleyway. What are you doing?

What troubled him was the way these Vermin were behaving. If he'd been a real human, he'd have stroked his chin or rubbed at his head trying to figure it out; as it happened, he wasn't, so he sat like a carving made from ice, his eyes straight ahead, watching the creatures, not blinking.

He wasn't known for being a team-player where he came from, but he was thankful he wasn't alone in this town. Mr Neil folded his hands on his lap, interlocked his fingers and concentrated. A blue-white light emanated from within, turning his skin translucent and showing the threadlike veins running through the diaphanous skin between his hands and fingers. He squeezed his hands together and a ball of light throbbed out from the gap between his thumb and forefinger like a bubble. It floated two inches in front of his face. The glow lighting his eyes. He stared deep into the bubble; his lips moved as if in silent prayer. Then it surged out through the glass window, like it wasn't there, and out into the grey sky.

Mr Neil smiled, although in the window's reflection, it didn't touch his blue-grey eyes with their crows-feet wrinkles that – like the real Mr Neil – lit up rooms with their enthusiasm and warmth. His thin lips now stretched in a permanent sneer, unlike the usual smile that for 44 years had rested pleasantly on his face. Still the Vermin waited across from him in the shadows of the alleyway. Who are you waiting for?

He heard an engine close by. Maybe in Broadleaf Square? He closed his eyes and opened his mind, listening. Whispers in the grey found their way to him. Three adults and two children were in that car. He opened his eyes. Why were they outside? The men in black suits and uniforms were supposed to have taken care of everyone in this town while they finished their business.

"Don't get out of the car, don't get out of the car, don't get out of the car," he muttered to himself, not caring if they got killed, but worried they would interrupt his business.

In his mind, he heard a man's voice say, *"Ready?"* followed by, *"Go."*

You stupid fuckers, he thought. Where are you planning to go? Can't you see there's nothing out there for you. There is no safety out there. You should have stayed in your homes like the men in uniforms told you to. The rage built. He stood and kicked the chair across the room. His dark-blue suit trousers ripped down the seam with the force, which made the rage inside even hotter. Idiot race. It was like a volcano building until it would finally erupt.

His fingertips glowed red like hot iron. He heard the click of car doors opening and he turned to the window; to wait and watch these humans run past. He waited. Seconds ticked by. They didn't appear. Instead, he heard the footfalls of animals approaching. Not the scurrying sound the Vermin makes. These footfalls were more elegant, poised.

A single red deer sauntered down the High Street. Mr Neil glanced to the alleyway where the Vermin cowered in the shadows. They were gone. Behind the deer were more. At least a dozen. Some had antlers and were large, while others were younger and smaller. Their orange-red fur was bright against the limestone buildings and wet cobbles. He saw white squares and diamonds on their backs.

He watched as they strolled down the High Street like a family doing a spot of lazy shopping on a Sunday afternoon. Their reflections in the shop windows were mesmerising. They passed in silence. Their heads raised high and proud. Alert eyes watching, while their tall ears flicked and listened for any sound. The places he'd visited had rarely amazed him, but today he stood in praise of these magnificent creatures who had taken back their habitat – for one day at least.

A child's scream broke the silence and the first deer stopped, its ears standing to attention. The scream came again and the deer launched themselves forward, prancing down the High Street, their hooves clattering like gunfire on the cobbles.

Mr Neil watched as the last one disappeared around the corner of Ironmonger Street and then turned away from the window and went down the low-ceilinged staircase that led to the alleyway entrance to the apartment. He cursed under his breath as he left the warmth of the apartment behind.

CHAPTER SEVEN – JACOB

They ran. Jacob held Sam to his chest, while Mike held Jack to his. Jack's tears had slowed to soft sobs after the initial wails when Mike had pulled him from the car. Nancy followed behind. They ran in crouched, long strides with quick glances to all sides and above. They went past St Michan's church, past its locked iron gate that led to the cemetery and up a one-way road at the back of the various fast food takeaways on the other side. Black bin bags had been ripped to shreds and pieces of meat and salad littered the floor. A large, white delivery van was left abandoned to the side with its delivery doors hanging open – the food inside defrosting and starting to give off a rank stench.

Jacob turned to check they were still together when he got to the top of the road. Sam's brown eyes peered out from under his wooly hat, which Jacob had pulled down.

"Nearly there, guys," he said.

"I hope you're right about this," Mike said to Nancy, as they huddled together close to the white-washed wall at the top of the road.

"I am," she replied. "It looks clear."

"Let's wait one more minute?" Jacob said.

Almshouse Street was a long road that ran next to the High Street. On both sides of the road were empty car parking spaces. Block paved slabs had replaced the cobbles of the paths of Broadleaf Square, and the road was dark tarmac with white-painted lines separating the parking bays. Tall, Georgian-style buildings with large sash windows and pretty white bay-windows loomed large on both sides. A mixture of rent per-month office space and independent retailers who couldn't afford the rent on the High Street. To the right, stood the old cinema, now a bar, and the theatre. Above the ground floor windows was an American-style cinema board with large white letters spelling out, 'Kinky Boots.'

Jacob could see the traffic lights at the top of Ironmonger Street, the street that connected both roads. The entrance to Locke's hospital was 10 feet in front of the lights, on their left. A set of narrow stone stairs with flower borders led to another set of stairs which would take them to the main entrance. A high stone wall ran across the front of the building. Five wooden benches sat empty under the wall and a war memorial, surrounded by black metal fencing, was quietly imposing. Large stained-glass windows, like those from a church or cathedral, looked out over where the cars usually parked, and a tall spire at the far-left of the building housed a blue and gold clock and a metal weathervane shaped like a knotted key. A tall white flagpole reached 50 feet into the sky. Once they were at the top of both sets of stairs, they would be visible to all eyes.

Nancy was right; the road was empty. There was no sign of the creatures. Still, Jacob was nervous. There were at least three alleyways leading down to the High Street where they could be hiding and watching and waiting. He didn't like it, but he could see no other choice. "Run, go, now," and as an afterthought, "quietly…"

They kept to the left hand-side path, away from the entrances to the alleyways and the correct side of the road for Locke's hospital. Jacob slipped on a wet paving slab but regained his balance. Nancy led this time, with Mike behind her and Jacob behind him. They ran in a crouch, keeping close to the stone wall to their left. The boys were quiet. Sam was heavy in Jacob's arms, but he held him tight, like the last drop of water in the desert. He caught up to Mike and, still moving, pulled back Jack's hood. Jack's little face smiled at him. They would make it. Jacob saw Nancy slow and press her back against the wet stone wall. Mike and Jacob arrived at the same time and pressed back against the wall too, making them look like soldiers from Black Hawk Down.

"What do you think?" Jacob asked Nancy.

"It seems clear," she answered, and then poked her head around the wall and up the stairs, "Yes, definitely clear."

"Okay, you go first – make sure you get the door unlocked and then come back down and we'll go together."

Nancy nodded, took a deep breath and then turned the corner. Jacob heard the little splashes of her footsteps as she climbed the steps. Jacob and Mike waited under the tall wall, their backs pressed back against it. Jack twisted in Mike's arms, and Jacob moved in front of him to calm him. Jack's cries started Sam off.

"Want to get down, daddy," he said.

"Not now, baby, okay? In a minute – daddy promises."

"Down… now…" Sam responded as Jack's cries got louder. He tried to wriggle free from Jacob's grip. Jacob held him tighter as he carried on trying to calm Jack too. He bit his lip to stop himself losing his temper.

"Okay, daddy put you down, but you must hold Mike's hand, okay?"

Sam shook his head.

"Then I won't let you down."

Sam screamed. Jack screamed. The echoes danced along the deserted street. Jacob felt sweat dripping down his forehead. Mike's eyes were wide and full of terror, more so than when they'd watched the creature's attack at the Police station. He could see thin red veins like lightning in the whites of Mike's eyes. Something touched Mike's shoulder. He jumped, then span around, feeling a trickle or warmth run down his leg, sure he would see one of those creatures on his shoulder with a dozen more staring down with their yellow eyes and razor-like teeth. Instead, he saw Nancy's pale face staring down at him with a knowing smile.

"Thank God," he said. "Are we in?"

"We are, come on let's get you all inside, before those things hear your boy's screams."

"Thank you, Nan–" he started, and then beyond her shoulder he saw something move on the roof of the old theatre opposite. He pushed Sam into her arms and she took him without question. It surprised Jacob to see Sam smile at her and not struggle.

"Come on, dude, let's get you inside," she said. And goddamn if he didn't giggle at that like it was one of the funniest things he'd ever heard.

Jacob felt his heart throb in his chest and then he reached and plucked Jack from Mike, who looked as relieved as if Jacob had just taken a ticking bomb from him.

"Thanks," Mike muttered, and together they ran up the steps. Jacob glanced down the street before entering through the large open doorway. He saw creatures writhing and jumping over each other as they scurried towards them. Jacob turned and closed the large solid-wood door behind them, careful not to make any loud sounds. He heard the lock catch with a soft click and leaned back against the door with Jack in his arms.

CHAPTER EIGHT – MR NEIL

Mr Neil stood in a dark alleyway watching the group. The two men and the woman crouched as they ran, keeping close to the wall before going up the steps and inside the ancient-looking building opposite. Where are you going?

Further down the road, past the traffic lights, he saw the scurrying cult of Vermin approaching, running and jumping and clawing and scratching each other in their rush to get to the sound. What was wrong with these humans, why didn't they listen to instructions, why didn't they stay inside their homes?

He'd come across the remains of the massacre at the police station earlier on his way into town. He had no feelings for these humans. Vermin themselves, he thought, but orders were orders and his orders were to help them.

Mr Neil had walked through piles of warm entrails and puddles of steaming blood, which curled and swirled into the cold air. The black tarmac of the car park shimmered pink in the daylight. One creature lay on the floor, still twitching, its back broken. He leered over it, studying it. It had changed, evolved. His cold eyes scanned the creature. It was bigger than any he'd seen before. It had also grown an extra pair of legs. The thick, black-brown fur was like porcupine spines up-close and underneath he could see dark-red leathery, wrinkled skin.

The sight of it caused him trouble, and after crunching its back under one big, brown boot, he had headed to the flat where he'd watched the deer. Now he was back outside, because of these stupid humans.

His comrades still hadn't appeared, even though he'd sent the signal. His straight face buckled, and he sneered as if he smelled something bad. He felt the red-hot anger bubble to the surface again. He'd have to improvise. He'd have to do something that none of his kind had done for centuries (except for the initial rites to get a body). He'd have to interact with the native inhabitants of this world.

CHAPTER NINE – NANCY

He was actually quite adorable. Those large, brown eyes swam with worry one moment and joy the next. She'd never seen eyes like them. And more than any male recently, he wanted to be with her for more than just one easy thing.

Sam hadn't let go of her hand since they'd entered Locke's hospital. His eyes wandered around the large building, taking in the wondrous sights. Old stone walls were cold to her touch as she walked around the inside of the vast ancient building with Sam following behind. The bottom of the walls were dark brown wood, similar to pews in a church, while four huge beams strode across the wooden roof of the hall. A large exposed-stone fireplace with ornate carvings stood silent on their right. In the centre of the room was a long solid-maple table with six black leather chairs running along either side with a single chair at each end. Mike sat in one of the chairs.

"Did you see them?" he asked.

Nancy shook her head. "How many?" she asked.

"Lots…" Mike leaned forward in the chair and put his head in his hands. "Is this place safe?"

"This room is. There are large, really heavy wooden doors we can shut to keep it that way too."

"Where?" asked Jacob. He joined Mike at the table and put Jack down in the middle of it. The little boy giggled and Sam, from beside Nancy, shushed him. Nancy saw Jacob smile and she thought it was a strong smile. A military smile.

Nancy pointed towards the end of the room. "There are two doors that end – one at the top of the stairs that lead up – and one at the top of the stairs that lead to the cellar. If we close and barricade both, nothing should be able to get into this room."

"Sounds like a plan…" said Mike, he massaged the centre of his forehead with his middle finger. "What do we use as barrica…"

Three sharp, loud knocks at the door interrupted Mike.

"Is that them?" Nancy asked.

"No – unless they've learnt how to knock."

"Then who is it?"

Jacob put a finger to his lips, and knelt next to Sam. "Keep quiet, baby, stay with Nancy, okay?" Sam nodded, and Jacob stood up. "And you," he started, looking at Jack. "You stay with Uncle Mike," Jacob lifted him from the table and passed him to Mike, kissing the boy's warm forehead before he did. "I'll go check it out."

Jacob walked towards the front porch where they had shut the big wooden door behind themselves. He opened it. It creaked the well-known creak from every horror movie ever made. Nancy watched Jacob step into the dimly-lit foyer and then the door closed behind him. Sam hugged her leg. She reached down and stroked his soft dark blond hair.

Muffled voices came from the other side of the big wooden door. Black metal arms reached across the dark wood, and large rusty-silver screwheads looked back at her. Jack cried and squirmed in Mike's arms. Sam's arms were locked around Nancy's right thigh. She exchanged looks with Mike. His hazel, rummy bloodshot eyes were dull. She looked towards the stained-glass windows. They were dark, only letting in a small amount of light. Send them away, Jacob, whoever it is, send them away.

The muffled voices stopped. Nancy tried to move towards the door, but Sam wouldn't release her leg. She looked to Mike for help. He sat with Jack on his lap staring into space. The door clicked and Jacob came back through followed by a man in a suit. His shirt was white and he wore a pale-blue tie. His short, brown hair was still neat despite his ruffled look. Jacob looked at Nancy, who without realising took a step in front of Sam.

"This is Mr Neil," Jacob said. "He was at the police station when the attack happened."

Nancy looked at the man. His face seemed hidden in the shadows behind Jacob, as if using him as a shield. Jacob walked to Mike and plucked the still-crying Jack from him, leaving Mr Neil exposed to their stares.

"Hello," he said.

CHAPTER 10

Tom was a writer. Although, it had been over a decade since his last hit. He had squirreled enough money away though to avoid having to get another job and to keep himself in Johnnie Walker Black Label.

On the day the Vermin arrived, he was sitting in his office at the back of his bungalow which overlooked the rear garden. The flowers had wilted, and the lawn looked colourless. Old wooden cabinets and bookcases full of classic books, contemporary books and gardening books surrounded him. He sat in his battered-leather Captain's chair at his enormous oak desk, his silver MacBook sitting in front of him, the cursor blinking on an empty word document.

The idea had come to him late last night when he was laying in bed alone, looking up at the swirling pattern on his ceiling. His first glorious idea in years. An overarching epic, combining the tales of classic myths such as Beowulf, King Arthur and The Song of Roland. He could have got out of bed, ran through the house and wrote, but he'd been in the game long enough to know what worked for him. No, he would sleep on it, let the idea settle and start in the morning.

The next day, he woke, made coffee and had now been sitting at his desk since 8.30 am. The screen was still blank.

He looked at the digital clock on the Mac screen; it was 5.37 pm. He'd moved from coffee to Johnnie Walker at 11am, hoping the golden liquid would unleash his inner writer – it hadn't, but he had a pleasant buzz on. The idea hadn't disappeared; it was still there in the back of his mind, but he couldn't put it down on paper. His fingers lingered over the glowing black keys. His old, stupid fingers. The skin fell flaccid from his thin bones and deep wrinkles ran across his knuckles. Something crashed in the trees and he saw the grey bodies of birds take off into the autumn sky.

Then he wrote, slowly at first, as if remembering how to do it, then quicker. The room filled with the clicks of the keys as the screen filled with flowing prose. He wrote, without rereading, for over an hour, until his mind ran clear. It felt like a purge. He smiled as he looked out the window into the dull-grey day. I'm back.

He stood and clicked his back, his hands on his hips rotating side-to-side. His glass was empty, and only an inch of liquid stood in the bottle on his desk. He wanted to celebrate, but knew he'd need more than what was left in the bottle. Hell, you don't celebrate alone, he thought, as he grabbed his black wool cardigan and wrapped it around himself. He shook off his brown leather slippers and found his shoes and slid them on. He looked back at the computer screen and saw the words floating in the word document. Another smile lit up his black-and-white-pepper stubbled face as he turned and left the house.

It was brisk outside. The chilly breeze bit into his bloodshot cheeks and made his eyes water. He pulled his cardigan tight around himself and set off down the street past the stone-faced houses on both sides and the naked trees with their black branches silhouetted against the ominous grey sky.

He said 'Hello,' to the people he walked past, including a young man with two children and turned left at the fire station. The gates were closed, and the building stood empty. Next to it, a tall tower used for exercises and drills also stood quiet in the afternoon, the occasional drip of water from a previous exercise breaking the silence.

A shout came from ahead and then the smell of rolled-up cigarettes breezed into Tom's nostrils. He saw three boyish men at the front of the pub.

They were standing near the entrance in between the wooden benches. Green umbrellas and a heavy silver chain cordoned the beer garden off from the road. A silver bucket full of sand and cigarette butts, smoked next to the entrance. Tom walked past the men, mumbling a hello and pushed the opaque glass door open and walked inside.

The pub was a throwback to what a pub should be, thought Tom. None of this poncy wood-effect flooring and strip lighting. Instead, there were black wood chairs surrounding black wood tables with paper beer mats and an old floral carpet. Above the fabric-covered red benches that stretched around the building, the semi-opaque windows were steamed up. He saw a young couple playing darts in the room's corner and the crash of pool balls in the room beyond. Even though no one had smoked in here for over a decade, the old fag smell still lingered in the carpets and furniture.

He pulled up a stool at the bar and perched on its green fabric seat waiting for the barmaid. His eyes scoured the bottles at the back of the bar, looking for the most expensive whisky they stocked. Tom smiled when he saw a bottle of Johnnie Walker Blue Label and with his mind made up, he glanced around the pub at the other patrons. Three men, older than him – though not by much – sat playing cards in the centre of the room. Past them, at the flashing lights of the gambler, was a middle-aged man in a flat cap. Above the man was a TV screen which showed a silent football match. A few people sat to the side, their eyes glued to the screen occasionally taking a swig of their lager or playing on their phones.

The barmaid arrived and he ordered his whiskey. She was a sour-looking thing with down-turned lips and dank blonde hair. She gave him the glass and he sniffed at the amber liquid before taking a sip. As he felt the warmth of the liquid run down his throat and into his belly, he heard a crash from the poolroom, followed by a shout. Then he heard another crash that sounded like the smash of a pool cue striking something hard. The barmaid shouted, and then a man covered in blood ran from the poolroom into the main bar. He took three steps and then collapsed on the sticky, floral-patterned floor.

Tom guessed there had been a fight, maybe a hustle gone wrong – but that sort of thing didn't happen in Westford, did it? Then he saw another man rush from the poolroom. Hanging onto his shoulder was a creature the size of a labrador with six legs and sharp-looking, black spikes coming from its body. Its sharp teeth, which stuck deep into the man's shoulder, reminded Tom of old Nosferatu movies.

The barmaid screamed and the man on the fruit machine rushed over and tried to pull the creature off him. As he struggled, Tom watched the pointed teeth rip through the flesh like a cheese-grater. The man screamed as blood gushed down his neck, onto his clothes and soaked into the floor. The light left his eyes and the man who'd removed the creature looked at the wriggling thing in his hands. It turned to look at him in his eyes, no further than six inches away. Tom stared dumbly as the creature smiled a gruesome blood-covered grin at the man and then launched itself at his face. He saw the needle-like teeth rip into the man's nose, shredding it like spaghetti before it moved in for a French kiss.

Tom saw movement from the corner of his eye in the darkened pool room and then three more of the creatures side-stepped, crab-like into the room. The barmaid screamed and he saw a black shape run up her body and bite at her neck. He turned to run for the door when he felt a tug at his trouser leg. He looked down into the glowing yellow eyes. His last thought before he felt the teeth was: 'But… my new book…'

Ms Bramley was hiding in her pantry among the jars and spices. She'd been baking a fresh batch of strawberry jam, ready for her grandchildren this afternoon. She'd had the wooden spoon in her mouth, checking if she needed any more sugar, when she heard a crash in her front porch. Ms Bramley had gone for the closest weapon she could find, which was a solid wooden rolling pin with remnants of flour and dough stuck to it.

Careful not to make a sound, she followed close to the wall and made her way to the hallway past the black and white photos of her beloved William, who had been gone for a decade. She glanced at the vases of dying flowers she was planning to replace this afternoon. Her slippers made no sound on the carpet.

Images of burglars in those terrible black hoodies the kids wore nowadays, brandishing sharp, silver knives ran through her mind. A shadow moved on the pale blue fluffy carpet ahead. They were in the house. She took a step back when she heard a muffled cry. Maybe one of them had caught themselves on a piece of broken glass. That will never come out of the carpet, was her next thought.

She peered around the corner of the exposed brick wall and saw a woman, no older than twenty-five, crawling along her carpet. Her egg-timer rang from the kitchen. The woman in her porch looked up towards the sound.

"Help me, please…"

Ms Bramley lowered the rolling pin and then sub-consciously wrung its neck. Oh God, if only William was here, he'd know what to do. She stepped out to help the woman, when she saw fat, crab-looking creatures nibbling and gnawing and biting at the woman's leg. The skin from her left calf fell to the floor like a flap of pig skin tangled in the shredded fabric from her jeans. They had eaten the flesh and muscle of the other leg up to the knee, leaving only the white bone and a few scraps of flesh that hung wilted like her flowers. It's so bright, she thought. The bone is bright white, like it's been washed in bleach.

Move. A voice inside her head that sounded like William said. Now, move. She dropped the rolling pin, and it landed with a soft whump on the fluffy carpet. The creatures, that until now hadn't noticed her, stopped their feasting and a dozen yellow eyes looked at her. MOVE.

She didn't hesitate. Ms Bramley ran towards the kitchen. When she got there, she saw more of the creatures on the window ledge outside. She looked towards the back porch and the lean-to. Dozens of the creatures were swarming over her summer garden. Without choice, and with the sounds of the creatures from the front rushing down the hall, she pulled a knife from a kitchen drawer and backed into the pantry. Only an old wooden door, less than an inch thick, with slats allowing light inside, separated her from the monsters outside.

The pantry smelled of cinnamon and allspice. She sat on the floor, her back against the wall. To her left and right were three shelves that housed spices, herbs and jars. The sound of the creature's footfalls changed. She heard the click, click, click of dozens of clawed feet on her red, quarry-tile kitchen floor. Then she heard sniffs at the base of the door, and fast-moving shadows underneath. I love you, Will, she whispered, closed her eyes and waited.

Fuck it, thought Adam. He'd been waiting overnight for his parents' to come home. He picked up his chipped and battered skateboard with luminous green wheels and stepped out the front door. They hadn't called. What sort of fucking parents did they think they were? What was he supposed to eat? There was food in the cupboards and fridge, but unused to doing anything for himself, the best he could do was make a bowl of cereal, and even then he left spilt milk over the kitchen sides and circular multi-grains on the floor.

He liked this time of year and with his parents' away for the day he went to the skatepark for the morning. It wasn't too cold yet for him, which was good, although he saw others wrapped in up their coats and scarves. The leaves had fallen from the trees, but he believed it was still warm enough to go out in a tee-shirt and jeans. He didn't notice the empty roads, streets and paths on the walk to the Recreation ground. Adam had his headphones in and was listening to Metallica at full volume.

Adam thought about his friends at college. Perhaps he should have gone there first and seen if anyone else wanted to bunk off with him – too late now. He approached the Recreation ground – 'the Rec' as the locals called it – and put his skateboard down on the yellow and orange leaf-strewn path. He got his balance and kicked on, building speed as he went. Green grass passed him in a blur on his right, while to his left, a row of red Victorian houses flashed by. He passed empty black metal benches and a colourful park that stood empty, the blue climbing frame reflecting the dull grey sky.

He jumped off his skateboard and kicked back to stop it as he neared the muddy path that led from the tarmac to the skatepark. Behind the skatepark was a bowling green surrounded by dark green hedges and a tennis court with a tatty-looking green net with holes in. The skatepark was empty. The graffitied wooden half-pipe had black skid marks and other scrapes, and he saw "Fuck Corbyn" in bright orange letters at the back of where the bikes launched themselves down. Adam thought someone would be here, anyone, even that dopey kid who always came on his scooter and worshipped him and his mates. But it was empty. He pulled out his headphones but could still hear the gruff voice of James and the crazy drumming of Lars. Not just the skatepark. The world was silent.

Adam ran up the smooth wood and caught the stiff metal lip at the top and pulled himself up. He turned around and stared out over Westford. The public car park was empty. He frowned. A shriek broke the silence. His gaze followed the rooftops towards the sound. It came from the police station. As he watched, he saw a Silver Nissan X-Trail speed away, leaving a line of damaged cars behind. Behind the Nissan, he saw a crowd of people running from the station and among, behind and above them, he saw black shapes running and attacking.

A man in a black coat ran across the road and onto the grass that led to the skatepark. Adam stared open-mouthed as he watched one creature – it looked like a gigantic rat, but it ran sideways like a crab – jump on his back and he saw a fine, red mist spurt into the air. He felt his bladder release and looked down at the wet stain that spread across the wood and trickled down over the metal lip. He listened to the screams and shrieks of the people at the police station and stood frozen to the spot.

Three of the creatures joined the other which was feasting on the man in the black coat on the grass. Stay silent, he told himself. He moved to his right, to duck and make himself as small as possible when he let go of his skateboard and it roared down the wooden halfpipe like a locomotive in the desert. He watched as it went up the other side and came back down again; only stopping when it left the wood and landed on the wet grass. Then he looked up.

The four creatures were already coming. They were 20 yards away and getting closer. He saw them nip and yap as they jumped over one another to get to him. He felt the remnants in his bladder release as he saw their glowing yellow eyes and their blood-dripping, needle-like teeth up close for the first time.

And then they were at the bottom of the ramp. He kicked at them as they climbed up the wood, sharp claws leaving scrapes in the soft wood. One attached itself to his black and white Converse when it bit through his toe as he attempted to kick it and he screamed. Tears ran down his face as the creature held on tight to his foot and he lost his balance and rolled down the ramp into the other creatures which jumped onto him...

All they left behind was a bright white skeleton with flaps of pink flesh in a puddle of coppery red and one blood-splattered, checkered black and white Converse trainer.

CHAPTER 11 – THE COUNCILLOR

Geoffrey Scott sat alone in his office in the town hall. Only a handful of staff had shown up this morning including Bill Hicks, the only other person who knew (nearly) as much as he did. This would all be over soon, he told himself, as he stared out the enormous sash window, over the empty street that led to the town bridge and the motorway. The road was usually bumper-to-bumper with cars making their way either in or out of town, but not this morning. He'd known it would be bad, but he didn't know it would be this bad.

They'd first contacted him two hours before the fireball hit on the outskirts of town, and since then – until two hours ago anyway – he'd been receiving updates. But he had heard nothing from the grey satellite phone that sat on his desk since the last update. Who they were was an unknown quantity, but they had all the official documents.

Geoffrey – Geoff, as his friends knew him – watched the bronze hands of the clock on his wall tick by. He ran a slab-like hand through his greying hair. What was going on out there? He liked to think, unlike other councillors who were in this game for their own personal aspirations and fame, that he cared about the people in his constituency. He wanted what was best for them, and he would listen to what they wanted and not make their decisions for them. Geoff was – as his wife liked to remind him often – one of the moral guys. If that was true, then why did this situation make him feel so shady?

He rolled up the sleeves of his plain white formal shirt, and then rolled them down again, before fiddling with his gold tie and buffing his glasses with a little black cloth. He couldn't contact them, could he? All the phone lines were down, he'd agreed to that – not that he thought he could stop them if he hadn't. That's why they'd given him the satellite phone. He didn't have their number, hadn't thought to ask for it either, and it didn't show up on the screen when they rang. The monotonous voice on the other end of the line would give him a two-minute update and would then hang up. Geoff hadn't expected the phone calls to stop. What did it mean? Or was there no further update?

His phone rang. Not the satellite phone, but the landline on his desk. He grabbed at it, dropping it as he bought it up to his ear and then catching it again. Finally he fumbled it to the side of his face and said: "Hello?"

"Geoff, it's me…"

"Bill? Are you calling internally?"

"Yes, boss, why?"

Geoff bit his lip to stop himself swearing down the phone at his younger colleague. "No reason, Bill. How's it going?"

"Not good, boss, not good at all…"

Geoff waited with the phone to his ear. "Care to elaborate, Bill?"

"Oh, yeah, sorry. The police, Geoff, at the station – they're gone."

"What do you mean gone?"

"Attacked… About an hour ago now. People didn't listen, they went out to get help, I guess, but, well… they're all dead."

"Hold up, Bill. What are you talking about?"

"All the officers and at least 20 to 30 residents – all dead."

"Attacked, are you sure? Where are the bodies? We can't just leave them out there."

"I don't know, I got a phone call from a local friend who saw it happen, but we have got no one left to investigate."

"Okay, thanks for letting me know, Bill. Give me 10 minutes, okay?"

"Yes, boss."

Geoff put the phone back on the receiver and leaned back in his cream leather chair. He spun himself around so he could look out the window again. What's going on out there? They had warned him there would be deaths, but the entire police force and 30 residents'? He knew he'd been told only what they thought he needed to know, but 30-plus deaths? They needed the army here. Bill said this was an attack. He didn't enjoy being kept in the dark.

He picked up the telephone and dialled Bill's internal number. "Bill, do we have any weapons?"

CHAPTER 12 – JACOB

Jacob watched as the man who'd introduced himself as Mr Neil shook hands with Mike followed by Nancy. Mike seemed excited about their unknown friend, but Jacob had seen Nancy's eyes when she'd looked at him. Her green eyes narrowed, full of suspicion and distrust, turning her face into a caricature of sorts. He'd stolen glances at her when he thought she wasn't looking.

He guessed she was at least 10 years younger than him, but her skin looked tired and her face creased when she smiled. She had black bags under her eyes and looked like she needed some proper sleep, not the sort where you passed out at the end of the night. If she cleaned herself up, she would be very attractive, but at the moment even her hair looked dull and straw-like. Sam was smitten with her though, but he thought he'd monitor her just in case.

Mr Neil took a seat at the table opposite Mike, who leaned forward like an excited child at school.

"What have you seen?" he asked.

"Those things, lots of them – they're all over the town…"

"Where were you when it started?" Mike asked.

"At home," he started. "I was about to head into the office. I'd been at home working yesterday and knew nothing was up until I drove into town this morning… then… and then, I saw those things attacking someone on my way in."

Nancy, who up until now had been standing with Sam, wandered over to the table and pulled up a chair. Sam followed behind her. Jacob smiled as he watched his eldest boy follow her, dragging a soft, brown toy hedgehog behind him along the wooden floor.

He watched Mr Neil look around the building, admiring the high ceilings and exposed wooden beams, and then Mr Neil spoke: "Do you know what they are?"

Jacob shook his head. "Not a clue. Me and my boys first saw them yesterday straight after that thing crashed near the quarry."

"The quarry?" Mr Neil enquired.

"Yes, you know, the one up near the Shell garage? Yesterday afternoon, a damn meteorite or something crashed there."

Mr Neil sat silent for a moment. Jacob joined the rest of them at the solid wood table and took Jack back and held him on his lap. "Whatever is going on out there, I know for sure it started then…"

"How did you make it this far into town? Those things were everywhere," asked Mr Neil.

Something about the way the question sounded made Jacob feel uneasy. He saw Nancy shift in her chair to the side of him and was sure she felt the same. It sounded more like an interview question you'd expect in an interrogation room at a police station.

Mike answered for them, "We sheltered at Jacob's till this morning, then we headed into town," Mike stopped and looked at the exposed ceiling beams. "We got as far as the police station… then there was… an incident."

"An incident?" enquired Mr Neil again.

"An attack… those things attacked a group of people," Jacob said, then wrapped his arms around Jack. "We saw at least two dozen people killed." He looked at Sam and smiled. "We escaped in Mike's car and tried to get out of town, but those creatures blocked us off."

"Blocked you off?" Why was everything this man said a question, wondered Jacob.

"Yes, blocked us off, there were hundreds of them all climbing over each other to get at us. We drove back into town and parked up, before running here."

"What's the plan now?" asked Mr Neil.

Jacob saw Nancy glance at Mike. "The plan is to stay here and wait it out… isn't it?" she said.

"It is," said Jacob. "In here we're safe, we just need to block the exits. In fact, Mike, Mr Neil, will you help me, while Nancy looks after the boys?"

"Hold up," Nancy started. "Why should I look after the boys? Because I'm a woman? Fuck that, none of you know this place like I do."

Mike smiled. Jacob looked across the table at her. "Mind your language in front of my children," and then added, "please…" at the end. "Not because you're a woman, no, but because Sam has taken a shine to you, and I believe if we left him here with anyone else, he would scream the house down and draw those things to us… it is a compliment, Sam rarely warms to people that quickly."

Nancy's features softened. She looked at Sam, who was standing by her side. His soft little hand resting on hers. She did something Jacob never expected – she picked Sam up and sat him on his lap. "Okay, little dude, you and me and your brother have a date down here, you okay with that?"

Sam turned to her and put his hands on her cheeks and nodded. Jacob stared open-mouthed. He didn't even act like that with his own mother. He watched Sam slink down into Nancy and get comfy on her, grabbing her arms to wrap them around him.

"Well, I guess that's settled. Sam, Jack and Nancy will stay down here, and we'll secure this old place."

Nancy watched Jacob, Mike and Mr Neil as they got up from the table and headed towards the old wooden door at the other side of the room. She'd told them the places that needed to be boarded up and checked.

Something about Mr Neil gave her the willies. Not just the way he answered in questions, but the way his mouth was two seconds too slow for his body – as if English wasn't his mother-tongue. She'd known enough foreigners to know when they were internally translating before they spoke, but she'd never seen it on someone with such an English name and with such an obvious English accent.

She had a read on Jacob and Mike – they wouldn't be her first choice of people to be in this situation with, but she sensed a strength in Jacob which came from his protectiveness of his children, and a wisdom and quietness to Mike that reminded her of her grandfather. Mr Neil though, he was something else. She's always been good at reading people, which was useful when you partied as much as she did. She always partied hard, but only with the right people – she could always tell when someone was dangerous. She thought Mr Neil was dangerous. Dangerous in a different way to Jacob. She knew he would fight for his children with his last breath and she sensed the same for Mike. But what did Mr Neil fight for?

The door closed behind the three men, and she was alone with the children. How had she gone from the last person anyone would leave their children with, to designated babysitter? With the men gone, she felt the return of the impending doom feeling that always accompanied the days after one of her binges. It was like a black hole that swallowed all her good thoughts and replaced them with a thousand what ifs? What if she hadn't made him wear a condom? What if that coke was cut with something else? She closed her eyes and leaned back in the chair, trying to control her breathing and slow her pulse. This wasn't the time, or place, for an anxiety attack. Nancy tried to focus on the positive things in her life. She opened her eyes, and Jack and Sam were studying her with smiles on their little faces.

Jack sat on the table in front of her, Sam was looking at her from her lap. They really were beautiful kids. Sam was sweet and innocent and looked the spitting image of Jacob with his brown-blond hair and dimple in his chin. Jacob was good looking, in that Westford townie kind of way. Jack was clearly Sam's brother, but the likeness to Jacob wasn't as strong. Milk had dried on the top of Jack's lip, which creased every time he smiled. To the side of his nose was a little brown beauty spot. He sat on the table pulling at his socks, trying to get them off. Sam giggled as he did and reached across to help him. Nancy lifted Sam and sat him next to his little brother on the table. They sat side-by-side and the resemblance was even more pronounced.

The boys helped push the feelings of dread away and she made funny faces at them. They giggled as she put her hand to her nose and wiggled her fingers and then hid her eyes with her hands and then reappeared. The boy's giggles chased away the anxiety like a song that takes you to a unique world.

"You wait there," she said, and stood, leaving both boys sitting in the middle of the huge wooden table. Nancy moved to the exposed stone fireplace and picked up an iron poker and started poking at the cold coals. She brought the poker up to eye level and rubbed her fingers into the black dust. With the dust on her fingers and with her back to the boys, she moved to a window to look at her reflection. She worked the coal-dust onto her face and around her eyes, aiming to turn herself into a panda for the boys.

Movement outside stopped her from working the black around her left eye. She watched as a dozen of the creatures slunk up the middle of the road. One left the pack and approached the door of the theatre across the road before returning. Then another left the group and approached the door of the estate agents opposite, before again returning to the group. What are they doing? Behind the pack of creatures, she saw something. Nancy couldn't define the shapes, they were like black fuzzy blurs of shadow. After a creature had approached a door, one of the fuzzy shadows would then move into position to the side of the door where it then disappeared, camouflaged into the shadows of the building.

Another creature broke from the pack and she saw its spiky porcupine-like spines as it made its way up the stairs towards the front door of the hospital. She stopped breathing. She wanted to run to the boys, to put her hands over their mouths to stop any noise but didn't dare move. It approached the door and she would later swear she felt its presence as it approached. After a moment it returned to the pack, its long rat-like tail trailing to its side, and she saw the shadow pass on its way to stand guard in the shadows at the door that led to the porch.

The pack was further down the road now, approaching the traffic lights and the crossing. Nancy bent her knees and lowered herself to the cold, dark-wood floor. She put her hands down for balance and held back a hiss as a splinter caught in the flap of skin between her fingers. The boys watched her as she slid on her butt across the floor to them. She looked up and beckoned them down to join her. Sam jumped and Nancy caught him and held him on her lap as she reached up to grab Jack, who was crawling to the edge. She grabbed him by his shoulders as he looked over the tip of the table.

Once she had them both at floor level with her, she whispered: "Let's play a game." Sam nodded excitedly. "It's a race – you see that door over there?" Nancy pointed, and both boys followed her finger to the large wooden door. "It's a crawling race, the first one to that door as quietly as possible wins. You ready?"

"I ready," Sam replied.

"Okay, don't forget to be a helpful big brother and help Jack…"

"Okay."

"Ready… steady…" Nancy took a quick glance back towards the entrance porch. "Go…"

Both boys moved along the floor towards the door, their knees sliding on the shiny wood like they were doing breaststroke. They were quieter than she'd hoped and she followed behind, looking over her shoulder towards the door to the porch. Looking at the door ahead that the men had gone through only five minutes earlier, she thought, please, don't come back through.

Sam was at the front, only 10 feet from the door with Jack on his heels. They were nearly there. Jack squealed. He rolled over onto his side, clutching his hand. She moved fast across the floor, her knees aching and hot. His cries echoed off the stone walls. She looked at his palm and saw a dark splinter the size of a push-pin protruding from his soft pink skin.

"Hold still, Jack," she said, as she tried with her long nails to pinch the tip and pull it free. Tears ran down his face. She wiped his tears with the back of her hands before kissing him on the palm. "It's okay, these are magic kisses – they'll make it feel better, baby."

Jack calmed, and she got the splinter out of his chubby little palm, leaving behind a tiny red dot where it had entered. She peppered it with more kisses and saw Sam had reached the door and was kneeling, watching her with a proud smile on his face.

"I win," he said.

Nancy laughed. "Yes you did, well done, Sam." She turned so she was on her butt and put Jack on her lap. Nancy bum-shuffled the last few feet until she was at the door. She reached up for the cold brass door handle and turned it till she heard it click. She leaned against the door, and it slowly opened. A rectangle of bright light grew on the floor next to her as the door opened and she shuffled through to the stone-floor corridor. They were alone, but she could hear the grunts of the men from above.

She pushed the door closed with her foot and leaned against a wall, her breath fast and her heart thumping in the silence. Sam and Jack cuddled into her and she sat holding them at the bottom of an ancient Game of Thrones-looking staircase with exposed stonework, wooden archways and a criss-crossing church-style window at the top. The staircase rounded a corner at the top and she heard the men's voices as they got closer on their way down.

Jacob came first and paused at the top of the stairs when he saw Nancy, Sam, and Jack at the bottom. Mike and Mr Neil stopped behind him, silhouetted against the window at the top.

CHAPTER 13 – THE COUNCILLOR

Geoff watched as Bill Hicks carried a black-fabric duffel bag into his office and put it on his desk with a dull thud.

"Do I want to know where you got that from?"

Bill shook his head and leaned over the bag, fumbling with a silver, four-digit padlock. He muttered under his breath as his fat fingers struggled with the dials. Geoff held back a laugh as he watched.

He had taken Bill on as – well, he didn't really know what his job title was – but he enjoyed having him around. Bill was 10 years younger and at least 10 kilos heavier. Geoff saw beads of sweat break out on his forehead as he struggled with the padlock.

Bill had been an editor for the local newspaper, but he lost his job when everything went digital and the stories changed. He looked like an editor – thin-rimmed glasses and balding grey hair – but his mind was sharp. He had his finger on the pulse, as his own father would say. He knew the people in his constituency. He knew what they wanted, what riled them, and he wrote speeches and pamphlets that Geoff was sure helped, more than any social media campaign, to get him re-elected. No-one else seemed to see what he saw, and one evening after a few drinks in the Baron Burghley, Geoff learned more about the man including a shooting hobby and an interest in modern culture that astounded him. He knew all the new bands and musicians as well as the old and had been a major part in the swing in the youngsters who had voted for him. Bill was a very worthy companion, and a fearsome adversary if it ever came to that. He had his own secrets, of which Geoff knew a few, and likewise, Bill knew a few too many of Geoff's for his own liking. Bill was the Lancelot to his King Arthur, minus the affair.

They were joined together and Geoff couldn't think of anyone he'd rather have on his side right now. Something was going on in his town.

They'd lied to him and people had died; been attacked and killed. That wasn't part of what he'd agreed to on the phone to that robotic voice. He'd never been in the army, had never shot a gun, but they were his people out there, they had voted for him to do his best for them.

Sitting inside this warm office while they were dying wasn't him doing his best for them.

Bill finally unlocked the padlock and pulled the sides of the bag apart. Geoff saw a gleam of black metal from inside the bag. Bill pulled out two black pistols. They had scuffs in the metal and he saw the words, FN HERSTAL BELGIUM in silver down the side. Geoff moved to touch one, and Bill stopped him. "Not yet, boss." He reached into the bag and pulled out a pair of blue latex gloves. "You must wear these every time you touch one of these guns, understand?"

Unused to being told what to do, Geoff took a breath and waited for the heat from his blood to cool, and then nodded at Bill. "Understood." He didn't want to ask why he had to wear gloves; but these guns were a necessity, even though every ounce of him wanted to put them straight back into the bag and never see them again. His brow furrowed as he watched Bill remove a larger weapon this time and place it on his desk. This one was newer and sleeker. It was a shotgun, that much he knew.

The stock was walnut, and the barrel was a matte-black metal with inch long – what he guessed to be – air holes. It was over a metre in length and when he put his gloves on and picked it up, he guessed it weighed at least three kilograms. Bill pulled out two red and yellow boxes, which Geoff assumed to be shotgun cartridges.

"Anything else?" Geoff asked, half joking. Bill smiled. "Don't tell me, a rocket launcher?" Bill's smile didn't change. Geoff's did. "Seriously, Bill, what else have you got in that duffel bag of death?"

"These," he replied and pulled out three ancient-looking, dark-green miniature pineapple-looking metal objects. He saw each had a rusted-red metal ring and a large lever along one side.

"Are they what I think they are?"

"Mills bombs," Bill replied. "World War Two grenades."

"Where did you get them?"

"You don't want to know, boss."

"Are they safe? They look older than you?"

Bill gave him a look. "As long as we don't remove the pins, they should be safe for another hundred years."

Geoff blew out his cheeks. "Fingers crossed we don't need any of these things, but as my dad used to say: 'Hope for the best, prepare for the worst...'" He looked over the table of weapons, a child-like love of guns, long since forgotten, made his heart beat fast and a giddiness like Christmas morning came over him.

Bill frowned at him. "Are we really going out there?"

Geoff put a hand on his shoulder. "We have to. What if it was your family out there, all alone? I'd rather have my throat slit than sitting in here not helping anyone if we can."

"I know, but… well, boss, look at us… two old men in cheap suits, one an elected councillor and the other a semi-retired editor – we're not exactly Rambo are we?"

Geoff chuckled. The image of Bill wearing a gun strapped around his podgy, pale belly and a bandana around his balding, greying head would live with him forever. "Heroes aren't always what they look like in the movies, Bill. Anyone can be a hero. It's not about what you look like being heroic, it's the fact that you had the chance to stay safe – safe and warm – warm and comfortable at home but chose to help others against all the odds. That's heroic, Bill, that's what makes a hero."

Bill gave him a sideways glance. "Did I write that speech?" he said, then his face creased and fell into a big, warm-hearted smile.

Geoff smacked him on the shoulder. "Come on, grab the guns. Let's do this."

Bill picked up each gun, turning them over in his hands before placing them back in the duffel-bag, which he then hooked over his shoulder. Geoff noticed him wince and pull at his back. Bill straightened himself and strode towards the door. Geoff followed.

They decided against taking a car, choosing to try to stay as quiet as possible as they snuck through the streets of Westford. Bill wore a big grey wooly hat and an olive-green Barbour jacket. The black strap of the duffel-bag looked like it was digging through the jacket, and Geoff saw the sweat and strained expression on his face.

"Do you want me to have a turn?" he asked.

Bill turned to him, his stubbled cheeks pink. "Actually, I would appreciate it." Geoff took the bag and watched Bill massage his shoulder.

The town centre was deserted, like a ghost town from the wild west novels he read as a boy.

"Awww, shit," Bill said. Geoff turned to him and put his finger to his mouth. "Deer scat, Boss, what the fuck is deer scat doing in the town centre… and on my shoe?"

Geoff knelt on the stone cobbles, feeling the cold through the thin material of his suit trousers. It was deer scat. He looked up to Bill and shrugged.

The shops hadn't opened, giving the town a late Sunday afternoon feel.

The world was grey and empty and silent. They backed away from the deer scat and stood under the brick roof of the alleyway they'd come from.

They leaned against the rain-stained, damp wall. Geoff lowered the bag to the ground and thought about the quickest way to the police station. They'd have to cross the High Street up the adjacent black alleyway, past Locke's hospital, up another dark alleyway and then along the path at the bottom of the Rec. He huffed out his cheeks at the thought of the wide-open spaces.

The Gothic-style buildings with silhouetted statues of weeping angels and gargoyles looking down on the cobbled, empty High Street was haunting. The vast windows of the flats above the closed shops were ominous. Geoff felt like he was being watched. It seemed as though there were only two colours in the world: grey and limestone-brown. And a deathly silence.

Geoff cocked his head towards the High Street. His eyes watered. His usual soft features were taut like a rubber band pulled too tight and ready to be released. We can't stand here like two scared children, he thought. If we don't start moving, we may as well have stayed at the office.

"Bill, get the pistols."

Bill nodded, reached down, opened the bag and pulled out the guns and the blue latex gloves. After he'd put his gloves on and handed the other pair to Geoff, he clicked off the safety of one of the guns, before passing it to Geoff, then he did the same with the other. He leaned into Geoff who was studying the gun in his gloved hands.

"It's simple, boss, point and shoot. Keep the safety off – if anything happens, I might not have a chance to turn it back on for you. But… the trigger is very, very sensitive, so only put your finger there when you need to shoot." Bill showed Geoff how he held his pistol and Geoff copied. "Good, just don't shoot me, okay?"

"No promises."

Bill pulled the bag from the floor and slung it over his shoulder. He motioned with one hand for Geoff to lead the way. Geoff left the dark of the passage and together they crossed the deserted High Street towards the black alleyway across from them. They ran like soldiers across a dangerous path, sideways, glancing left and right with their pistols in front of them pointed towards the ground.

The entrance to the alleyway was sandwiched between an independent bookshop with exposed beams and mock-Tudor frontage to the left and a HSBC bank to the right. The usual A-frame signs that advertised the shops up the alley, that Geoff passed every day on his walk through the High Street, were noticeable by their absence. He stared dumbly at a spot on the wall he'd never seen before which was usually blocked by the A-frame.

The herbal aroma of the natural health and medicine shop that hid up the alley lingered on the air, not as strong as most days, just a shadow of the normal pungent odour. They stopped with their backs against the stone wall at the entrance to the alley, Geoff on the left and Bill on the right, like two 1970s detectives. Bill nodded at Geoff and counted down. Three… two… one… on his fingers. They rounded the corner with their guns raised. Geoff heard something shuffling, but saw nothing. He looked at Bill, who nodded again before taking the lead and entering the alley.

They drifted, careful not to make any noise as they passed the locked up herbal store on their left. Above them, the pitch-black roof of the alleyway gave way to a bright white sky. The passage was still except for their own light footfalls. A large black-metal drainpipe hung from a wall to their right, behind it the mucky water had stained the stone green. At the bottom, sitting on the drain, was a pile of slight bones like the remains of sticky BBQ ribs. Just a few pieces of tendon-like pieces of flesh hung to them. The green wastewater had mixed with the blood and insides of intestines to create a gloopy, brown mess.

The sound of Bill retching pulled Geoff from the grisly scene in front of him. He turned and saw Bill leaning over with one hand on his knees and the other supporting himself against the wall. The duffel bag hung from his side. Geoff didn't want to, but pulled his fingers to his lips to shush him again. Bill rolled his eyes, looked to the sky and took three deep breaths. When he looked back, Geoff gave him a thumbs-up and Bill gave him the middle-finger back.

The alley opened up towards the top so they wouldn't have to walk single-file any longer. They held their guns pointed towards the ground as they passed the closed sandwich shop to their right. Geoff peered in through the window and saw white plastic boxes that usually contained food, smashed on the floor and remnants of ham, chicken, onion and peppers scattered on the sides and up the walls. A poster with a smiling young boy advertising a musical at the Corn Exchange stared back at him when he moved back from the window.

It's like a post-apocalyptic novel, he thought. Something he'd expect to read by Stephen King or Richard Matheson at his book club. This was no radiation leak. They'd lied to him and his staff – his friends had been alone with no help all night and morning.

They had to keep moving. They might not be able to fight off what was happening, but they could try to help as many people as possible.

"Bill, are you ready?"

Bill wiped away spittle from his top lip and wiped it on the wall. "I'm ready. The police station?"

Geoff nodded, and together they approached the top of the passage which opened to Almshouse Street. He peered around the corner of the alleyway, feeling like a ridiculous private eye, and down the narrow road with its kebab shops and bakeries towards Broad Leaf Square, and then to his right up the wide road which was eerily quiet and empty with just two cars in the usually full parking spaces on either side of the road. He saw the tall office buildings opposite with their shutters drawn and further up the road the metal weathervane of Locke's hospital.

Nothing moved, and for a moment it appeared even the clouds in the sky had frozen in place. Was this happening everywhere, he wondered.

"Let's go," he said. "Stay close to the buildings."

Geoff went first, keeping close to the old-stone walls of the bank to his right. The ATM blinked at him. Another opening led to a betting shop and a hairdresser, and he darted across the opening and leaned back against the safety and shadows of another wall. He lifted his hand to Bill and motioned for him to run across.

Bill's eyes were wide, darting from left to right, and Geoff expected his were the same, as if they'd been shooting double espressos all morning. Better to be wired and alert than the other, he thought. They carried on past the big red doors of the Corn Exchange with the large black-metal gates padlocked in front. Posters of pantomimes, stand-up comics and other gigs stared out at them from inside the dark.

He could see the traffic lights now they had come around the side of the building. They were on green. Across from them, he thought he saw movement in one window of the old hospital. He put his arm back and pushed Bill against the wall.

"What?" Bill asked.

"Ssshhh…" Geoff said and pointed to Locke's hospital. They studied the building across the road. Nothing moved. The traffic lights changed to red. They sidestepped along the wall to the T-junction of the crossing. They would be in the open for 10 seconds as they ran across the road towards the darkness of yet another alley. Geoff noticed the grey sky above had taken on a yellowish tint. A sign of a storm, his dad had always told him.

"I will run across first and when I'm there, you follow, okay?" Geoff said.

Bill nodded. He was running on the spot and wringing his hands. Geoff didn't know whether his fear was from running or the queer atmosphere of the day, but he felt it too.

He looked both ways from under the shadow of the building they were hiding against, closed his eyes, whispered a prayer, opened his eyes and ran.

His heart thumped in his chest and every breath hurt as he made it across the road and stood on top of a rusted-metal cellar door on the path in front of the converted pub on the opposite side of the road to where Bill still stood. He needed to go for a slash. He wasn't sure how long he could hold the need to piss in. Bill ran across the road, his jowls wobbling and his man-boobs bouncing under his heavy coat. In his right hand he held the duffel bag. He moved fast for a fat man. Arriving next to Geoff, he bent down with his hands on his knees, trying to catch his breath. Two beads of sweat dripped down the side of his face. Geoff reached out to pat him on the back, when a scratching sound from the alley to the side of the pub made him stop with his arm hanging in the air. Bill looked up and together they flattened themselves against the building.

It was a tick, tick, tick and then a drip, drip, drip of monotonous, metronomic scratching; as if a mechanical toy had gotten stuck on its back.

"What the fuck is that?" Bill whispered.

Geoff shuffled along the wall, past the limestone window sill, and craned the side of his head as close to the opening of the alleyway as he dared. He couldn't tell if it was mechanical or natural. The tick-like scratches were sharp sounding, like flint against a rock. However, the drip-like sound after was muffled as if someone had dropped a raw steak on a lino-floor. The sound was familiar to Geoff. He remembered his uncle's house in the countryside. He had taken Geoff on hunts when he was younger, however, Geoff had never been allowed to carry a gun. Behind the house was a wooden hut where his uncle would tie the kills to the rafters to let them bleed out. The floor would be slippery with metallic-smelling blood that he could taste on the air.

He snuck a glance around the corner and withdrew instantly. Bill touched his shoulder, and he flinched. He struggled to compute what he'd seen up the alleyway. Bill went to look himself.

"Don't," Geoff said weakly, but it was too late.

"Wh…" Bill started, before trailing off. His shoulders slumped and Geoff thought his legs would give way before he got back to the wall. Tears spiked in his eyes, and his mouth settled on a tight-lipped grimace.

"Bill, are you okay?"

"Those poor people…"

"I know, Bill, I know…"

"What could do that?"

"I don't know. How many were there?"

"Five or six, don't make me look again… can we go another way, Geoff?"

Geoff looked into Bill's pleading eyes. Tears dripped down his splotchy, pale face. He was biting his lip so hard Geoff thought he would draw blood - it gave a new meaning to the British-style stiff upper lip. "It's a long way to go out in the open. I think this is the only way."

"No, it can't be. I can't walk underneath them, Geoff… I can't… don't make me."

"You can, Bill. I'll be in front of you... don't look and just follow, okay?" He reached and took Bill's wrist. "We need to go now."

Bill picked up the duffel bag, and with Geoff's hand still on his wrist they rounded the corner, Geoff in front and Bill behind. "Keep your eyes on the floor," he instructed.

The drip, tick, drip, tick echoed off the icy stone walls of the alleyway. Five paces ahead of them was the first body. It hung from above, the legs trussed with a thick gold-metal chain which hung from high above over the top of the wall of the alley. The features of the face, even upside down, were set in a terrified grimace. Bloodshot eyes bulged out of the sockets and arms, half-eaten to the elbow-joint, hung loosely and were pointing at the floor where a puddle of entrails, intestines and blood pooled. The tick-sound came from one chain which had become tangled and made one of the six bodies twist mechanically in the air. The drip came from the contents of another one of the body's stomachs, a coil of yellow-pink sagging and twisted intestines had leaked where the pressure had caused the muscle to tear.

The alleyway smelled of shit, bile and vomit all laced together with an underlying stench of blood. Geoff ambled. The last thing he wanted was to slip and end up lying on the floor, looking up at the poor souls who hung above. He stopped as he approached the first body. He backed against the wall and shimmied around the puddle of gore on the floor. Bill followed – Geoff's hand gripped his wrist tighter now. It was a gruesome slalom, and Geoff wanted to get rid of his boots as soon as possible. The cramped alleyway seemed to close in tighter with the weight of the dead above them.

He refused to look at the last four bodies hanging above, instead using the putrid puddles to guide him. He saw a part-digested French-fry and his stomach lurched and he tasted sour bile. With his left hand he covered his nose and mouth and carried on leading Bill past the bodies towards the top of the alleyway.

When they went past the last body, they hopped the last two steps to the end of the alley. They took deep breaths of fresh air and looked back down the alleyway. From their elevated position, they could see the chains clearly. They were attached as one to a piece of bent and serrated-looking rusted piece of rebar at the top of the left-hand-side wall and then moved out like a spider web and wrapped around a further black length of rebar that stretched along the length of the alley.

"What could have done that?" asked Bill.

Geoff shook his head. "I don't know."

"Should we get them down?"

"I can't see how we can..." He turned away from the opening of the

58

alley and looked out over the empty car park and the Rec opposite.

The yellow and orange leaves contrasted against the green and brown field, which added colour to the otherwise cold and dead landscape. A thousand skeleton-like fingers stretched into the sky from the trees that lined the edges of both sides of the grass. The black paths were empty, as was the skate park, although he saw a black form lying on the ground. They only needed to follow the path, and it would take them to the police station.

A tall stone wall lined the path to their left with deep recesses and old green-wooden doors locked tight. They kept close as they approached the police station along the empty road. Across from them, a wide turn with large oak trees on either side led to the tennis courts and the bowling green. The police station stood silent on the corner.

The car park was empty. A brown wooden picket fence that surrounded it had fallen in one place – it looked as though it had been trampled into the mud. The station was a modern building compared to the rest of Westford's centre. It was two storeys tall with three gigantic windows on each level to the side of the steps that led to the large double blue doors. On the steps lay a half-eaten body. From where they stood, they could make out the mustard-yellow of a woollen coat and the exposed flesh of an arm extended down the steps.

They crossed the road in a jog and stood behind the vast oak tree. Bill's face was pale. Geoff stared at the body on the steps. Black puddles slunk across the ground. What happened here? Scattered remnants of autumn coats and carrier bags danced lazily in the breeze, their ends stuck in puddles and danced like a charmed snake. The weight of the gun felt good in his hands.

The body on the steps twitched. The extended arm shuddered. From the centre, a black creature lifted its head and sniffed at the air. Geoff ducked behind the tree, pushing himself up against Bill. He dared another glance. The creature had gone back to its feast, the body juddering as it nipped at flesh. He looked past the feeding creature and the twitching body. The door was closed, but he hoped it might be open. Where's safer than a police station? If they could get inside, they could lock the doors and find the radio room. The windows had bars over them. They just needed to get past the creature.

Using his hands, Geoff tried to explain the plan. Bill looked at him blankly. Geoff pointed at the police station again. Bill shook his head. Geoff nodded. He bent down and picked up a large rock from the dirt under the tree. He mimicked throwing it. Bill looked at the rock in his hand, then back to Geoff. Bill rolled his eyes, then took the rock. Geoff pointed towards the tennis courts and nodded. Bill weighed the distance in his mind. In an ideal world, Geoff thought, it would go over the crisscrossing green fence and onto the courts. Bill got in position, trying to use the cover of the tree, and then pelted the rock across the road.

It didn't make it over the fence – but it went through one of the diamond-shaped holes, landing with a soft bounce. Shit, the tennis courts were synthetic, which absorbed the sound. Then a ping broke the silence. It had hit the metal end which held the tattered net.

They ducked back behind the tree. Geoff looked around the side of the trunk towards the police station steps. The body was still. He couldn't see the creature. Bill shrugged at him and then mouthed: "Should we run?" Geoff checked the car park again. It was empty. Nothing moved except the pieces of clothing flickering like a candle in the breeze.

Something rustled above them in the tree. With no leaves for cover, they saw the creature above them almost camouflaged against the branches. They froze. It was on one of the top branches, at least 50 feet in the sky against the yellow-grey. They stared up as the creature drifted, purposely, with a sideways gait like a crab towards the end of the branch. Its weight caused the branch to bow at the end. It didn't know they were below. Geoff and Bil held their breath.

It jumped across the road, seeming to float in the sky like a leaf on the wind, and landed silently on the top of the stone wall of the extensive car park which led to the tennis courts. Still, they didn't move. It was twice the size of a rat and had hollow-looking spikes sticking up from its back. They watched as it slunk across the top of the wall, its feet leaving red stains on the grey stone.

Geoff tapped Bill's shoulder and nodded towards the station. They went around the tree trunk, turning their backs on the creature until they were facing the station. Geoff gave Bill a thumbs up. They sprinted across the muddy grass towards the gap in the fallen fence. Geoff looked behind him. The creature had disappeared from the wall.

Soft mud turned to splintered wood, turned to concrete as they entered the car park. They splashed through black puddles towards the steps. Geoff took them two at a time, jumping over the body. Blank blue eyes stared up at him. He reached the door first. It was locked. He looked back to check on Bill and behind him he saw two of the creatures stalking them from the other side of the fence.

The creatures approached the gap in the fence, even though they could have jumped it. They're playing with us, Geoff thought. Behind the creatures, on the roofs of the houses beyond, he saw inky shadows moving. There must be thousands of them.

Bill joined him at the top of the steps and they pushed and hammered against the blue door. Bill aimed his pistol, took a step back and then shot at the lock. The crash echoed. The door didn't give. Geoff watched as the creatures entered the car park. Their teeth were thin and sharp, and yellow eyes glinted in the grey. He looked up the building. There was a concrete balcony with blue-metal railings that led to a window. If they could climb, they could smash the window and board it up behind them. He wouldn't be able to lift Bill to reach it – Bill would have to push him up, and then he would run through the building and unlock the front door.

"Bill, the balcony. Give me a leg-up."

Bill looked up at the balcony and moved into place, putting the gun down the back of his jeans. Geoff raised his leg and put his red-stained and dripping boot into Bill's interlocked hands. With a grunt and a strength that surprised Geoff, Bill launched him into the sky. He caught the cold metal of one railing and pulled himself up, using Bill's wide shoulders for leverage. Without pausing, he raised the butt of his gun and smashed the window on the balcony. Again, the stillness of the day was shattered with the tinkling of broken glass. He looked behind him at the car park and saw the two creatures 20 feet from Bill. He ducked his head and dipped his shoulders before barging through the splinters of glass and cracked wood. It tore at his skin and cut the top of his head, but still he ran.

Having been in the police station before, he knew the way to the front door. He sprinted out of the office he'd landed in, skidded around a corner and jumped down the white stairs, landing with a grunt at the bottom. He picked himself up and ran to the desk and ruffled through paperwork and searched for the keys. Geoff pushed over a metal rack and ransacked the drawers beneath. Bill screamed from the other side of the door. Geoff looked up and saw the keys protruding from the lock. He sprinted around the side of the desk as another scream pierced the air, followed by a gunshot.

"Bill, hold on – I'm coming."

He reached the door and twisted the keys in the lock. Geoff heard a click and pulled. Still the door didn't budge. He looked up and saw a six-inch black-metal bolt. He reached and pulled it across and opened the door.

Bill fell backwards through the door. One of the creatures was attached to the lower half of his leg. The creature oozed purple blood out of a hole to the side of its body. Geoff took a step towards it and punted it like a rugby ball. The creature took a three-inch piece of flesh from Bill's calf with it, as it flew down the steps and into the car park. Bill screamed. Geoff reached under Bill's armpits and dragged him into the police station. Then he closed the door and bolted it again. Blood pooled under Bill's right leg.

"I'll be right back." He ran up the stairs towards the office he'd come through. At the window another creature stared in, testing the sharp shards of glass with its claws. Geoff ran at the creature with his gun raised. He fired twice, the first shot went wide spraying white splinters of paint and plaster over the creature and the second shot skimmed off the left side of its head. It didn't shriek or cry out. Geoff picked up a wooden chair that sat in front of the desk and launched it at the creature. It connected, and the chair and the creature fell to the floor. He ran to the window and peered down. Both creatures were at the top of the steps. Geoff turned around, searching for something to board the window with. The desk was wide and long. If he could turn it lengthways, it would cover most of the window. He ran his arm down the desk knocking paperwork and pictures flying, then he tipped the desk onto its side and pushed it up against the window. It covered the window, but with one push the creatures would be back inside. He stood with his back against the desk and surveyed the room again. A large, grey-metal cabinet stood in the corner. If he could push it over, it would be sturdy enough so he could at least check on Bill.

Using strength he didn't know he possessed, he shimmied the cabinet away from the wall and using his shoulders, moved it along the carpet towards the upturned desk. Once in place, he pushed and checked the sturdiness of his makeshift blockage. It should hold for now. He backed out of the trashed office, and with the keys he had brought up from downstairs, searched for the correct one for the office. Geoff locked the door on the third attempt and staggered down the corridor back towards Bill.

He left blood trails down the stair rails and as he reached Bill at the bottom, he fell to the floor next to his friend and passed out.

CHAPTER 14 – MR NEIL

Mr Neil looked past Jacob, who stood in front of him on the stairs, and at the girl and the two children on the stone floor at the bottom. Something's happened. Things were moving faster than they'd done before. The Vermin were more aggressive than usual. He'd heard legends passed down from hunter to hunter about them changing and evolving suddenly. Was he witnessing one of these moments?

Jacob sprinted down the stairs to his children, leaving Mr Neil and Mike staring after them. Mike looked at him and shrugged. Mr Neil searched his body's memories and returned the shrug while holding his hands out open, palms up.

They'd boarded the windows and the door to the room above, so the staircase was only lit by the stained-glass window behind them. An image of a once-bright, forlorn-looking saint stared down at them judgmentally. He heard Jacob at the bottom of the stairs whispering to his children. He saw the look between Jacob and the girl and thought they might be *mates* in the animal sense of the word.

Mike moved past him and down the stairs. Mr Neil followed, wanting to hear what happened, but trying not to show too much interest.

As he put his foot down on one of the stone steps, a shot echoed from outside. He turned towards the window and then back to the people at the bottom. Wide eyes stared back at him. They didn't move, waiting for another sound. They looked like petrified wood, unbreathing and long dead. Silence returned, only broken by a giggle from Sam.

"Musical statues," the boy giggled.

"That's right, baby, musical statues – your go again," Jacob whispered.

The boy grinned and stood up straight on one foot, using his hand for balance to stop himself from moving. He puffed his chest out, and the girl and Jacob lost their serious expressions and smiled at each other. Another shot rang out in the grey, empty world outside. Sam tripped and fell, and Jacob caught him before his head hit the floor. His face creased, wrinkles forming at his eyes as tears fell.

Jacob stroked the boy's hair and Nancy leaned in and rubbed his back. Jack watched them from Nancy's lap with a bubbly, wet smile. Another gunshot cracked the air, and they huddled together. Jacob enveloped the three of them in his arms. They looked towards the window and Nancy asked: "What's happening?"

"I don't know."

Mr Neil did. They weren't the only ones who'd ignored the advice to stay inside. With the change in the Vermin's behaviour, perhaps that was for the best. If this other group had a gun, maybe they should try to find them. Whether a human weapon would work on the Vermin was another question, but he'd rather have one weapon than none, especially seeing his comrades were yet to make their appearance. He smiled. Maybe the person with the gun was one of his comrades?

"Why are you smiling?" Mike asked him.

Mr Neil flushed red. Shit. Thinking fast, he replied: "It means there's someone else out there – someone with a weapon."

Silence. They looked at one another. He'd gotten away with it. Mr Neil decided the time to press on had come. "What did you see?" he asked Nancy. "You saw something, otherwise you would still be in the other room, am I right?"

"Those things came back, but there was something else." She looked uneasily to the door to the primary room. "They were like shadows of the creatures. They shimmered and then got lost among the shadows. They're in every doorway, watching… I know it."

Mr Neil pondered this information. These shadow-Vermin, as Nancy had described them, were new to him. Was this the next step of their evolution? He needed to contact his superiors. Someone who may know was going on.

"These things, they're in every doorway? You're sure?" he asked.

She nodded. "They're watching everywhere – what the fuck are these things?"

Jacob interrupted: "I don't know, and I don't think anyone in this room knows, but we have bigger problems. We're no longer hiding; we're trapped. I don't know about anyone else, but I have seen no food or water yet, you?"

Mr Neil had never been interrupted when speaking before, especially by a member of a species lower than himself. He glared at Jacob. These humans didn't know their place, there was a rebellious streak that ran through all of them. He sensed it in the man's mind he'd taken over; in the struggle to make the man commit the murder that let him, and in their sheer inability to carry out the simplest of orders. The situation was going south.

These particular humans were filthy, he could smell the stench of the remnants of chemicals coming from the woman's pores, and the children… the children… They shit and pissed in paper undergarments and waited to be changed by their elders. How had this species survived? They were disgusting and stupid. They'd escaped being trapped, only to trap themselves in an unknown building instead – now with no means for escape. At least the Vermin outside had a purpose. They were an enemy he had respect for. These humans were nothing, yet they had taken over this world and succeeded where countless others had tried and failed.

These four would be no help to him, but whoever was outside with the weapon just might. He'll need these four to get to them, and they just may be perfect as bait to help him slink through.

"Whoever that was, they have weapons. Perhaps we should think about leaving here and making our way to them?" he said.

"No. I didn't risk my children's lives to find safety, only to go chasing after someone with a gun back outside… They could be as dangerous as those things…"

"Maybe he's right," Mike started. "Jacob, I understand what you're saying, but look where we are. We have no food, no water, and we're trapped. If we stay here, we must leave within 24 hours anyway. Maybe we should take the chance."

"We haven't searched this place properly." Jacob turned to Nancy. "And Nancy used to work here, she knows where stuff is in here. I don't think we should give up on the safety of this place yet… And what about those shadow-creatures in every doorway? How long would we last out there?"

"It's true, the old sister who ran this place used to tell me stories about secret passageways and stuff – and I do know where the supplies are. I'm with Jacob. I say we stay." Nancy smiled at Jacob and hugged Jack close to her chest.

Mr Neil clenched his fists together. They were so stupid – they would listen to this chemical-smelling girl over him. Didn't they understand the situation? They were nothing, not even a microsecond of time in the universe. He didn't have time for this. If the Vermin were evolving, he couldn't sit around here with these stinking creatures. But he needed them; he needed their knowledge. The older man next to him touched his elbow. He turned to him and was led back up the stairs and around the corner at the top.

"I understand what you're saying, Mr Neil, but I also understand where Jacob is coming from," Mike leaned in closer to him. "We can't stay here for long either way, and I know I would feel safer with a gun than without."

Mr Neil nodded and Mike carried on. "Let's get the children safe, find some food and water, and then you and me go out there? That gunfire came from the police station, I'm certain of it, which means maybe an officer, or two survived. Maybe they locked themselves in and have an arsenal with them?"

"The police station. Are you sure?"

"Definitely, and they're more likely to let us in if there's only two of us, as opposed to two children and a junkie girl," his eyes had a wicked glint to them. "Yes, I know she's a junkie too – I think even Jacob does deep down."

Mr Neil took a second to search in his memory for the term, 'Junkie,' and his eyes opened wide when he found it. Yes, that was what the chemical smell was. We have drugs on our world too, he thought, but they're harder to get than here.

"Why don't we just go?" Mr Neil asked.

Mike frowned. Aatami thought he had gone too far. After a moment, Mike shook his head. "I can't… Jacob helped me and I want to help him, regardless if I don't agree with him."

Mr Neil put a hand on the old man's shoulder. "It's okay, we'll wait."

Mike folded in front of his eyes. He reached out and used Mr Neil's body to hold himself up. Mr Neil knew if he'd pushed, Mike would have left them now, but Mr Neil had a plan. By making Mike think he had made his own decision, he would be easier to conflict later and together they would leave and find the weapons at the police station. For now they would sit tight, explore this ancient building and who knew, the junkie-girl may even be telling the truth. Perhaps there was a secret tunnel that would lead him to where he needed to go. Patience was one of the most sought-after traits where he was from, and he liked to think he'd perfected the art.

"Are you okay to go back to them?" he asked Mike.

Mike reached out and touched his arm. "Yes, thank you, Mr Neil, let's go."

You're mine, he thought, as they rounded the corner and went back down the stone stairs.

"We shouldn't go back in there," Nancy said, glancing towards the large wooden door that led to the primary room.

"Don't worry, we won't," Jacob replied. He wasn't a fool. Nancy wasn't the type of woman he would let near his children in other circumstances, but she was the only mother-type figure available and if he knew one thing, at times like these, children needed a woman's motherly ways, more than a father's fun and games. "So, these secret passages, did the Sister say where they are?"

"It's always been a mystery. There are passages from Burghley House that lead to many places in Westford including here, the Priory, several churches and the Monk hotel."

"Wow, how have I never heard of these?"

"They have searched for them but were never found, so people figured they're just a myth." Jacob raised his eyebrows. "What? Because I'm a party girl I'm not allowed to know about the history of this town?"

Jacob raised his hands in front of him. "Sorry."

Nancy laughed as Jack nuzzled into her, and Sam fought for space to have a cuddle too. "Don't worry, I get it all the time." She placed a hand over his, and he let it rest there for a minute longer than necessary. Behind them they heard the echoing footsteps of Mike and Mr Neil as they came down the stairs.

"Everything okay?" Jacob asked without looking up.

"Fine… fine…" said Mike.

Nancy spoke again. "The Sister always said that the secret passages weren't easy to find – that there were certain clues to follow."

"Clues?" asked Mike.

"Yes, like a treasure hunt."

"We don't have time for games," said Mike. "We need to find a way out."

"Did the Sister give a hint or a starting point for these clues?" asked Jacob.

Nancy shook her head. "I never asked, just overheard them talking on one tour that came through."

"Well, they're definitely not above us, so that leaves down below." Jacob nodded towards the blocked wooden door to the cellar. "Mike, will you stay with the boys this time while Nancy, Mr Neil and I check it out?"

"Of course, Jacob," the old man replied.

Jacob went to the door and tried to shove the old church-style pew from in front of it. He grunted and looked towards Mr Neil who came over and helped. Nancy pulled from the other end. It made a loud scrape as the solid wood legs finally moved, and they all heaved together. They twisted it to the side, with Nancy's end against the wall, while the men's side pivoted out at an angle.

"That should be enough," Jacob said, as he reached for the dull-gold doorknob and twisted. It opened, creating an eight-inch crack of blackness that they could squeeze through into the cellar. He felt the coldness of the air escaping from the dark, and it brought his skin out in gooseflesh. Jacob turned back towards Mike, who sat in the middle of both his boys making his thumb disappear. He listened to the happy giggles of the boys as he turned back and slid through the gap into the darkness.

Nancy and Jacob lit the way using the torches on their mobile phones. The light was harsh, white and artificial in the natural dark below. The stone stairs were narrow; Jacob's size 10s too large by an inch, and his toes hung over the precipice. Each of their steps echoed in the darkness below. They heard a drip, drip, drip in the dark somewhere towards the back of the room.

The torches threw out wide beams of light. The room was cavernous, with big stone arches separating one room from the next. It was like a crypt. A pile of mould-stained wooden boxes slunk in the far corner of the first room, but nothing else. The pale stone walls shone in the torchlight, a wet reflection that refracted back. Jacob reached out and put his palm against the closest wall. "It's wet," he said.

Mr Neil and Nancy touched the wall too.

Jacob's mind flooded with images of horses and carts above, of hunters unloading carcasses of deer and rabbits down to keep cool. Of cheeses, butters and milk kept as fresh as possible. He sniffed, and it smelled faintly of the sea. Straw on the floor helped to grip on the slippery cobbles. There must be a cellar door above towards the edge of the building that opened towards the street for unloading, and if there was, then the stories of secret passages, may be true. Black splotches stained the cobbles. His chest tightened, and his throat grew small when he swallowed. Dry blood?

"Should we split up?" Mr Neil asked.

"Uhm... do you think that's wise?" Jacob asked.

"It seems like an enormous place... we might get through it quicker if we spread out."

"But you don't have a torch."

"I'll take yours, and then you and her can stay together?"

Nancy and Jacob looked at each other – they smiled; although they disagreed with splitting up, neither wanted to be alone down here.

Jacob handed his phone to Mr Neil, who took it and shone it around the dark cellar. "If I go that way, you guys can check out the rooms down there?" He pointed to the distance.

Nancy grabbed hold of Jacob, fitting her left arm through the hook in his right arm. It felt good to have bodily contact with someone warm down here in the cold dark. Jacob had become disorientated, and no longer knew which end of the building they were heading towards, but they needed to check out this cellar.

"If anything happens, call out, we'll be able to follow the echoes and find each other," said Jacob.

"Okay," Mr Neil replied. He stood, as if on attention, waiting for Jacob and the girl to leave towards the darkness. The surrounding light faded as their torch lit up a pathway away from him.

As soon as the light had faded, and he could no longer hear the echoes of their footfalls, he lowered himself to the icy floor and sat cross-legged like a yogi. He placed the phone flat on the ground, so the bright white light only escaped from the sides and he closed his eyes. He blanked out the cold on his bottom. A moment later an electrical hum came from his hands, which he held open, palms up, resting on his lap, followed by a glowing purple ball of light that throbbed from the size of a penny to a side plate. The centre of the light was bright, while the surrounding purple was deeper, leading to the fuzzy edges which grew, then shrunk in a steady beat. When Mr Neil opened his eyes, the purple reflected from the whites.

The ball of light floated in his lap, six inches above his open hands, and then raised to in front of his face. He whispered something, and it floated higher into the air. He stood, picked up the phone and watched as it made its way consciously around the walls of the cellar, lighting up the leaking stained and wet stone walls.

Aatami, in Mr Neil's body, followed the silent purple glow as it left the room and went into the next one which looked identical to the room he'd just come from. Identical. Everything in this world was identical. Shops were shops; identical in what they did, just not what they sold. Cars, bikes and buses all did the same job, they just looked different. And humans, well they were more alike to each other than anything else, each had their own mindless worries, their own small selfish thoughts, their own doubts and the same arrogance. But, and it was a big but, to save his world, he needed to save this one, just like the ones he'd saved before. Didn't mean he had to like it though, did it?

The purple ball of light floated around the edge of the room, only stopping to inspect a wall, but then started moving again. He was now entering the third room and getting closer to the direction Jacob and Nancy had gone. The cellar was silent, except for his own deep breaths when the ball of light stopped, and he thought it had found what he was looking for. Could that idiot junkie be right?

The light exited this room and entered another, Mr Neil lost it as it buzzed around the corner of a wall he hadn't seen. He inspected it with the torch and saw it was a fake wall that without closer inspection, he wouldn't have realised had a slim, dark passageway behind it. It was like a mirage in the wall, something only visible if you knew it was there. From inside, the purple glow led deep into a hidden tunnel. He felt no breeze as he entered sideways, leading along with his right shoulder.

He could leave. Now he knew these people had survived by blind luck, he could leave them to carry on surviving without him. There was nothing special or magical in their survival, nothing he could use in the long term or short term to defeat the Vermin. He could follow this passage to wherever it led and find his comrades and finish the job they were here for. The humans would think he'd either got lost in the tunnels or found his way out. Either way it didn't matter, he would be out there and they would be in here.

He felt a blinding pain of light in his shoulder. Something sharp sticking out from the wall had first scratched, then tore and ripped through the flesh where his arm and shoulder met and then lodged between the bones. Aatami moved gingerly, testing how stuck he was, and he felt a thousand nerve endings touch the ice-like lightning of whatever had impaled him. He took a sharp intake of breath and tried to settle his ever-faster heartbeat. He felt the blood pulsing through his suddenly red-hot ears. The purple light was fading ahead, and he'd dropped the phone when he'd impaled himself. It now sat torch light down in a puddle on the stone floor. He whispered into the dark, and the purple glow faded.

Mr Neil kicked out at the phone, trying to flip it over and give himself more light. He sent it further down the passageway. Fuck…

"Jacob… Nancy…?" He waited for the echoes to travel away from him down the thin passageway. His blood, that had been flowing down his shoulder and onto the floor, slowed to a drip, drip, drip. The rhythmic thudding of his pulse in his ears was the only sound left when the dripping slowed to once every 30 seconds and the echoes of his voice had died in the dark.

Fuck… He didn't know what was worse; the fact he'd have to wait for a junkie human to save him or the fact that he may just die here, alone in the dark without a body nearby to inhabit next. His vision acclimatised to the dark. There was nothing to see. He waited as the life of the man whose body he was in, dripped away into a dark pool on the floor and mingled with the ancient soft moss and ran through little channels in the cobbled-stone floor to an unknown river or pool somewhere further downstream and outside to where he was trying to go. If he could get free, he could heal himself, but not while he was still impaled. He lost consciousness, as the pulse in his ears stopped and he was left pinned to the wall in silent darkness.

CHAPTER 15 – THE COUNCILLOR

Geoff woke on the cold, polished grey floor. He was laying with his head on Bill's lap. His shirt had risen and the exposed flesh of his lower back felt numb from the icy floor. Bill was asleep. He had moved them up against the big white station desk while Geoff had been out and he now sat with his back propped up against it. His left leg was raised and sat atop a blue plastic box with the remains of Bill's coat wrapped around the calf. Bill had bandaged it himself, even though he was the injured one. The bandage had changed colour with the blood that had soaked it.

"Bill?" Geoff said, scared that the grey-ashen colour of Bill's skin foretold the passing of his friend.

Bill opened his eyes and looked down at Geoff. "I thought I'd lost you, boss."

"Never mind me, Bill, what about you? How long was I out for?"

"An hour or so, I think. I'm not sure, I've been a bit in and out of it, boss." Bill's eyes rolled back to show their yellowy-whites and then rolled forward again. "It's good to have you back," he said with a thin smile.

"It's good to be back. I take it from the silence they haven't got in?"

"No, it's been quiet since you passed out, kinda like they lost interest," Bill's head lolled forward and then snapped up again. "What were those things, boss?"

"I don't know, Bill, but thank God we brought those guns. I don't know what's going on, but we need to do something, the entire town is in danger."

"I don't think I can, boss, my leg…"

Geoff sat, careful not to lean on Bill. His back creaked and his legs cracked as he stood. He massaged his aching muscles and shook out the stiffness from sleeping on the cold, hard floor. The guns were at Bill's side and he smiled at his injured friend, before kneeling next to him.

He could smell the leg before he pulled the sticky, heavy coat away from it. A rotting, metallic meaty smell mixed in with the earthy odour of the wax coat. If he'd only been out an hour, then rot shouldn't have set in already. Did those things carry something? An infection of some sort, rabies maybe? Fuck, what have you got yourself into?

Bill tried to stay still as Geoff unwrapped the coat, but he lurched back against the desk as the first piece peeled away. The movement triggered a coughing fit that went on for 30 seconds. Geoff leaned away and dodged the flying spittle, his face flushed red after, ashamed. Bill needed his help, but he was already treating him like a leper. Something contagious to be avoided. He swallowed back the urge to avoid something potentially deadly and leaned forward over Bill again.

"It's okay, Bill, we'll get you some help."

The police station was silent except for the tick of the hand of the enormous clock behind the desk. They must hold medicine, antibiotics, something here in case of emergencies. It wasn't a city centre police station, that was for sure, but for emergencies they must have medicine, food, drink and weapons, a small arsenal maybe to go with the two pistols, shotgun and grenades.

"Bill, listen to me. I'll be right back, but I need to explore this place, I need to get food and water – will you be okay?"

Bill nodded, and on the last nod his chin fell and came to rest on his chest. Soft snores joined the tick, tick, tick of the clock. Geoff put the back of his hand against Bill's forehead. It was hot and clammy. An infection was working its way through his body fast.

He'd been here before, for photo opportunities, but once, years ago, he'd been shown around by the new chief inspector. The reception area was sterile, empty. A row of blue metal chairs was fixed to the wall opposite, with a barred window above. The walls were white and the tiled floor dark grey. He closed his eyes, trying to remember the route they'd walked and the rooms they had shown him, but came up blank. On the walls were blue stickers with arrows pointing in different directions: Toilets, interrogation room, locker room, temporary holding cells, offices and accommodation. The arrows for the offices and accommodation led upstairs, while the others pointed past the desk and towards the back of the ground floor of the building. With no power, the building was lit by emergency strip lighting, which hurt his eyes and reflected off the polished floor. He wished there was a manual, a way to know what to do in every situation, but life is life... There are no manuals.

"I'm just as likely to find medicine that will kill him or make him worse than to find the right antibiotics. But if I do nothing, he's as good as dead already," he muttered to himself, more to avoid the unsettling silence than anything else. "But then what, Geoff? Are you going to take him with you when you leave? Because you need to leave, you know that, don't you?"

Fuck, he hated himself sometimes. He knew he'd have to leave, of course he did. he would get Bill comfortable, maybe move him up to one of the offices that looks out over the Rec and set him up with a walky-talky. Geoff hoped he would last that long, but then he would have to leave, to check on his *flock*. Could he call them his flock if he was their councilman, not their priest? He thought he could call them what he wanted and the *flock* sounded right, it sounded righteous. And, boy, could he feel a righteous fire starting to burn inside him to sort this out and save his town.

He came to a plain-off-white door to his right with a thin, frosted window four inches wide running down the middle. A blue sticker sat above the window, just above head height. White letters spelled 'Locker room.' Geoff smiled. As good a place as any to start, and maybe, with a little of luck, one of the officers had a chest infection and kept antibiotics in their locker.

He turned the silver doorknob, it turned, and opened inwards. The room smelled of eucalyptus shower gel, anti-perspirant deodorant and something mildewy and wet beneath lingering on the still air. The pale-yellow tiles reminded him of a leisure centre swimming pool full of children running around in dirty swimming nappies. It was a room that wanted to be a clean place, but always came up wanting when compared to a bathroom at home.

A dirty white towel lay on one of the wooden benches that sat around the room in front of the dark blue metal lockers. One corner trailed to the ground and wept in a little puddle of water. All the lockers were shut, but Geoff smiled when he saw no padlocks on any of them. An officer would be seriously stupid to steal from a colleague in a police station. The lockers didn't have names on them, so he figured it was a free-for-all with whoever was on duty on the day. How many would be on duty in quiet Westford on a Monday morning?

He walked past the central bank of lockers the room ran around in an L-shape to where he assumed the showers were. Geoff could hear in his mind the sounds of PE changing rooms and the banter that came with it. But today it was silent except for the steady drip of a shower or a tap coming from the room beyond.

Geoff counted seven lockers on his right, running along the wall. Past the centre, on his left, was a row of toilet cubicles and a large mirror with three sinks. He guessed you could get to the shower room from the end of the central bank of lockers or from the sink and toilet area. There was no natural light entering the room, and in the emergency lighting it was dimmer than he'd imagined.

He tried the first locker on his right. It swung open with a noisy creak, but it was empty except for a balled-up receipt. He tried the next one and the next, but they were also empty except for the musty smell of wet towels. The fourth one was full: A pair of dark blue jeans, a black tee shirt and a checkered shirt hung from three hangers. At the bottom was a pair of tan boots and a dark green wash bag. Geoff pulled out the wash bag, unzipped it and rummaged through the contents. He lined up a mini bottle of yellow shower gel, a mini can of shaving foam, a toothbrush, a straight razor with a walnut handle and two tin-foil pill packets. Black writing across the foil said Propranolol. He sighed and creased his nose. Propranolol was something he was all too familiar with from his daughters troubled life so far. They would be no use to Bill. He pocketed them anyway along with the straight razor and kept on opening the doors of the lockers. A few of the lockers contained random items: an odd sock, a hairbrush and a rusted set of nail clippers, but nothing else of any use. The other lockers didn't contain any antibiotics. He sat on a bench with his back to the lockers in the centre of the room. He blew out his cheeks and stroked his grey-stubbled chin with his fingers. There would definitely be no antibiotics in the interrogation rooms, holding cells or toilets, so that left him with the only other option: Back upstairs to the offices and the accommodation rooms. Back the way he came. He had no interest in going into the showers, the steady drip didn't entice him to investigate as he remembered a particular scene from a book, and two subsequent films, that featured a young girl and lots of blood.

The corridor was as silent as he'd left it. The shiny grey floor reflected the emergency lighting. There was no smell, not even cleaning supplies. It was a long, wide corridor with three off-white doors on either side with blue stickers. At the end of the corridor was another grey wall and the alternative to go either left or right. He had a fleeting memory of a visit from before and of an officer telling him: "No point going down there, councillor, just the cells and toilets."

He turned back the way he came and made his way to Bill. At least he could check on him again before he went upstairs. As he rounded the corner towards the officer's front desk, he heard voices. Two voices. Geoff stopped just before he came into view of the front entrance. He ducked down and poked his head around the wall. The front foyer was empty, the door was shut and locked. Two voices? One sounded like Bill, the other was harsh and raspy, almost childlike if said child had ripped open his larynx with his fingernails. He stayed where he was, his head cocked towards the voices, listening.

"Let me in, I can save you," the raspy voice said.

"No, I don't want to, I won't let you…"

"It wasn't me who made the birds fall from the sky," the voice continued, "it's not just the Vermin that's out there you know…"

"What else is out there?" Bill's voice was shaking.

"The Beast, the one that controls the Vermin – he's always watching, he's been waiting, but I can stop him."

"I… I… I can't, I won't kill him even if it lets you in. I won't kill him."

"We'll see, he's listening you know, from just around the corner. Maybe if I ask him to let me in at the cost of your life your friend won't be so… stubborn."

Geoff gasped. The hairs on his arms stood up like long grass in the wind. He took a breath and stepped around the corner, pulling the gun from his belt as he did. Bill was alone. His eyes were closed and he was snoring. His eyelids flickered as if in a dream. An ashy-hue had settled over his skin. If it wasn't for the soft snores and the rise of his chest, he looked dead. He approached, holding the gun in both hands, keeping it pointed at the ground as he'd seen officers do in movies.

"Bill? Are you awake?"

Bill kept on snoring. Geoff leaned over him. A strange nutty odour, similar to almonds, came from his wound. He nudged him and Bill's eyes opened, looked around and then closed again, seemingly not seeing Geoff standing next to him. The infection was moving fast. Would antibiotics even do anything?

"Hold on, Bill," He turned towards the stairs and took them two at a time.

Geoff reached the top, saw the blue plastic sticker signs and ran towards the offices. He passed the room he'd boarded up and locked and moved onto the next one. Panic set in. He ran when he would have walked. His breath came in sharp hisses. His mind was racing, his senses heightened. His skin felt icy, but when he put his hand to it, he pulled it away, dripping with sweat. The tips of his fingers tingled. His breath got even shallower. It was coming, whatever it was, it was coming. It was already here. Was it already here? He put an arm against the wall to steady himself but missed it and slipped down it. His vision doubled and a dizziness came over him. It was here, it was inside, it had always been inside. He couldn't do this. He couldn't save Bill. he couldn't save himself. It was already here. It would kill him. It had killed Bill. Was Bill dead? No, he was snoring downstairs. Was he? Are you sure? Are you sure you're still alive? A black shadow, ever growing, swallowed the last of his mind. Terror. Cold. Silence. The smell of almonds. Blood. Infection. Death. Can't breathe.

He fell to the floor on all fours – retching, trying to breathe. Oily sweat soaked his shirt. It was cold. He couldn't take in any breaths. Geoff let more and more out of his empty lungs. He folded in two on to his side on the floor and lay there hugging himself. Waiting for it to pass. Sure if it did, he would find out he had died. This was hell. His vision blurred, the outer parts like a vignette. A figure approached. It looked like Bill. His breath caught and he sucked it in.

"Bill?" The black of a sole of a shoe came down into his vision and he passed out.

Rope dug into his wrists. His arms were tied behind his back to a bench in the locker room. He couldn't move his arms. Geoff sat with his back straight and his feet crossed and tied to the silver metal bars under the wooden bench. Across from him sat Bill.

His eyes were yellow and his skin looked thin, like greaseproof paper. How are you walking around? The smell of almonds followed him, and another smell almost chemical-like; ammonia? How are you not dead? Bill didn't raise his eyes to look at Geoff. He seemed to avoid his gaze. What's going on here? He remembered that other raspy voice. Has the infection sent you crazy?

"Hey, Bill…" he started, "who was your friend you were talking to in the foyer?"

Bill didn't look up. He didn't answer. It was only then Geoff saw Bill was turning something over in his hands. He recognised the walnut-handle. It was the straight-razor.

"Bill? I don't know what's going on, but you don't have to do this… I can get you help." Geoff heard the pleading in his voice and hated himself for it.

Bill said nothing. Geoff saw a thin line of bright greenish-yellow pus trail down Bill's bloodied trouser leg. It looked thick and creamy. The rest of the trouser leg was crusted over. How long had he been out? How long had they been in the police station? Antibiotics…

"Bill, we just need to find some antibiotics, we'll be able to knock out the infection."

Bill smiled, it was a rueful smile that didn't touch his eyes.

"I wish it was that easy, boss," he said, his voice breaking. "I don't want to, Geoff, you know I love you like an older brother."

"What are you talking about, Bill? You don't need to do anything…" Geoff kept his eyes on Bill, urging him to look into his own eyes. "Look at me, Bill. We'll find a way to fix this together, starting with fixing you and then fixing the rest of the town."

Bill chuckled, but then looked to his side. Geoff saw him bite his bottom lip, trying to control the tears that he could see forming in his yellow infected eyes.

"I don't understand it, boss, I don't know why it wants me to do what it wants me to do, but it can heal me and save the town… tell me, would you do it if it meant sacrificing just one life, you would, wouldn't you?"

"What are you talking about, Bill, you're sick. One of those things has left an infection inside of you. You're sick, that's all – it's fever."

"I don't think so, Geoff, not this time. I can sense it, it's so powerful… I'm going to go now, boss. I'm sorry, but it's for the best of Westford." He looked up into Geoff's eyes for the first time, and Geoff saw the sorrow in them. "Do it," Bill spat. His mouth opened into a twisted grin, showing his teeth.

"Bill," Geoff screamed. He scrambled on the bench, but the ropes were too tight. The best he could do was shuffle his body from side to side. Geoff saw thick screwheads in the wood. Bill stood opposite him. His skin was turning pink and healthy again. Then the eyes changed colour. Geoff saw a green light behind them. He screamed and fought as Bill opened the straight-razor and approached. He looked up at his old friend. He wouldn't cry. He wouldn't beg.

With a flick of his wrist, Bill opened the thin skin of Geoff's throat in one long paper-cut-like line which was thin and black at first before it folded open. Hot metallic-smelling blood erupted out of the wound and covered Bill from head to toe. She watched as the life left the man's body. She didn't know who he was, nor did she care. She didn't care about the man whose body she was now in control of either. She had work to do.

PART TWO

CHAPTER ONE – BILL

The town was in a shit state. She'd never known it to happen so fast. Could it mean the Beast was here? In other worlds it was an insidious takeover, something they could covertly stop, but here it was like an all-out, full-blown invasion. There was no subtlety, no cuteness from the Vermin. No one had seen the Beast for centuries. If it was here, something big was happening. This wasn't a standard hive-style invasion.

Where were her Comrades? She'd had one body, but she lost it in the attack at the police station. So, she'd waited like a ghost, wandering the halls of a long-abandoned house. Then the two men entered. It hadn't taken her long to sow the seeds of doubt, and sensing death approaching, it hadn't been hard to coerce the man into letting her in, and with the other man's death, she had locked herself in tight to this body.

The black bag containing primitive explosives had been a pleasant surprise, as had the two pistols and the shotgun. Armed, she now needed to find her Comrades and work on a plan. They needed to get a warning back to command. They needed back-up.

She was on the top floor in the office the man called Geoff had boarded up. The stench of death that reminded her of battlefields and war was on the breeze that blew in through the smashed window. The Vermin had gone, but she knew the shadow Vermin still kept watch, so she moved silently through the office towards the window. She wanted to see what was happening outside. She couldn't sense her Comrades yet, but if she could see outside, she could send out a beacon to find them and to show them her location.

She peered around the desk blocking the window and looked out into the empty world. Nothing moved. Across the road, past the dull, leafless trees, was the sizeable piece of grassland the man called the Rec. She saw red tarmac tennis courts which contrasted against the green of the grass and the grey of the sky. Nothing was bright. Was it always this grey, this lifeless? The cloud that hung heavy on the day, did it ever clear and let the sunlight through? She longed for her own world.

A ball of glowing green light materialised between her hands. It throbbed as if it had a heartbeat. She turned her right hand, so the palm was face up. With a flick of her fingers the ball lifted into the air, floated between the gap in the window and split in two. One of the green orbs shot into the sky above the police station, while the other moved towards the town centre.

Dinah, for that was her name, watched the green light as it moved along the old stone wall and down the alleyway where she sensed death. She entered the ball of light, seeing what it saw – flesh and gore with bodies hanging above. This wasn't the Vermin. The Beast was here. Back in the office, a slight smile stretched over Bill's face.

CHAPTER TWO – JACOB

Jacob and Nancy heard the echoes of Mr Neil and followed them back through the cavernous maze of the cellar.

"Mr Neil? Where are you?" Nancy called. There was no reply. Perhaps he was lost. The dark of the cellar suited him. She sensed a darkness in him. Something not quite right, not wholly good.

They'd found little on their search of the back rooms of the cellar. A few boxes were scattered in the corner of one of the rooms, but they were empty. If there was a passageway, it was well hidden. There had been no white rectangular light that could have been the hinges of a cellar door to the world above.

"Mr Neil," Jacob called this time, his deeper voice reverberating off the icy stone walls. Every room they passed through was empty. The glow of Mr Neil's phone torch was nowhere to be seen. Jacob put out an arm to stop Nancy.

"Listen," he said. "Do you hear that?"

They stood side-by-side stock still. Listening for any sounds that came from one of the rooms.

"I don… "

Jacob put his fingers to his lips. "There it is again. Did you hear it?"

"What?" she replied, but then she heard it. A scraping sound. "Is it one of those things?"

"No, at least I hope not." He pointed the torch through to another room. "I think it came from over there."

Nancy linked her arm back through his and they moved together with the torch held out in front of them. Shadows enveloped them from behind as they moved forward. They walked through the archway and into the other room. It was empty. They turned in a small circle, checking all the walls, but there was nothing there. Then they heard the scrape again.

"I don't get it, now it's back that way?" Nancy said.

"Let's take a step at a time towards it."

They moved as one in the sound's direction and then stopped and waited for it again. Jacob could hear Nancy breathing, then he felt her tighten her grip on his arm. They took another step towards the sound. This time, as they stood in silence, Jacob turned off the torch.

"It'll heighten our sense of sound."

"But it's so dark," she said, holding on to him tighter.

The scrape seemed louder in the pitch black. Jacob heard Nancy's breath quicken. He tried to control his. The darkness was absolute. He didn't know if his eyes were open or closed, but it increased his other senses. He could smell the earthiness of the cellar he had lost before and the scrape, when it came, was in a clear direction. Time stopped, as one step at a time, they made their way through the black.

"It's right in front of us," Nancy spoke, causing Jacob to jump back a pace. "And I feel a breeze – do you feel it?"

Jacob raised his right hand in front of him as if he were a blind man. His palm was sweaty and warm, but as he held it out, he felt the flicker of an icy breeze on his hand. "I feel it. Should I turn the torch back on?"

"Yes, point it right in front of us."

He unlocked the screen, and the glow lit up his face. He turned to Nancy and smiled. With a few taps on the screen, the bright white of the torchlight lit up the space in front of them. He heard Nancy gasp. He moved backs and shone the beam along the wall.

"I'll be damned." He took a step to the side, just before the entrance to the room, and shook his head. "It's a hidden passage – from any other angle you can't see it, unless you are in this exact position head-on."

Nancy followed Jacob and saw it too. Jacob shone his light down the concealed passageway. Ten metres down he saw the silhouette of a man. His skin turned cold and clammy. It was as though someone had hung him on a coat hanger. The scrape was the toe of one of the man's shoes against the cobblestones.

"Mr Neil, is that you? Are you okay?" No answer. He turned the torch to both sides of the passageway walls and followed it down. "It gets narrower the further you get in," he said. "Mr Neil, are you stuck?"

Nancy slid under Jacob's arm and peered down the passage. "I can squeeze down there, Jacob." She looked at him earnestly. "If he's stuck, he needs help, and you won't fit." She didn't want to help him, but she couldn't leave him there. Alone in the dark.

Jacob closed his eyes and blew out a breath. "I don't like it. Why is his body sitting like that?"

"That's what I will find out. Give me your phone," she answered.

Jacob relented and held out the phone. "I'll be right here. If it gets too tight, don't get stuck yourself."

She stood on her tiptoes and leaned in and kissed him on his cheek. His eyes opened wide.

"Thanks for caring. I mean that, it means a lot." And with those last words, and with the touch of her lips still lingering on his cheeks, she turned and started down the alleyway towards the body.

He heard them, but he couldn't move. He couldn't make a sound. If he spent any more energy, he would die. These bodies were weak and fragile, yet robust at the same time. He knew if he waited and if someone came, this body could fix itself and with a little of his own magic, he could fix himself even faster.

He'd turned his leg into a pendulum using a rusted nail in the wall and the fabric of the trouser leg. Every 30 seconds his foot would scrape against the floor, and he hoped it was loud enough for someone to hear. If he died, he would be trapped within a certain range of this building and he wasn't hopeful he'd be able to coerce anyone else to let him into their body.

He needed to survive, and his survival now depended on the humans he'd decided were expendable. If he'd had irony on his world, he would have grinned for he wasn't always serious and without humour – he made his wife and children smile when he was with them.

It had worked. They were coming. Jacob wouldn't fit. He didn't have much faith in the junkie girl. He thought she would talk Jacob into leaving him, and who could blame her. And yet, from his left, he heard the scuffs and grunts of someone approaching. Not only hadn't she argued, but she'd come at once. Had he misjudged her, or judged her too soon? Had he been too quick to write off their entire race?

There was something else, another reason he needed to live. He'd felt one of his Comrades – one of them was close. From this distance, he couldn't tell who, and it didn't matter. If he could heal himself, he could release his pulse and find them. Together they could regroup and come up with a plan. He hoped they'd fared better than he had.

From down the passageway he could hear the girl's breathing now. She was getting closer. He hoped she had water. His throat was dry and his shoulder was numb, both of which were bliss compared to the sting of his frayed nerves every time he moved. The pain would get worse before it got better. She would have to rip him down. The metal bar had cut through his flesh and lodged itself between his shoulder bones. He would have to be pulled free. The bone would splinter and chip, and the exposed nerves would spread electricity through his veins. Would he survive that pain?

"Mr Neil, is that you? It's me, Nancy."

He turned his head and was blinded by a brilliant white light. Mr Neil saw all the features of her face drop at once as she saw him.

"That bad, huh?" he mumbled.

"Are you hurt or just stuck?"

"Both. I've lost a lot of blood, something jabbed me. It's still got me hooked."

"I can't get around you to look, this passage is too small. Do you know what it is, how bad it is?"

"Metal, maybe rebar... it's pretty bad."

Her eyes changed. Nancy's features hardened, and he realised how tough she was. He had underestimated her. "What were you doing down here on your own? Why didn't you call us?"

"I was checking it wasn't just a dead end."

Her eyes narrowed. He realised she trusted him as little as he trusted her.

"Well, Jacob isn't going to fit down here, so if you can handle being rescued by a girl let's get on with it."

He had the impression she would like the pain she was about to impress upon him. Was there a choice? "Do it," he whispered. "Nancy... do it fast and do it hard."

She squeezed in closer to him. He could smell the drugs coming from her body, they were weaker now, more diluted by her own scent. She wasn't afraid.

"Look at me," she said, and touched his sweaty cheek. "On three, I am going to yank hard. Now tell me, when I yank, should I pull down or up, as well as to the side?"

He thought about the question. The metal had entered him from above his shoulder blade before moving down and lodging itself between the two bones in his shoulder.

"Down and towards you. And Nancy... do it hard. The metal has got stuck between my bones."

He thought he saw the briefest flicker of doubt in her eyes, but then it was gone. She moved her arms around his body in an awkward sideways cuddle, before interlocking her fingers under his right armpit.

"Ready?" she said. "One, tw..."

Pain flashed through his mind. A blinding white pain shot from his shoulder, through his body, and erupted in his mind. He heard the creak and crunch as dull ridges in the metal lodged against the bone and scratched down, taking out little notches he felt but would never see. His fingers and toes splayed open with shock. A film of oily sweat broke out over his body. He flashed red hot and then cold. Then he felt a release. The metal was out.

His shoulder was free. He slumped to the floor on top of Nancy. Spittle fell from his mouth as he held onto consciousness like an alcoholic holding onto the last drop of whisky. He lost the fight, but a hard slap brought him back to. He was on top of Nancy as his weight had pinned her down. She tried to push him up, but only his chest moved higher.

"Get off me," she screamed.

"Nancy?" Jacob shouted from the entrance of the passage.

At the sound of Jacob's voice, Mr Neil found a source of energy. It was a sensation he'd never felt before. Adrenaline. He heard the whump, whump, whump from his fast-beating pulse in his ears. He pushed himself up from on top of Nancy, who took a deep breath and said: "Thanks." She got to her feet, and they stood in the harsh white of the phone's torch. He leaned on her, and she took his weight.

"Are you okay?" she asked, her own face had turned grey. "The sound of your bone…"

"I'm okay," he replied. "Let's get out of here."

Nancy went first with the phone out in front of her to avoid another accident, while Mr Neil stayed close with his good arm wrapped around her shoulders and neck. It amazed him his feet were walking. Adrenaline, he thought, I'll have to remember this stuff. The passage got wider as they got closer to the entrance. They could see the whites of Jacob's eyes at the end, staring at them.

"What happened?"

They emerged from the passageway and collapsed to the floor in a heap. Jacob knelt next to them. He took the phone and inspected Mr Neil.

"Your shoulder."

"It'll be okay, I just need to rest." He turned to Nancy and said: "Thank you, you saved me." And with that he passed out again.

It was a fever dream. He'd never dreamt before. His body ran hot and then cold. thick sweat emerged from every pore and soaked his body. His limbs shook. Aatami opened his eyes. He was on the stone floor in the corridor with the staircase. On turning his head, he saw Jacob, Nancy, Mike and the two boys sat on the stairs. None of them spoke. Jacob sat with his head in his hands, and Nancy dozed on his shoulder.

"Hey," he said, the sound of his hoarse, weak voice scared him.

Nancy opened her eyes and raised her head. Jacob jumped from the stairs and rushed to his side.

"You're awake? We didn't know if you were too far gone?" Jacob said.

"Water?"

"I'll get some, drink it slow though, we don't have much left and you've been out for a while." Jacob turned to the stairs and reached to Mike, who passed him a couple of half-full bottles of water, careful not to wake the sleeping child on his lap. Mike ruffled Sam's hair as he did. Jacob said, "Stay with uncle Mike for me a little longer. Mr Neil's poorly, okay?" Sam nodded sleepily at him. "Good boy."

Nancy knelt next to Mr Neil and poured the water slowly into Mr Neil's mouth, careful not to waste any. She inspected Mr Neil's shoulder. She had bandaged it as good as she could with what she had in her handbag – which was a purple scrunchie and a small yellow-silk scarf. A dented metal hip flask containing vodka – a gift from her dad – had proved useful as she poured the alcohol over the wound. Because of his position in the passage, his blood had started to clot. She thought he would live. They just needed to watch for infection.

She knew the difference between an adrenaline comedown and an infection, and, so far, Mr Neil was a very lucky man.

"You're going to be okay," she said. "You're very lucky to be alive, but you will be okay."

Maybe he was still dreaming? Nancy had saved him once and then continued to save him. Was this humanity? A natural caring for your fellow person, without prejudice and with deep compassion. If he'd been injured in his world, he'd be left to care for himself. A form of Ka. If he made it through, there'd be trials to see if he could still contribute, and if he couldn't, he would be sent to the wilderness.

"Thank you," he said.

"It's nothing."

"Luckily for you, Nancy seems somewhat skilled in treating people, and that handbag of hers is full of useful supplies." Jacob pulled out a foil packet and popped two blue pills through the tinfoil. "Take these…" he said, offering the water again.

Mr Neil swallowed the pills and laid his head back. Someone had created a pillow for him from a jacket. The sensation at the back of his mind was still there. One of his Comrades was close, but he couldn't send out his light to find them, not in front of Jacob, Nancy, Mike or the boys. His magic wasn't strong enough, yet. He'd have to give it some time. His shoulder throbbed, but otherwise felt numb. Probably whatever those pills were. His magic wasn't strong enough to send out a pulse, however, it was strong enough to increase the speed of his recovery. Warmth spread through his body.

"Rest," Nancy said and touched his chest.

Jacob and Nancy joined Mike and the boys back at the stairs. They walked past them and made their way to the top and around the corner, out of sight. Mr Neil closed his eyes and fell back into a dream-filled sleep.

Nancy took Jacob's hand. "We don't have enough water or food, we're still in the same position we were in, only now, if we don't get help, that man down there may die."

Jacob rubbed his stubbled cheeks with his other hand and pursed his lips. He knew the situation, he didn't need to be told, but that didn't help. Jacob already knew what she was going to suggest.

"I can fit."

He sighed. "I know you can, but look what happened to Mr Neil... what if that happens to you? No one can come in after you. I'm too big, as is Mike, and the boys are too young."

"I'll be careful. Trust me, I don't want to go, but if I don't, we'll have no choice but to either go outside or starve."

He shook his head. "I don't like it, there has to be another way?"

"We've barely got any water left, and even less food..." She reached up and cupped his chin in her hand and turned his gaze towards her. "I can do this. I don't need to ask permission, you know?"

"I know."

"You're a kind man, Jacob. A wonderful dad, you remind me of mine. He was a moral guy, but always struggled to make a hard choice, so I will make this one for all of us... I'm going."

He reached out and touched her cheek. It was warm and homely. She'd changed in the few hours they'd known each other. She wasn't who he'd thought she was, and he felt a flash of guilt for judging someone so fast. "Maybe after this, you'll let me take you for a drink?" he asked.

She stood on her tiptoes to reach him and put her other hand on his cheek. He moved in closer with one hand on her cheek and the other on her side, and they kissed. He felt calm despite the stirring inside. A sense of something natural and meant to be. He opened his eyes as she pulled away from the kiss. Hers were already open, piercing hazel looking deep inside him. She smiled and turned from him and went back down the stairs. Jacob sighed, swallowed and took a moment before following her down towards Mike, Sam and Jack. Thoughts of something he'd once read lingering in the back of his mind. *The third love is the one that feels like home with no rhyme or reason; the love that isn't like a thunderstorm at sea – but rather the quiet peace of the ocean the night after. The one we never see coming. The one that lasts. The one that shows us why it never worked out before.*

With each step he took down to his children, he let the kiss fade but kept it in his memory. He couldn't do this now. After this was over, maybe, but right now all he could do was keep everyone safe. The feelings for Nancy wouldn't go away. They'd still be there waiting for him after this was over. There was a time for love, and perhaps there was no better time for it than now, but he had responsibilities. Fatherly responsibilities.

Nancy was already at the bottom of the stairs. Was she going so soon? She was rummaging through her handbag, pulling out objects and putting them in her jeans and coat pockets. He watched her from above. She moved with purpose as if she stopped now, she'd change her mind. Sam and Jack were both asleep. Mike watched Nancy and turned his head to Jacob and mouthed: "What's going on?"

He came down two more steps and sat. Jacob looked at both his boys, safe and comfortable on Mike. An immense sense of gratitude came over him. A gratitude towards all the people in this room. "She's going through the passage."

Mike nodded. "I thought as much. What are we going to do?"

"Wait, I guess." Jacob leaned his head back against the stone wall.

CHAPTER THREE – DINAH/BILL

No one came. Eyes blank and seeing through the green orb, she saw nothing move in the town centre. She could sense one of her Comrades close by, but she couldn't zone in on them. The signal (for lack of a better word) was weak, as if their energy was depleted.

Had the Vermin wiped her team out? She'd already lost one body. Was it possible, if not probable, that they'd been targeted as they came into being. Were the spirits of her Comrades still lurking, waiting for a host to inhabit? It was only luck that she got this new body. The Vermin could have travelled to any time or place, but they'd come here to this town at this time on this world. This wasn't a standard invasion – the Beast must be here.

No one came. Eyes blank and seeing through the green orb, she saw nothing move in the town centre. She could sense one of her Comrades close by, but she couldn't zone in on them. The signal (for lack of a better word) was weak, as if their energy was depleted.

Had the Vermin wiped her team out? She'd already lost one body. Was it possible, if not probable, that they'd been targeted as they came into being. Were the spirits of her Comrades still lurking, waiting for a host to inhabit? It was only luck that she got this new body. The Vermin could have travelled to any time or place, but they'd come here to this town at this time on this world. This wasn't a standard invasion – the Beast must be here.

If she could find just one of her Comrades, she'd feel better, stronger. She was the strongest of the five, but that didn't count for much if she came upon the Beast alone. Her magic would be like a slowly trickling stream opposed to the power of the ocean. Strength in numbers.

She had seen none of the Vermin from the top floor office window. They would station the shadow Vermin in every doorway, watching. If she moved, they'd attack and, sensing who she was, they'd attack in numbers like they had the first time in her first body. The policeman's body. The reason the Vermin had attacked the police station was her. Like a shark smelling blood, they'd known she was there. The streets were quiet now for this reason. The dead man had put out a message to stay indoors and the residents' seemed to have done just that... or they were all dead.

If she couldn't go out on the streets, could she go under the streets? Closing her eyes, she took control of the orb which was hovering above Broad Leaf square. It hummed in the air and then zoomed down towards the cobbled floor before finding a drain. It swooshed between the black metal bars and entered the subterranean world of Westford.

Among the channels of the rank sewerage system which she followed back to the police station, she sensed a larger space, a dry space without running water. Her light found a way through a crack and entered a tunnel. She left the orb to explore as she came back to Bill's body. A smile passed over her face. A hidden underground system? She searched the man's mind and found a few snippets of conversation with the dead man in his office.

"It's a myth, Bill, you know better than that." Geoff's body was leaner and his hair a little darker.

"I know, but wouldn't it be cool? It would make a splendid story and would be great for the next election. I can see the headlines: 'Local councillor finds hidden historical passages and commits funds to explore'. It would show the locals how much you care about the place."

Geoff leaned back in his chair. "It would be great for tourism too, but they're a myth. There are no hidden tunnels, otherwise they'd have been found already. You sound like my daughter."

"There's a book, I have it in my bag; it says that one tunnel leads from the Monk Hotel all the way up to Burghley House, imagine it..."

"Bill, it's a brilliant idea, it really is. But we need something more concrete than myths of underground tunnels to win the next election. Please, let's move on."

The door to Geoff's office opened without announcement and a moody-looking teenage girl walked in. She walked around the desk and draped her arms around Geoff's neck. She looked up at Bill and gave him a wink.

"Hi, Daddy. You know you love me, right?"

"How much do you need?" he sighed.

"A hundred, please, Daddy, it's for a new dress for the party..."

Geoff reached into his trouser pocket and pulled out a brown leather wallet. Inside were a selection of notes. He pulled out five and counted them into her hands. She kissed him on the cheek and giggled: "Thanks, Daddy."

If only you knew where that money was really going, thought Bill.

Then the memory ended.

Not a lot to go on, she thought. But it's something, and down below my light has found the tunnels. They are real. Soon the orb will return, having mapped out the maze below. Dinah sat down behind the large wooden desk and leaned back in the brown leather reclining chair. She waited. One thing she was good at was waiting patiently for the right moment.

CHAPTER FOUR – NANCY

It was dark in the tunnel. Damp dust and wet mould tipped every wall she'd touched. She moved her hand to her finger and pulled it away, grimacing.

Behind her, at the entrance, stood Jacob on his own. She'd turned around once, but wouldn't turn again. She would keep on moving forward. She wanted to go, not because she was the only one who would fit, but because it's what her dad would have done. After disappointing him for so long, she wanted him to be proud of her; she wanted to be someone more than just his junkie daughter.

The passage got thinner as she got deeper. The two inches she'd had on either side was down to just one. Silver dust flecked and floated in front of the flash of the torch in front of her. Nancy could see the stained and bloodied piece of black metal rebar that had punctured Mr Neil. Beneath the rebar she could see a puddle. The passage smelled of earth and damp. She reached out and touched the old stone wall to her side. It felt cold and wet and crumbled under her touch.

In 50 yards she'd have to turn sideways to get through the thinnest part of the tunnel. Above her black beams, splintered and cracked, held up the packed-in dirt. Her heartbeat pounded in her chest and her mouth went dry. She felt a tremor through her body, but closed her eyes, took a deep breath and steadied herself.

"Are you okay?" Jacob asked. As he did, a few pieces of dirt fell from above and into her hair. She scrambled and flicked her hair. Her skin flushed as she swallowed a piece of dirt and choked – or at least felt as if she was choking; for as soon as the sensation appeared, it disappeared. Her breaths came fast and shallow, and white lights exploded in the dark before her like fireworks.

"Nancy?" he called again.

She turned towards him, her left shoulder bumping into the wall just inches from where the rebar impaled Mr Neil. The realisation of the close call of impaling herself snapped her out of the panic rising inside her.

"Stop shouting," she whispered. "It's not stable… I'm fine."

Nancy imagined the sad puppy-dog look on his face and longed to go towards him and the safety of the old building, but they were depending on her now. She needed to follow the passage and find help.

The piece of metal stuck out the wall opposite her as she kept it to her front and moved along the wall with her back against it. Once she passed the metal, she kept moving. The tunnel had a gentle curve she hadn't noticed until she looked behind her and realised she couldn't see the entrance anymore. She was alone. Surrounded by compacted dirt.

Sideways, with her back against the wall, both sides pressed in around her, crushing her breasts. She felt the chilly dampness of the walls through her clothes and deep into her body down to her bones. Nancy fought to control her breathing, to keep calm.

The white light from the phone lit up the stone walls and the dirt above her head, but it didn't throw light any further than six feet ahead of her. The wall pushed against her back, jutting out. Sharp stones dug into her lower back near the kidneys. Her breath caught in her throat as she got stuck. Her right foot refused to move and cross over her left. The whump, whump, whump of her heartbeat increased like a train pulling out of the station. She wiggled her foot. Her shoe came loose. She slipped it back into the warmth and tried again. Turning it to an odd angle. The wall let go, and she stumbled a few steps further into the dark.

She stopped and leaned her head against the wall. Controlling her breathing. Fighting back tears. She'd never been a crier, hadn't even cried the first time her father found out about her drug use and sent her to rehab. She was a realist. *Fuck, the situations you get yourself into, you useless girl.* How long had she been in the passage? *Not as long as it took you to get into a mess with the wrong guy.* Ha! Good old internal monologue. She thought the voice had gone after that first stint in rehab, but after six weeks it raised its smiling head. *Go on, Nancy, just a little bump, why not? Or just a small glass of wine?*

She no longer believed it would ever go away, but she could quieten it by doing what it says. The drugs must nearly be out of her system, if it was talking again now. Egging her on to find more. *Fuck that stupid guy and his snotty kids, fuck the dying man and the weird neighbour, let's get out of here and find a party…*

"Shut up," she whispered. The echo spirited itself off the walls and into the dark ahead, and after a second, came back speeding past her like a hurricane towards Jacob at the entrance to the passage. Nancy saw a wall ahead. Please don't be a dead end, not after all of this. *Dead end, sounds just like your life, ha!*

Nancy flashed the torch towards the end of the tunnel. Something deflected her light from a rectangular piece of wall. It was three-inches high by 12 inches long at chest height. She was too far away to see what it was. Then the tunnel grew wider and released her from the side. Taking a deep breath, enjoying the sensation of her diaphragm expanding, she walked the last few feet. Dead end!

The stone wall felt cold and dry beneath her fingers. She dragged her hands over the smooth rock and then settled on the ice-cold metal. It was corroded in the corners, as if becoming one with the stone and the earth. She could feel engraved letters under her fingers. She shone the light onto the plaque. It was brass. The letters that had once been engraved into the brown metal had long since eroded, leaving behind sharp tears and a greenish-white not-quite rust that coloured her fingers. Arrows. She was certain she saw the shape of two arrows – like the ones from a bow and arrow – one pointing left and the other right. The words above were well worn, but underneath one said 'Tristan's arrows,' and underneath the other, 'Fail-not.' She moved the torch to the right and then to the left. Nancy saw a darkness in both directions. *Whichever one you choose will be wrong, Nancy. You're going to die down here.*

Which way had she come? She tried to picture the tunnel as if she was on the ground floor. Was she still under the old hospital? Which way had the tunnel curved? Above her, was there grey daylight of the street or the gloomy interior of Locke's hospital, or had she gone farther than she thought?

Nancy didn't fancy going back through the tight tunnel. She shone the torch down both passages. They looked identical. Green moss-covered cobbles; black dirt above held up with beams and dripping wet stone walls on either side. She felt the cold shadows surround her when she moved the torch. She licked the tip of her index finger, a trick her dad had taught her, and held it up to both passages. Her finger felt an icy breeze towards the right tunnel and she was sure she felt it caress her face like frostbitten fingers.

With one last glance behind her, she took a step down the right tunnel, the one which said, 'Tristan's arrows.' It was much the same as the last tunnel, only wider. The stories were genuine – there were secret passages under Westford. So many times she'd been told they were just a myth, but here she was. No one had set foot down here for centuries, or decades at least. With the thrill of exploring, the voice at the back of her mind had been silenced, as had the usual cravings.

A scuttling sound ahead made her stop. She froze in place. Sweat breaking out on her forehead. The sound came again. The thought of running came, but she couldn't move her feet. It was if she'd stepped into quick-dry cement. She held the torch still – afraid to move it and guide the sound closer. Her breath turned into vapour in front of her.

The sound came again, further away this time. Was it going in the opposite direction? It could be a rat, or a mouse? She felt stupid for being so full of fear. It was moving away, but in the dark she couldn't tell how far. She expected to see a pair of glowing yellow eyes in the dark at any moment. The fear was more annoying than the other voice. Shut up, shut up, shut up, she wanted to scream. The torch turned itself off. She was left in pitch black. Her heart missed a beat before returning to a steady, if fast, beat. Nancy turned the screen and saw the battery was down to 10 per cent. The phone must have an automatic turn off to conserve power. The screen was dimmer too, barely throwing out any light into the black.

She reached into the back pocket of her jeans and pulled out a gold zippo lighter. The smell of petrol filled the tunnel as she flicked it and lit up the passage in orange, flickering light. The shadows bounced and spat against the oddly-shaped stone as if the walls were alive. Her breathing was shallow and fast. The breeze from the tunnel made the flame bend towards her. She moved. The urge to get out and back into an open-space, ideally above ground, was larger than the urge to stand still, waiting to be saved. There was no one to save her. She'd never been the sort to ask for help, anyway.

She moved forward with more urgency than before. If her lighter ran out of fuel, she would be in pitch black. The passage didn't seem to go anywhere. The lighter was getting hot in her hand and she needed to stop and let it cool down. Should she turn back towards the T-junction with the brass sign? The cobbles were making her feet ache. How far until she came to another turning? Something fell from above and landed on her shoulder. She shook it off. *Was it possible to be lost, when you didn't know where you were to begin with? Stop it, shut up, take a breath and start again.* Keep cool. She remembered a scientific paper she'd read about miners while studying at university. If these tunnels had stood for this long, empty and unused, could the disruption she was causing bring them down on top of her?

She stumbled over a jutting cobble and fell to the ground, ripping a hole in the knee of her jeans and dropping the phone with a screen-splintering crunch. The lighter landed with a ting and then a soft thump as it came to lie in spongy moss somewhere in front of her.

"Fuck." Her voice echoed down the dark and came back past her on the chilly breeze. Pieces of dirt fell from above. She lay in the dark with her hands covering her head.

When it was apparent she hadn't caused a cave-in, and she got back some of her motor functions, she reached out feeling among the soft damp moss and the cold hardness of the cobbled floor. Her fingernails scraped against the dirt between the stones and finally came upon the metal zippo lighter. She flicked the flint and smiled when she saw the sparks and the warm orange flame a second later.

The mobile phone was in front of her, its screen smashed into a thousand tiny cobweb cracks but still working. She picked it up and put it in her pocket and then climbed to a kneeling position. Her right knee stung. Nancy stood and straightened her jacket and strode down the tunnel with the zippo lighter in her right hand leading the way. An orange glow lit the walls, and angry shadows danced on the stone walls. Her left hand was in front of her, reaching into the dark for any unseen obstacles.

She carried on in this way until the zippo burned her hand again. This tunnel was never ending. Have I walked past the way out without even realising – just like the way the entrance to this passage was hidden? Keep going, you've come this far. A rather helpful voice she hadn't heard for a long time spoke.

"I will," she replied to the dark. She flicked the flint again and carried on into the black. Unaware of the eyes watching her.

Jacob headed back up the stairs. He'd stood in the entrance for 10 minutes after he'd lost sight of Nancy. Her kiss upstairs still lingered on his memory, as did the way she'd cuddled the boys and kept them safe. Come back to me, he thought. We haven't even had a chance to see if this is real or simply a result of the situation, and I want to know. I need to know. If you could be my unintended and unlooked for love, I need to know.

It had been years since he'd been with a woman. Despite having shared a bed with his ex until six months ago, they hadn't shared a sexual relationship for two years before the final separation. He missed the soft touch of someone he loved, and the returned touch that showed someone cared for him too. But the boys came first, would always come first.

Were her eyes playing tricks on her? She rubbed at them as the leftover glow of green light stuck in her mind after it had gone. It had looked like a glowing green orb, but that was crazy. But then she saw it again. She flicked the lid of the zippo shut, expelling the flame and watched. Yes, at the end of the passage, in the black, was a floating, glowing green ball of light like something from Harry Potter.

She sensed intelligence from it as she watched it work its way along, lighting up a stone wall with its eerie radiance. It wasn't over 20 feet in front of her. The hairs on her arms raised as if there was an electric charge in the tunnel. Then it disappeared, as if something tall had stepped in front of it, and she realised there must be a turn in the passage.

Nancy jogged to catch up with it with her right hand out in front and the left dragging along the stone to keep within touching distance of the wall. Got to take a chance, the voice said. Before you're stuck down here forever. Running in the dark was enlightening. With every step, she felt the claustrophobia and the fear depart. As she ran, she felt the ever-strengthening breeze against her forehead and cheeks. There was a way out ahead, she knew it.

Her left arm fell into space and she realised she'd reached the turn in the tunnel. She didn't stop in time and ran into a solid stone wall. Her arm stopped her from crunching her face against the rock. She reached into her pocket, breathing harsh breaths of damp air, and pulled out the zippo. She flicked the flint and saw to her left a large, stone archway opening. Following the fresh air that came on the breeze, she walked through the crumbling archway.

She was in a cavernous circular room the size of a grand hall from a castle with a ceiling as high as two double-decker buses. The orange flame flickered in the increasing breeze. The room smelled damp and earthy. As her eyes adjusted, she saw eight dark beams as wide as school desks reaching from the edge of the room and up into the vaulted ceiling, meeting in the middle. In the centre, hanging down like a stalactite, was an off-white crystallised figure. An outstretched arm pointed accusingly towards a spot in the shadows.

"What the fuck?"

The white crystal took on a green hue and she saw the orb floating behind it. The way it inspected the form reminded her of a crime scene investigator. It circled slowly, moving up and down the crystallised figure as if scanning it. She clicked the zippo lid shut and took three steps back into the shadow of the archway. There she stood, watching. As she watched, she saw the figure held a bow pulled taut, but there was no arrow. Was this Tristan?

The orb was definitely intelligent, or being controlled like a drone by someone intelligent. Could it be a drone from the army looking for survivors? The centre glowed brighter than the outer, which turned a darker green, fuzzy at the edges. It was at least the size of a football. Was it solid or not? Nancy couldn't decide. No sound came from it as it moved around the stalactite figure. Nancy thought it should have hummed or something.

It stopped at the tip of the bow. Sharp splinters of salt-like crystal shot out from the figure like frozen lightning. With the light from the orb at the thinnest part of the off-white crystal, she thought she saw something inside. A dark form that looked hauntingly like a real hand. The green orb stopped, throbbed outwards like a heart, and then flashed down to the floor and through a dark doorway opposite she hadn't seen earlier. She was left in the dark, green light flashed in her eyes like the memory of headlights on an unlit road and then she was alone.

Once she was sure it was gone, Nancy headed deeper into the room and stood underneath the figure in the centre. She craned her neck and saw the space where the arrow should go in the bow. The bow itself wasn't there, just the crystal shape of one, as if it had been there. On the figure's back, with the opening pointing to the ground, was an empty quiver. Nancy stepped back and heard a crack as if she'd stood on a twig. She kneeled and inspected the ground. Nancy frowned, looking at a blue and white-coloured feather fletching of an arrow buried among the moss. She pulled it free and saw the light-wood shaft and a dull metal arrowhead. Inspecting it in her hands, another arrowhead glinted in the flickering flame below. This one's shaft had snapped in half, but the arrowhead was sharp. She put both into her jeans pocket and stood, ready to follow the orb.

CHAPTER FIVE – DINAH/BILL

Her orb returned. Dinah soaked in the information as it became one with her. Not just tunnels down below but rooms, huge cavernous rooms. The orb had found a stalactite crystallised form hanging from the ceiling with organic material inside. She frowned. It couldn't be the Beast or the Vermin otherwise they would have swarmed the tunnels, and there had only been two other life-forms down below, a girl who was hiding in the shadows and the other a small creature which could be one of the Vermin.

The questions of *what* was in this town changed to *where* was she? What was this place? She knew places where evil had recently attracted the Vermin, which was why they came from their dimension, attracted to the remnants of the act itself. Like an echo of evil. She searched the man's memories for any recent events in this town.

An incident six weeks ago involving a missing boy who had since been found; an animal attack on a woman at an old man's home in the countryside and several other disappearances; a sinkhole at Westford Water caught her attention. If her superiors were more proactive, as she suggested countless times, and less reactive, they may have been able to stop this before it happened. Was this what attracted the Vermin and the Beast? And had whatever was underneath this town attracted the first attacks that drew the Vermin here?

The tunnels went deep into the earth, deeper than her power allowed her light to go. As an adolescent girl she'd heard stories, myths and legends about a world that was the First World; the world where everything began. All other worlds were copies of this world, like a pantomime stage with a different cast each time. But buried in this world was the first true evil. True evil that her distant ancestors defeated. As in most worlds with the same legends, she thought her world was the First World, but what if she was wrong? What if this world was the First World? The one true evil could be buried beneath her feet and the people here, these humans, could they really be the first people? Had the evil that caused the echo been searching to release its Master and was The Beast now doing the same?

She could no longer wait. If her suspicions proved true, the entire universe and not just this world, this town, was in danger. The only other life-form, besides the Vermin, she had come across was the girl down in the tunnels. What was she doing down there alone? She would need to go down into the tunnels and find her.

The black duffel bag was heavy, but she wanted the weapons inside it. The three ancient-looking rusted grenades, a heavy shotgun and two pistols were her sole arsenal to take on the Vermin outside. She put one of the loaded pistols down the back of her jeans. There was a full box of shotgun shells and two magazines – one for each pistol – on top of the ones already loaded.

She summoned the light and the green orb floated in front of her. She spoke to it using her mind and the orb floated along the corridor. Dinah followed. She needed to find an entrance to the tunnels and to find the girl. Her light led the way, and she hoped she wouldn't be outside too long. The shadow Vermin would see her as soon as she left the police station.

Blood stains had dried black on the grey floor of the front entrance. She walked past them and towards the enormous doors. The green orb stopped and waited for her to unlock the door. She grasped the fabric straps of the bag and hoisted it over her shoulder, ready to run. A few Vermin wouldn't be a problem. She could take care of them, but she didn't want to expel any of her power. She would use the rudimentary guns of the humans if she had to.

The door creaked as it opened. Her orb floated out into the grey of the day. She followed at a jog behind it, out into the car park. The green light didn't follow paths or roads, so she found herself on the grass verge running through the gap in the fallen wooden fence. It crossed the road and passed the cars that sat empty like discarded beer cans. Dinah turned and looked up over the police station. The other orb she'd sent out was following them from above.

There was a large opening in the wall opposite and she puffed out her cheeks when the green light went through it.

She was in a gravelled car park at the back of a building that led to Broad Leaf Square. There was space for at least 25 cars. But besides two cars, they were all empty. She picked up the sensation again of one of her Comrades. One of them had been here in this car park and maybe the building itself.

Dinah followed the orb through the car park and down a set of stone stairs to the back of the building. To her right was an empty bike rack with white paint peeling off the metal, leaving blood-red rust behind. She followed down another set of stairs and found herself in a narrow garden. A block-paved patio with weeds growing between the cracks led the way down a further set of stairs. On her right was a muddy area with massive trees and shrubs, and to her left she saw into the empty dark rooms of the building.

The sense that her Comrade had been here was stronger. The back of the building loomed large with crumbling gargoyle heads looking down at her as she approached. A wide window spread along the back of the building, but the blinds were down. To her left, where the orb was hovering, was a modern-looking door. To its right, at shoulder height, attached to the wall was a small black box with two unblinking lights. Fob entry, a quick search of the man's mind told her. There was no lock to pick.

The green orb floated next to her. She got into position in front of the door when she heard a scuttling sound from the top of the stone stairs behind her. There was no need to look. She knew what was coming. She balanced herself and kicked the door where she guessed the bolt would be. It held firm. She kicked again, this time a thin slice of wood splintered off, but the door didn't give. The scuttling sound grew louder. Sharp claws on concrete. Dinah threw her shoulder at the door, but it didn't move. She pulled the pistol from the back of her jeans and brought the black butt down on the window. Nothing. "Fuck."

Wasting a bullet to get into the building would never have crossed her mind, if it wasn't for the ever-growing clicking of claws that grew closer each second. Without a lock to shoot, she pointed the gun at the glass. The gunshot echoed in the small courtyard garden. A bullet hole appeared perfectly round in the glass and from it, spider web cracks shot to the edges. She hit the glass with the butt of her gun and the glass fell inside with a sharp crash. A few stray nuggets of sharp glass caught in the sides of the door, but she didn't have time to clean them off before she pushed herself, head and top half first, through the hole. She put her hands out to cushion her fall and felt shards of glass cut into her palms. Her legs crumpled inside the building after her and with nothing at hand to block the window and with the sounds of the Vermin almost upon her, she followed the glowing green orb into the building.

Dinah was in a reception area with elegant deep-red wallpaper with a gold flower pattern, two cream leather chairs and a vast pine desk with a monitor and a phone. She counted three white doors and a spiral staircase with blue carpet leading to three further floors. Her gaze followed the staircase to the galleried landing areas. With the lights off, and the blinds down, it was dark inside. Serviced offices, the man's mind told her.

Her green light stayed near the door she'd come through, hovering at head height. She could hear the Vermin on the other side. It was a sturdy security door that hadn't budged with the thuds of the Vermin attacking it. She listened to the orb. It wanted to go back the way they had come. The way to the tunnels was under this building. There was a cellar, and the door was in the porch she'd just come through. The porch with the smashed window allowing the Vermin inside.

There was no other way down to the cellar, her light would have told her if there was. She could move on to the front entrance, following the ball of glowing green back outside, but didn't know how far she'd have to go to find another entrance to the tunnels below. Could she open the security door and let the Vermin in and somehow find a way past them? She'd have mere seconds from the door opening before they swamped the room and not enough gunpowder to stop them all. She refused to use her magic… yet.

The grenades. She didn't know how powerful the explosion would be but hoped it would be enough to blow apart the Vermin and offer her the chance to run past and to the cellar door. The heavy bag was on her shoulder. She placed it on the floor and undid the zip. Pulling out a grenade, she smiled as she felt the weight of it in her palm. A rudimentary weapon for a basic species, but it would do the job.

She searched Bill's memories like an instruction manual. Pull the pin, let go of the lever and throw. There was some other important information buried in the blur of his memories, but she didn't understand the specifics. She only got fragments. Was the grenade a fragmentation grenade? If so, why did that matter? She let go of the memory and studied the object in her hand. It was old. Would it still work? As she turned it over feeling its weight, she realised she couldn't open the door, they would be too strong and she wouldn't be able to close it again. It would have to be thrown from somewhere else. Upstairs?

The grand staircase squeaked as she made her way up. A grotesque, bright multi-colour oil painting of what she guessed was supposed to be flowers, but in which she saw blue mis-shaped monsters, looking down at her from the wall. The blinds weren't shut on the wide window on the first-floor landing. She had to bend to look out.

Below, she saw a dozen of the Vermin clambering over each other to get through the smashed window. She estimated at least a dozen more were already inside the building. If she dropped the grenade down she would get the Vermin outside, but not the ones inside. It would take 10 seconds to get from the landing, down the stairs and to the door once the grenade went off. The grenade needed to explode from inside the porch. Would she be able to throw it accurately enough? She didn't think so, not with the Vermin snapping below her, trying to get at her. She had seconds once she opened the window to throw the grenade and close it again. Even then, the Vermin would smash through the window and she'd have no choice but to go for the security door and the cellar. If she had something long enough, she could roll it down into the porch through the smashed window. She peered up at the top of the building. Running along the ceiling was a black drainpipe. A smile crossed Bill's face. She'd need to get their attention, so she had the chance to move whatever chute she used into place, before rolling the grenade down, otherwise she'd never get it past them.

Dinah marked the spot in her mind and followed the stairs up past the second floor to the third. On this floor there were three white doors. Two of the offices would overlook the front of the building while the other, the side. She tried the door to the side office first. It opened. Empty tables sat disorganised in the middle of the room. It smelled stale and unused. One window looked out to the side with a view of a stone wall of the next building. She thought she'd have time to open the window and pull off a piece of the black drain before the Vermin heard her. Then she'd have to move fast. She still held the grenade in her hand. The duffel bag sat next to the security door downstairs, ready to grab as she ran through.

She breathed the fresh air from outside as she opened the sash window. This wasn't the trickiest maneuver she'd ever pulled on a battlefield, but it was in the top three. She leaned out the window and twisted her body to get at the black plastic drainpipe. The grenade almost slipped from her hand, so she slid it carefully into her jacket pocket. The drainpipe was slotted together in three parts, each two metres long. It was a long way down to the gravelled ground below. Thin, metal semi-circular clips held the drainpipe to the wall, screwed in with small rusted screws. If she could release the one at this level, she was certain she could pull the one below free as well. Four metres of drainpipe would be more than enough to reach from the first floor into the porch.

She pulled the drainpipe away from the wall and smiled as she saw the clip move and with one last tug, it pinged off and fell to the ground. The top of the drainpipe was slotted into the guttering that ran along the width of the building, and with some wiggling she got that loose too. A noise. A scrambling of claws over the gravel towards the end of the building. With a yank she pulled the drainpipe towards her and the brittle plastic snapped somewhere below. She prayed it would still be long enough as she walked backwards pulling the pipe inside the office. She was almost out the door on the other side of the room when the snapped end came through the window. It clattered to the floor as she dropped it and ran and shut the window. Black shapes appeared as shadows on the floor of the office as she looked over her shoulder, dragging the drainpipe behind her.

The drainpipe wasn't heavy just awkward as she ran with it down the stairs. The plastic made a soft thud down each carpeted stair. She held one end under her arm as the other rat-a-tat-tatted down the stairs behind her. She didn't need to lift it over the bannister because of the width of the staircase.

When she reached the first-floor landing, she peeked out the window and saw most of the Vermin had left the courtyard. A crash upstairs confirmed this as the window broke. She'd closed the door to the office and thought she had two minutes before that gave way too.

The window on the landing opened with a stiff push. Dinah moved into position with the drainpipe sticking out behind her and slowly slid it through Bill's hands, out the window and towards the door below. It was plenty long enough, and after a minute, careful to balance the drainpipe as it wobbled in her hands, it slotted through the smashed window into the downstairs porch. She gave it one last shove, and reached into her jacket pocket for the weight that had been bouncing comfortingly against her side.

The inside of the pipe was dark and smelled earthy. Coming up it, she heard the chattering and the movement of the Vermin below. She pulled the grenade from her pocket, pulled the pin out, which took more effort than she'd thought, and then let go of the lever as she pushed it down the drainpipe.

CHAPTER SIX – AATAMI

The being inside Mr. Neil was dreaming. He was back on his own world. The sky had an eerie purple glow. The pink long-grass field he lay in had blue-bark trees and a mirage-like border surrounding. His name was Aatami, and in a blue-wood hut to the left corner of the pink field, played his two children and his wife.

Overhead yellow lines, like sparklers, crisscrossed across the purple. His brothers and sisters who had gained Citizenship, were free to explore this world and make their own way. One more mission and he and his family would be one of them. No more little blue hut, no more days spent staring out into freedom.

It was a system that had been in place for thousands of years. The only thing he had ever known. He was a soldier, but not a career soldier, despite the propaganda they had fed him since he first escaped the egg. Only his wife and children mattered to him. Even on missions, he didn't care about the worlds he was saving. They were a valiant people, defending other worlds, but underneath they were a bigoted species, believing the other species they saved were below them. Aatami was no different. He despised the other life-forms he came across, thinking them stupid and arrogant. If he had a choice, he would leave them to their own devices and not intervene, but he was a good soldier – he had skills that set him apart from others – and followed orders so one day his family would be Citizens.

He rose from the ground. The pink grass was six feet tall, but he stood 10 feet taller. His long arms with their thin hands and slender fingers stroked the top of the grass as he walked towards the hut. A glowing white orb shot down from the sky and towards the hut. He watched his wife and their two children run inside. His last mission had arrived. He heard their excited voices from inside as he approached. The door opened automatically as he got closer, and he stepped inside to the light.

Aatami opened Mr Neil's eyes. He lay on the icy stone floor of the passageway that led to the stairs and the cellar. Jacob, Mike and the boys were asleep on the stairs. Weak reddish-pink light flooded the room. How long had he been out? Had he dreamed Nancy going down to the tunnel alone?

"Jacob," he whispered. "Jacob…"

Jacob stirred. He released himself from the cuddling boys and came to him. Jacob rubbed at his eyes. They were red. He reached down and checked Mr. Neil's wound. Mr. Neil closed his eyes, waiting for the pain. Jacob moved back with a sharp intake of breath.

"Your wound… it's healed."

Mr. Neil looked at Jacob and reached out to him. He held his wrist and said: "I didn't know if I would heal but, now I have, I need to tell you something."

"What… I don't understand… what do you mean? How can you be healed?"

Mr. Neil sat holding Jacob's wrist. "I'm not from here, Jacob." He held Jacob's puzzled gaze. "I was sent here to eradicate the Vermin problem."

"Sent?"

"Where's Nancy? What time is it? Did she go down into the tunnels?"

"What do you mean sent? Who by?" Mr Neil didn't answer. Jacob checked his watch. "It's just after four. She's been down there for an hour."

"If I tell you, you can't tell anyone – not yet, anyway."

Jacob looked towards Sam and Jack. "If it helps us, then yes. Are you part of the army?"

Mr. Neil shook his head and then stood and turned to the cellar door. "Follow me, we don't want to wake up your boys."

Jacob followed Aatami into the dark cellar. He pulled out his phone and turned on the torch. The gloom of the cellar was lit up by artificial white light in a five metre circle around them.

"What I am about to tell you has never been told to anyone before that I know of."

Jacob nodded. "Okay."

"Yours isn't the only world with life. There are 73 other worlds…" He let the words hang in the air, waiting for Jacob to talk.

Jacob laughed. "You're an alien?"

"No, Jacob." He searched through Mr. Neil's memories. "I believe you'd call them other dimensions. My name is Aatami, and I'm from another dimension: Same planet, different world."

"Right, of course you are, and the Vermin?"

"Similar thing, another dimension… world, not mine or yours. They follow the Beast, an ancient evil. They attack after an echo of terror."

"You're kidding right, trying to throw some levity on the situation? I don't find this funny – I've got kids upstairs." Jacob turned to leave. Aatami grabbed his wrist and pulled him back so he was facing him.

"I'm not kidding, Jacob. You saw the meteor – is it that hard to believe?"

"Well, yes."

"Jacob, something happened here, not so long ago, which attracted the Beast and the Vermin. I'm not part of your army and I'm not kidding."

"An echo of terror? Nothing happened here, this is Westford, it's a quiet town, nothing ever happens here! I'm just trying to raise my boys as well as I can… this is crazy."

Aatami searched the memories again. "What about the sinkhole at Westford Water and the animal attacks?"

"What about them?" He shrugged. "I read about them in the news."

"That sounds like the sort of thing that would attract the Vermin."

"Wait… Aatami? Is that right?"

"Yes."

"Who are you?"

"I'm an Exo. We hunt the Vermin and the Beast. Stopping them before they release the One."

"The One? What's that? Worse than the Beast?"

"All our worlds were an experiment, like a petri dish. A few drops of DNA on each planet and then the Maker sat back and watched. Each world evolved at a different rate with different species. Does that make sense?"

"Not really, but go on…"

"Did you ever wonder where your myths and legends came from? The Greek gods, the Nordic gods? I've searched this body's memories you have a similar story, your Maker is simply called God, and the being we call the One, you call Satan."

"God and Satan…" Jacob snorted. "This is insane!"

"Myths and legends, Jacob. Myths and legends. Did you never wonder where the original stories came from?"

"It's what we get taught at school, it's nothing more than that. Christmas, Easter, all that shit… they're just stories, excuses to buy people presents they'll never use. I'm sorry, you're talking to the wrong person. This is bonkers."

"Watch." Mr Neil put his palms together and after a second a glowing orb appeared, lighting up Jacob's face in a purple hue. His eyes went wide and his mouth froze in an 'O'.

"It's real, Jacob, and there is another story. One of the 73 worlds is the original world, the template for all the others and if this world gets destroyed… the universe dies…" Jacob's face didn't move. "Jacob, did you hear me?"

"What is that thing?"

"As an Exo we have what you call magic, but we call science. They bound this orb to me when I was born. It's a sentient being, but without me it can't live and likewise, I without it, wouldn't survive."

"You're telling the truth?"

Aatami nodded.

"And this one true world, that's your world right?"

"That's always been the assumption, yes."

Jacob bristled. "Assumed by who, you?" He took a step back from Aatami. "Believe it or not, Aatami... did I say that right?" Aatami nodded. "I bet each civilization on their own world would have the same assumption. On this world we have Christians, Catholics, Muslims, a whole plethora of religions, with each believing their God is the one and that their way is right. Add in 72 other worlds and you get one big mess of beliefs. How do you know what your telling me is true? Did you read it from a book? Well guess what, we have books too; each religion each with their own holy book. Now, I know this isn't the time to get into a whole belief argument... but what exactly can you do to help us here and now!"

Mr. Neil smiled. "I like you, Jacob, if there are more people like you on this world then maybe I was wrong all this time. What can *we* do? We know how to kill them, how to eradicate them so they won't come back..."

"And the Beast and the One?"

Mr. Neil reached out and put a hand on Jacob's shoulder. "We can fight."

"We? Are there other Exo's here in Westford?"

"They sent me as part of a team of five. We were supposed to meet in the town centre, but no one turned up. But I can sense one close by."

"With the others, can you win?"

"We can fight," he repeated.

CHAPTER SEVEN – NANCY

There were five tunnels she'd counted as she felt blindly around the edge of the room, using her hands to see. The orb had gone down one of these tunnels. However, in the dark she had turned herself around and no longer knew which. She'd have to pick a tunnel and take the chance. The stalactite figure above loomed like an unseen monster in the dark. The arrowheads dug into her thigh.

Her lucky number had always been number three, just like her dad, so she set off around the room again using the wall for balance. She passed one void in the dark, a second and then a third. She stood in front of it. No one else needed to be here with her to tell her this tunnel could be her doom or her salvation.

The black was all-encompassing. It didn't come in shades of grey but was a solid thing. An entity into itself. The darkness had never bothered her before, in fact she had often sought it out. When her mother died, followed shortly after by her older brother, she sat in the dark for hours. Thoughts of death weren't what she needed now, so she shook her head, encouraging them to leave. A trick an old counsellor had taught her. She could hear her voice: *'Shake those thoughts away, Nancy, when they come just shake them away as if they're a solid thing in your mind.'* So that is what she did, and they left her alone, for now.

It was a wide tunnel. She extended both arms to her sides and did not touch the walls. The air was stale. She stumbled in the dark, unaware that she had passed another passage which led back the way she came. She carried on.

As the time passed and the trickle of hope she had left evaporated like mist in the morning, she heard the echo of what sounded like an explosion from behind. Traces of dirt fell from the ceiling above. She crouched to her knees, put her hands over her head and waited for death. Nancy realised for the first time in a very long time, she wanted to live.

Her arms were covered in dust and debris, but the roof hadn't fallen. Nancy coughed and spat onto the floor. She grabbed the Zippo from her pocket and sparked it up. Grey specks of dust floated in the tunnel. From behind her, she heard something move. It scuttled along the ground towards her. She couldn't see through the falling dust and the short orange circle of light the Zippo emitted. As she turned in one direction and then the other, the tunnel fell silent. Was that an explos....

A black shape launched itself at her from the black. Orange flames flickered in the glowing yellow eyes and razor-sharp teeth spat at her. Nancy reached into her pocket and pulled out the broken arrow. She held it in front of her as the Vermin crashed down on top of her with a shriek. The Zippo fell to the floor beside her, still alight. She felt warmth run down her top. The thing was struggling, and its mouth was snapping at her neck. She held its head up with her left hand while she stabbed and stabbed with the arrow in her right hand, finding flesh time and time again and feeling the gush of something hot and sticky down her arm. Still, its sharp teeth snapped inches away from her exposed throat. Her arms grew tired. Her face moist with the rancid heat of the creature's breath. With one last stab she felt her hand enter the creature, she ripped through its insides and gagged on the stench from it. The Vermin snapped at her one more time and then grew still. She could still feel the slight rise of its chest as it lay dying on top of her. Nancy didn't let go of the creature's neck, nor did she stop ripping its insides out and onto the ground next to them. She tasted acid in her throat. Then she screamed. A guttural cry of victory, a howl of defiance. Dirt fell onto her from the roof, and she stopped. Nancy pushed the creature off her, picked up the burning hot Zippo and stood over it, her arm dripping gross blood to the floor. She'd lost the arrowhead inside the creature. She bent over the creature, inspecting it.

Nancy had severed one of its gnarled and twisted pink legs. On the floor, reflecting the orange flame, was a puddle of gore and intestines. The Zippo burnt her hand, and she hissed. Back in the pitch black she stumbled down the tunnel into the blackness.

CHAPTER EIGHT – DINAH

She was halfway down the wide winding staircase when she heard the blast from both behind and in front of her. Glass shattered, and wood splintered. The loud crash sent projectiles hurtling through the doors, the windows, and the bodies of the Vermin. She jumped the last three steps and landed mid-run, hurtling towards the duffel bag, the green orb and the grisly vista in front of her, and through the broken security door.

Vermin lay on the floor. Two bodies twitched with the potential of life, but it had ripped the others to shreds. She didn't stop to count how many she'd taken out. The smell of the explosion and the smoke still lingered in the porchway. The green orb moved through the air, leading her towards the door that led to the cellar. It was still intact to the right of the wall opposite the entrance.

The sound of Vermin approaching, attracted by the explosion, came through the shredded door. Dinah grabbed the old brass door handle and turned. She exhaled loudly as it opened. The green light floated down the stairs and she followed, closing the door behind her.

There was no emergency lighting. The only light emanated from the glow of her orb, sending everything into an ethereal green. To her left, inset to the wall, was a range of cleaning products. She could smell bleach. A solid-looking wooden broom would make a good obstruction, but she didn't know how much time she had. Scuttling sounds, and the tinkling of claws on broken glass, were already coming from the other side. The stairs were narrow stone, and she held her hands out as she raced down them to keep up with the light.

Downstairs, the room opened into a high-ceilinged space with a dusty block-paved floor and exposed brick walls. Archways separated the room into at least three other sections. White boxes of paperwork with red writing stood to all sides of the cellar. In the green glow, it looked as though she had trapped herself in a room with no way out, but the orb floated through to the rear. She followed, pushing boxes out the way which landed with a dull whump and pieces of paper falling to the floor.

To the back of the rear room, she saw an exposed stone wall with rocks, ranging in size from dinner plates to coffee cups, jutting out at odd angles. The stones shone distinct shades of green, like algae in a flowing river. Her orb stopped and hovered next to a stone that shone brighter than the others. It was the size of a standard brick. Its edges looked artificial, sharp and straight, as compared to the other rounded stones. She touched it. The surface was warm, and she felt it give when she added pressure. It moved inwards and to the right as if on a hinge and disappeared, leaving a hole behind. Dinah reached her hand through.

Brick-dust clung to her clammy skin. The floor of the small hole was smooth. Her arm was in to her elbow when she touched something ice cold, and from its surface, she knew it was metal. She pushed, and it moved back. It was a button. She pushed it again until she heard a click and the button stayed in place, recessed against the wall.

A rudimentary mechanical sound came from behind the wall. The sound of non-motorized and non-electrical metal and stone elements moving into place. A thunk came from the stone wall an inch to the right of the hole. She saw a crack of pitch black appear around the stones and a flurry of dust fell to the floor which, when cleared, left the outline of a door. The green orb throbbed excitedly. There was no handle, so Dinah pushed against the door shape with her shoulder. It moved backwards as if on rails. It went five feet into the wall and stopped. As she turned back to the room, to her left and right, were dark entrances to passageways underneath the building.

The green orb lingered in the centre of the entrance, seeming to contemplate which tunnel to take, before it throbbed twice and took the left one. Dinah followed with the duffel bag still on her shoulder and a pistol in the back of her jeans. Two grenades left. The idea of letting one of them off down here worried her. Would the passage take the blast or would it cause a cave-in? She hoped she wouldn't have to find out.

The tunnel was old, but solid. The stone walls lit up green as if she was seeing the world through night vision goggles. With each step she kicked up centuries old dust that hovered an inch above the ground before settling again. Behind her, she left solid black footsteps on the floor. How deep into these tunnels was the girl? Ahead of her, the green orb stopped and throbbed.

She stepped through an unseen entrance into a large open room. The wall to the right was more dirt than stone. Oddly-shaped stones, elongated and round, stuck out from the wall. The orb scanned the scene from left to right and when she pulled back, she saw the full image.

They were skeletons. Human, beast and bird skeletons that were placed into the dirt to create a scene akin to old cave paintings. Two human adults, with large craniums, crouched next to the skeleton of a young baby. The bones of the infant had become one with the dirt, but there was no doubting the size of the skull and the tiny curved spine. To the right of the humans were four stalking skeletal animals much larger than the humans with enormous swooping tails, four large, thin bones that must be wings and long skulls with large nostril holes and five curved horns. Their skulls were full of sharp teeth that seemed too far apart and appeared to laugh from the wall. Above were the thin bones of a massive hawk whose wings spread at least seven foot across the top right of the vista. It spread its talons open and came down with death from above upon the laughing dragons. Words written on the walls, faded red, spelled: *Our Hero, Beowulf.*

It couldn't be, could it? The Tomb of Heroes. The mythical tomb of all 73 world's heroes surrounding the cage of the One. Behind the humans was a skeleton that held Dinah's gaze. It was impossible, and confirmed it. There was no way it should be there.

It rose at least 10 feet from the base of the wall. Each bone was a winding mass, like the roots of a tree trunk three inches thick. She'd never seen one in actual life; they were creatures of legend, but the way they positioned the body and the make-up of the bones made her sure. She was looking at an Angel. There was another name for them on her world, but here they were called Angels. And that name seemed perfect for what she was seeing.

Who were the couple and who was the baby? What was an Angel doing on this world, in the flesh, if not one of the archangels who put the One in his cage? She heard a crack behind her, and the scuttling claws of the Vermin echoed from behind. They had broken through. The orb whizzed off towards the end of the room and another tunnel. Dinah ran behind. The sound of the Vermin was like an arrow in the dark, straight and constant, always behind her. But then she thought she heard it from in front. Could they have gotten around her through another tunnel? No, she didn't think so, otherwise the orb wouldn't have gone that way. But they're faster than you… spoke a voice inside. The orb shot off to the left, and she saw the tunnel split in two. She kept pace, always two metres behind, and then ran into something solid crouched on the floor.

The shape moaned as Dinah rolled over onto her side and came to a stop on her back on the hard, icy floor. She heard muffled tears. The green orb came back and lit up the passage. It was the youthful girl. She had been sitting on the floor with her back against the wall. The tunnel was wide, and it was luck she'd ran into her otherwise she'd have ran right past her. The girl didn't look up. Dinah could smell one of her Comrades on her.

"Hello?" Bill said. The girl didn't answer.

Something in the body's memory was sparking, trying to get her attention. She looked through the memories. There was nothing special she could see. Just memories of the man she'd killed and his daughter. His daughter. Nancy.

"Nancy?"

The girl looked up from the arms crossed in front of her face. "Bill? Is that you? What are you doing down here?"

"Looking for you…"

"But how did you know I was down here? Where's my dad?"

Bill stood. "Nancy, we need to get you out of here, they're coming, the Vermin."

Nancy's eyes grew wide and in the green light, glowed wet. Bill saw the girl was shaking. She approached and pulled her to her feet. She put an arm on each shoulder and looked at her. "We need to get out of here, Nancy. Do you remember the way you came?" From this close, the smell of her comrade was strong.

"I… I… the battery on the phone died, I had no torch and then my lighter ran out… I thought I was going to die down here in the dark."

We still might, Dinah thought.

"What is that thing?" Nancy asked, looking behind Bill. "Is it a drone? Who's controlling it?"

"I'll explain that later. Which way did you come from?"

"I can't remember, I got turned around in the dark…" Her eyes lit up. "There was a massive room, it had something coming from the ceiling; if we can get back and with the light from that thing, I would remember, I'm sure."

Without blinking, Bill spoke to the orb, which throbbed and drifted through the tunnel.

"Where's it going?" Nancy asked.

"I don't know," said Bill. "Let's follow it though."

"Bill, where is my dad? Is he okay?"

Sensing she wouldn't ever get the girl out of the tunnel if she told the truth, Bill said: "Yes, Nancy, your dad is fine. He's just worried about you, we all were."

CHAPTER NINE – JACOB

Jacob sat on the stairs sandwiched between Sam and Jack. They were all that mattered. He hadn't told Mike about his conversation with Mr Neil. It was crazy, but he believed him just the same. Nancy had picked up on something about him from the first moment and he guessed, somewhere inside, he had too. Was that why he had let him in? Had he sensed he could help save his children? They were trapped like rats. Someone needed to help before they starved or were attacked.

Sam had told him he was hungry five minutes ago, and it broke his heart to tell him they had nothing to eat. The little boy's eyes had grown wet with tears, and he nodded his head. You are too young to be brave about things like not eating, you should be eating anything and everything you want, he thought. It was his duty, his responsibility to care for and protect these boys and he was failing. He'd led them into a dead-end. Somewhere to die.

Mr Neil lay on the floor, resting after their conversation in the cellar. He looked asleep. What would Mike say if he told him about their conversation? He would give it another hour to see if Nancy came back, and if she didn't, they would need to talk about options. In an hour it would be dark outside. He didn't think the streetlights would turn on this evening. He pondered what Mr Neil had said. Multiple dimensions. God and Satan. The Beast and the Vermin. The One. It sounded like science fiction. But the Vermin were real, as was that glowing orb Mr Neil had summoned from thin air. How could they survive the Beast, the Vermin or Satan, never mind defeat them? What about God? Where did he fit? If the minions of hell were loose on this earth, where were the Angels and the forces of good? He wasn't a religious man, but he remembered the biblical stories from school. He'd always liked the idea of something bigger than himself and the epic battles between good and evil. But he never thought he'd be in the middle of one. If others knew what he was coming to think of as the truth, what would they say? Would it just be another offshoot of a religion? Another case of my God is bigger than yours? Another reason to kill each other? What if they were just an experiment from a mad scientist of a God? One of 73 petri dishes sitting on the sides in a lab. At least the meaning of life would be answered, but he didn't think many people would take it too well. But wasn't that exactly what they'd been doing as a human race, playing God with AI and other technology.

What would the Beast and Satan want with 73 petri dish worlds? Then he remembered what Aatami had said. His species hunts and kills the Vermin. What if each world is something bigger, what if without one there would be no other? The Exos hold back the Vermin, while another race on another world creates art and beauty, and another one creates magic. But with one world gone, everything is thrown out of balance. Is that what the universe is? Balance? The individual makes the whole...

How much hatred must one have to want to destroy something so wholly? He could understand a lust for power, lust for control, but a lust for nothingness? Just wanton destruction. Why? His head was swimming with philosophy, religion and physics. He pulled both boys tighter to him and kissed each on their foreheads.

"Are you okay, Jacob?" Mike asked from the top of the stairs. "If I didn't know any better, just now you looked like a man contemplating the meaning of life and coming up short and with an urge to go potty."

Jacob chuckled. "You're a poet, Mike."

"I try. But seriously, are you okay?"

"I will be once we get out of here."

"And when will that be?"

"We need to wait on Nancy ... she'll be back."

"And if she isn't?"

"She will be..."

Mike nodded and Jacob was thankful he hadn't pushed. The last thing they needed was to argue between themselves. "One of us could go on a food run while waiting."

Jacob shook his head. "No, we can't. Mr Neil is in no shape to move. I can't leave the boys and you won't make it five steps before those things get you."

"So our hope rests solely on that girl's shoulders?"

"For the moment, yes."

Mike sat on the top step. "I don't know about you, but I wish I'd brought a book or something..."

Should he tell him? The window was open. Mr Neil could show him the glowing orb and explain everything. But where would that get them? Nowhere. Let Mr Neil rest, and when Nancy comes back, tell them altogether. Mr Neil has to have a plan. Where are his 'comrades?' He looked over at the sleeping man. Is he communicating with them now, telepathically? Bringing them to him so they can do what they're meant to do and go home. He hoped so. The town would mourn, but then recover. After all, isn't that what humans do?

"You okay, Jacob? I lost you again for a moment."

"I'm fine, just thinking."

"Don't go hurting yourself," Mike said. "Get some rest."

The door to the cellar opened, and Nancy stepped out. Jacob jumped to his feet. Mike rose slowly. Her hair was thick with dirt and cobwebs. The whites of her eyes were bright against the dirt of her cheeks and forehead. Gore soaked her clothes, and she smelled rank. As she stepped forward, a man – another stranger – stepped out of the shadows. Mr Neil opened his eyes and stood. To Jacob, he looked like he was about to salute.

"Nancy? Are you okay?" asked Jacob, rushing over to her. Nancy put an arm out, and he took it and put it around his shoulder. "You look exhausted."

"Oh thanks, and here I was thinking I looked like I was stepping out to prom."

Jacob smiled and led her to the stairs. He helped her down and she sat next to Sam and Jack who both grinned at her. She reached across and ruffled their hair. "You two are a sight for sore eyes."

"You smell funny," Sam said.

Jacob turned from her and back to the man in the doorway. He reached out with his hand. "Thank you…?"

Bill took Jacob's hand. "Bill, I'm a friend of Nancy's father."

"Wow, okay, that was a stroke of luck being down in the tunnels…"

Mr Neil moved towards Bill and stuck his hand out. Jacob watched, expecting lightning to shoot from their fingers or something as they shook hands. When nothing happened, Jacob's shoulders slumped, but as Mr Neil turned he nodded to him. Jacob smiled. He knew it was one of Mr Neil's comrades.

Mike came down the stairs and also shook Bill's hand. He then turned to Mr Neil. "My gosh, you were on death's door not two hours ago. Whatever she gave you must have done the trick – I'm glad you're better." Mike touched him on his shoulder.

"Thank you, Mike," Mr Neil replied.

"It's incredible," said Nancy. "I didn't think you would pull through. What happened?"

"Oh I'm as strong as a goat, some rest was all I needed."

Jacob saw the look Nancy and Mike shared. He felt the desperation from Mr Neil and Bill to be alone. Had anyone else noticed?

A heavy-looking black duffel bag hung from Bill's wide shoulders and past his protruding belly. *How did you get through the tunnel? Mr Neil tried, and he's at least three stone skinnier than you and he got impaled on a piece of rebar.*

"Nancy, what happened to you? Did you find any food?" Mike asked when the silence got too much.

She hung her head, shaking it side-to-side. Mike walked over to her and put a hand on her shoulder. "One of those things attacked me. I killed it, but it nearly got me." She pulled out the complete arrow. "I killed it with one of these. There's tunnel upon tunnel down there, and something else too."

"What?" Jacob asked.

"I don't know. It was like a frozen figure hanging from the ceiling – it had a bow and arrow. Well, it didn't, not anymore, anyway. And then Bill found me, and his orb thing – it's like a drone, I guess."

At the mention of the orb, Mr Neil and Jacob looked at each other. Then Mr Neil looked at Bill with an eyebrow comically raised.

"What about food?" asked Mike.

"None, I'm sorry."

"Don't worry, dear, we're just glad you're back and safe."

"Do you have any water?" Bill asked.

"We have a couple of bottles upstairs. Mike, Mr Neil, Bill care to join me? Nancy, you rest up and look after the boys." He figured she was too tired to argue and he was right.

He leaned over and kissed the boys on the top of their heads and without thinking did the same to Nancy.

The upstairs room had exposed floorboards, two stained-glass windows to each wall and a black wood table in the middle. It smelled of dust and old paperback books. On the table was the case of water that Jacob had found earlier. Six bottles remained. He opened one of the bottles and passed it around the group. They took small gulps, careful to avoid drinking more than their share. Mr Neil and Bill held eye contact across the table, and Jacob imagined a silent communication between them. Mike didn't seem to notice.

"Mike," started Jacob, "we need to talk... Mr Neil it's probably best if you begin."

As Mr Neil spoke, Jacob took it all in again. Bill didn't interrupt Aatami. Mike pulled a chair back from the table and sat. His eyes grew wider as Aatami spoke. He had no questions like he once had. Once Mr Neil had finished he looked at Bill, who nodded his head.

"Mike, Jacob, you must know we have never broken our cover before while on a mission. This is a new and deadly situation we haven't come across before. No one has faced the Beast for centuries – maybe longer."

Jacob looked at Mike. "Are you okay?"

"As crazy as it sounds, I am. It's hard not to believe it with those things outside and if I believe that, I believe the rest."

Mike impressed Jacob. It was another wonderful human trait, the willingness to believe. Belief was faith, he thought. His confidence was growing in the situation, but there was still one problem. "Okay, so we believe... Now what do we do? We need to get out of here. If we stay much longer, we're as good as dead."

Bill put the duffel bag on the table and opened it. Jacob, Mike and Mr Neil leaned over to look inside.

"Guns?" asked Mike.

"Two pistols, one shotgun and two grenades," replied Bill.

"You want to fight your way out?" asked Jacob.

"We can't all go into the tunnels and add to that the Vermin are now down there That leaves us with the front door."

"The Vermin are in the tunnels?" said Mr Neil.

"They broke through where I entered from."

Jacob looked at Bill, his eyes wide. "They could get into here?"

"Eventually, yes," replied Bill. "But not for a while. I have left something that should put them off the trail, but not for long... we need to leave."

"But where are we going?" asked Mike.

"With Aatami and I together, our 'magic' is stronger. We can scan more of the town and find the Beast. We can find the hive of the Vermin and our other comrades."

"Find the Beast? I've got two children. I can't take them closer to him."

"Jacob's right," said Aatami.

Bill turned on her comrade. "RIGHT! RIGHT? Have you forgotten your mission, have you forgotten who your superior is?"

Aatami shrunk back. "We need to talk to command..."

"COMMAND? Aatami I am your commander while we are on mission, do you understand?"

"Bu–"

"If you interrupt me again I will make sure the command hears about it when we get back and this 'special last mission' will become your 'special middle mission'. Do you understand comrade?"

Aatami nodded meekly. Jacob tried to catch his eye, but Aatami kept his firmly on the table. Jacob couldn't take his children, or Nancy, closer to the

Beast, he wouldn't.

"Give us a gun and we'll make our own way."

"Out of the question – I will not give away any of our weapons."

Jacob looked to Aatami for backup, but he wouldn't look at him. Mike shrugged from across the table. "Then we have no choice; we will come with you, but we will leave for safety the first chance we get, agreed?"

"Affirmative," answered Bill.

"What about Nancy?" asked Mike on the way down the stairs. "Shouldn't we tell her?"

Jacob looked at Nancy. She was asleep with her head back on the stone wall. Sam and Jack looked bored. "Let's wait."

"But she needs to know that's not Bill... that's not her dad's friend."

"I know, but if that's not Bill, where is her dad?"

Mike put a hand on Jacob's arm. "Do you think?"

"It's a definite possibility."

"Fuck," Mike muttered.

"We need to keep everyone calm. If we're going out there, we need everyone focused... no mess-ups."

"I don't like this... I don't trust Dinah; I trust Aatami, but Dinah..." He shook his head. "There's something off about her, something a bit to Colonel Kurtz, if you know what I mean?"

Jacob knew exactly what he meant. Aatami seemed like a reluctant soldier, someone fighting someone else's war, someone with empathy. Dinah was something more, something dangerous. A career soldier, perhaps? Or simply unhinged? But Dinah had the weapons.

"I keep thinking about the fireball," Jacob started. "And the birds falling from the sky. Have you noticed that there are no bodies? Where did the bodies of the birds go? When that thing crashed I swore I saw the tops of the trees bending and moving; it was like when the T-Rex appeared in Jurassic Park. How big is the Beast? Can they even stop it?"

"If it is that big, it seems like a suicide mission?"

"That's my worry, we need to talk to Aatami alone. I'm worried Dinah has a Colonel Kurtz complex that will get us all killed."

CHAPTER 10 – DINAH

Who did these humans think they were? Trying to order her around. She had led great armies to fantastic victories; she had fought off the Vermin time and time again. Who was Aatami to question her in front of these creatures? And how dare they talk to her as if she was their equal? If the great Beast was here on this world, she would fight him off, she would be the saviour of this world, all worlds and be honoured on every world.

She was alone in the room upstairs. First Jacob and Mike left and then she flicked her wrist towards Aatami and he left too.

For the moment she needed Aatami - not for his skills, but for his power. After that, maybe Aatami would have an accident just before they travelled back to their own world. A soldier in the field, unable to follow his commander's orders, was a danger.

She stared out the stainedglass window. It was nearly fully dark. The world had become a dark blue of shapes without the orange glow of the streetlights.

What were the human's names? She hadn't bothered to listen to the introductions. Stupid simple names with no meaning. Maybe she should kill the two children now. Have it done with? That would be a mercy for the adults. They didn't need anyone slowing them down. Yes, that would be a mercy. And it would leave her able to concentrate on the battle at hand. But, if you're going to kill the children, you may as well kill all of them: what are human adults anyway if nothing but bigger, pinker, human babies? Full of self-importance and confidence in their place in the universe. Yes, she would kill them all and be done with it. No one would question her when she got back to her world if she was now Dinah, the Killer of the Beast.

CHAPTER 11 – NANCY

Bill was acting strange. The Bill she knew who came to her dad's house to drink beer and watch football was a sweet guy, a caring guy, who always asked how she was. Quick to smile with a sharp wit from years working with words. This Bill passed her on the stairs with barely a glance. He made his way through the two boys as if they were rats, as if being touched by one of them would be fatal. Bill loved children.

Mike and Jacob sat further up the stairs in a deep conversation. At one point she was sure she heard her name in whispered tones. Having your eyes closed and pretending to be asleep was as good as pretending to be drunk to get to know how someone would treat you when you were vulnerable. When she'd started one of her many jobs in sales, she realised early the benefits of people thinking you were stupid and slow. Not quite with it.

Her mission in the tunnels had been a failure. She hadn't found a way out, instead she'd bought a strange-acting Bill into the group and led the Vermin through the tunnels to them. Yes, they hadn't arrived yet, but she knew they would soon enough. She'd condemned them to death – it was just a choice of whether to sit and wait for it in here, or to face it head-on out there. If it was just her, she would have gone already.

She watched Bill and Mr Neil. They were rummaging through the duffel bag Bill had bought with him from the tunnels. The two men didn't act like strangers. Mr Neil seemed to defer to Bill. Sam and Jack were playing at the bottom of the stairs and she watched them with a slight smile spreading across her face. Would she have been a good mum, she wondered. She watched as Mr Neil and Bill removed two pistols and a shotgun from the bag followed by a box of shotgun shells, two magazines and two small pineapple-shaped green objects. She saw the pin at the top.

"Grenades?" she asked.

Bill didn't look at her, but Mr Neil did. "Fragmentation grenades, old ones by the look of it, but they could come in useful."

"Is that what I heard when I was down in the tunnel?"

Bill nodded.

"Are we going somewhere?"

"Talk to Jacob, Nancy," Mr Neil said, not unkindly. Her life had turned inside out. Bill, the friendly old friend of her dad was cold towards her, while Mr Neil, the ultimate weirdo from earlier, was now being kind.

"Bill, do you have a minute, please?" she asked.

"Not now, maybe later."

"It's about my dad."

"What about him?"

"Is he okay?"

"He's fine."

"You're sure?"

"Certain"

"Where is he?"

"At the police station."

Something walked over her grave. The police station… but everyone there was dead. Jacob and Mike had seen it happen. Nancy remembered the gunshots. They came from that direction. Perhaps there were people there now. Maybe they'd found a way to board themselves in.

"Is that where we're going?"

"No."

"Why not? Are there others there?"

"Not anymore."

"Where did they go?"

"They left."

"Are they safe?"

"Yes."

"Where are we going?"

"Don't know yet."

She frowned. Why was he so cryptic? Where was her dad? Was he okay? She saw Mr Neil give her an apologetic smile. Jacob and Mike had stopped talking and looked away when she looked up the stairs towards them.

"Will someone tell me what the fuck is going on!"

The only noise came from Sam and Jack, who continued to play with the little stones they'd found near the wall. *Clack. Clack.* The stones hit each other on the stone floor. Sam picked them up and threw them again, *clack, clack,* before kicking them towards the stairs. Jack's face fell and then he squealed. Jacob made his way down and picked him off the floor. The little boy wrapped his arms and his legs around his father.

Nancy looked up at Jacob. "Please, I'm not a little girl, someone tell me what's going on."

"We're getting ready to leave," said Mike. "That's why we're tense. We can't stay here any longer, we have no food and only a few bottles of water left. Bill has weapons, so we're going out the front door."

"That's it? That's all?"

Mike nodded.

Nancy looked to Jacob. "You promise?" She saw something flicker in his eyes, but then it was gone.

"Promise," he said. "We didn't want to get you and the boys scared was all."

"Scared? I'm not a little girl, or someone who needs protecting – never leave me out of one of those conversations again, you hear me?"

She felt something touch her knee. It was Sam. "No be sad, Nancy," he said. "No sad." He shook his little head, and then he pushed through her bent knees and cuddled her. She held him in her arms and looked up to Jacob who held Jack in his. *Please be telling the truth, I won't be able to handle it if you've lied to me.*

They stood together. Four men, one woman and two little boys in the small unlit corridor they'd been in for what seemed like days but turned out to be only hours. It was nighttime outside. It was dark inside. They agreed they couldn't spend the night in the old hospital. With the tunnels now swarming with Vermin, they could be overwhelmed and trapped within moments.

The tunnels, which had promised safety, now offered only death. They would have to go overground again. Nancy touched the arrowhead poking out of her jeans pocket; it felt reassuringly sharp. She wasn't sure where they were going, but hoped it was somewhere high. She let her reservations about Bill go, so they were lingering only lightly at the back of her mind.

Sam and Jack stayed close to her, as Jacob, Mr Neil, Bill and Mike went ahead. Was she pissed about being the designated babysitter? Yes. But would she protect Jacob's boy's as if they were her own? Yes. Not just because of the attraction between her and Jacob, but because they were children without their mother. And no woman could let a motherless child go into the unknown without holding their hand. Who would wipe away their tears if they cried, who would hold them when they got scared?

Jacob held the shotgun, while Mr Neil and Bill held the pistols to their sides. Mike held the black duffel bag with the ammo and grenades slung over his shoulder and the remaining mobile phone with its harsh torchlight.

"Don't shoot unless we're attacked. Understand?" said Bill.

The men nodded. Jacob turned back to Nancy and the boys. He knelt and hugged each boy, telling them, "Stay with Nancy," before kissing them on their foreheads. He stood in front of Nancy and moved his hand to her cheek.

"I'll keep them safe, I promise," she said.

He kissed her on her lips and he took her hand. After a moment of getting lost in the warmth of his touch, she opened her eyes. He pulled away with her hand still holding onto his, not willing to let him go. "It'll be okay," he said to the three of them.

Nancy picked Jack from the floor and held her hand out to Sam. He took it and she saw him fighting back tears. She squeezed his hand in hers. "Just a little game, baby boy. A little game in the dark – it's like a race, we just have to keep up with your daddy, okay?"

Jacob turned and spoke over his shoulder, "I'm right here, Sam, daddy's not going anywhere." He looked at Nancy. "Ready?"

"Ready?"

They opened the door into the principal room of Locke's hospital. The torchlight lit up the long table in the middle, which reflected white on the polished wood. The windows were black. No streetlights had turned on. The entire town of Westford stood dark and silent behind the two solid wooden doors they were now approaching. Jacob and Mr Neil went to the left of the door, while Bill and Mike went to the right. Bill reached out and twisted the brass doorknob. He pulled it open and Jacob and Mr Neil swung into the foyer with their guns raised. It was empty.

"We go together, okay?" Jacob said, as they squeezed into the small porch which reminded Nancy of the entrance to a church.

"Are you sure we shouldn't go to the police station?" asked Mike.

"Trust me, there's no one there any more," replied Bill.

"And you're sure about where we *are* going?" asked Nancy.

"There was no sign of the Vermin up there when I was at the police station earlier… it's where people were trying to get to for safety."

"Okay, let's go."

Jacob opened the door and one by one, silently they entered the dark and deserted town.

CHAPTER 12 – AATAMI

Aatami was worried. The ritual to take over a body had never caused him guilt before. It had simply been part of the process. When he looked into Dinah's mind, he saw the man he had killed to take control of Bill's body. He didn't need to be a mind-reader to put the pieces together. Dinah had killed Nancy's father.

That wasn't the only worry. Something about Dinah felt wrong. He remembered an old story about a commander who lost it when in the field. In the story, the commander lost all sense, the mission took precedence over everything. Many Exos died, and a great many locals too. Had the excitement of coming face to face with the Beast tipped Dinah over the edge? Was she so out for the scalp of him that she would sacrifice everything and everyone in her way? He could see the lust for glory in Bill's blue eyes.

He looked back to Nancy, who carried Jack in one arm while holding hands with Sam with the other. She'd saved him and she had now taken over the safety of two boys who 12 hours ago she didn't know existed. Jacob and Mike were good men. Smart and brave. They had no magic like him and Dinah, but here they were, ready to fight for each other. Dinah would sacrifice him without blinking.

They stayed close to the tall buildings on Almshouse Street. walking crouched, military-style in a row with Dinah to the front and Mike to the rear, behind Nancy and the boys. Dinah had cut her mind off from him. She was leading them towards the hive. He spoke telepathically to her, hoping she would hear. "We can't take them up the alleyway, they don't need to see the death I saw in your mind."

"Understood," came the swift reply, and it relieved him when she kept her word and walked past the dark alley. A puddle of blood had pooled at the bottom with oil-like streams seeping through the cobbles, out onto the road and down the drain. The sky was clear and a blue half-moon reflected in the dark red pool.

They kept moving. The only sound an occasional scuff from one of their shoes on a protruding cobble. Across the road from the old museum, and a closed Indian restaurant on their right, was a one-way road. Keeping close to the stone wall they followed it up the hill to a T-junction onto the main road, which if they went left led past the car park towards the police station. They went right, heading away from the town centre.

Two sets of unblinking traffic lights sat along the road. They approached the posh private school to their right and Aatami looked up at the metal bridge that crossed the road some 20 feet above which led to the signposted sports fields. The stars above blinked in the night sky. Aatami didn't think he had ever seen such a clear sky, not even on his own world.

He frowned. The thought of his own world made him sad. His wife and two children were waiting for him to return. They had been full of excitement about their newly-gained Citizenship before he'd left. The longer he stayed on this world, the worse he thought his chances of returning to his were. He lingered on the memory of each of their faces a moment longer, before blocking them out and coming back to the mission.

Dinah hadn't told him where they were going. He bit his lip. Something felt wrong. They should have seen at least one of the Vermin by now. He was sure the shadow Vermin had even left their sentry positions at the base of every doorway. This was unlike any mission he'd been on. The Vermin weren't acting like they did on other worlds, in other skirmishes. This was something new, and something big. He was certain there was something special about this world, and about this town.

Ahead, Dinah raised one hand to the air. They stopped in a line, moving closer from the back to the front; huddled together. They rounded a corner and crouched behind a brick wall in an old terraced house's front courtyard.

'Can you summon your light?' he heard Dinah in his mind, while to the group she spoke out loud, "Stop… I hear something ahead."

Aatami reached inside himself. He had enough power to summon his light, but he was unsure how long it would last, and how far away from him it would reach.

'I can, but not for long – I'm still not fully recovered.' Feeling flushed from deceit, he said to the group: "I'll go and check it out."

"No, you won't," said Nancy. "I don't know what happened, but your miraculous recovery might just be shock or something – you can't go."

"Really, I feel fine," he whispered. *'She won't let me go…'*

'Are you so spineless, Aatami? You've been too long in the company of these pests.'

"I am fine Nancy, now let me go…" He brushed past her and felt his cheeks flush with guilt and stupidity as he realised Dinah had goaded him so easily. He turned back to her as he crept past the others and out the front gate and mouthed: "I'm sorry."

A row of gloomy houses spread far up the hill on both sides of the road. Cars, some parked, some crashed, sat on the road and on the curb. As he moved further up the hill, he saw a car's emergency lights flashing orange every other second, creating a strobe-like effect in the glass of the windows and doors of the houses. Nancy and the group were at the bottom of the hill, at least 100 yards away.

He ducked around a corner with his back against a wall to a similar courtyard to the one he'd left the others crouched in. Aatami concentrated in a yoga-style pose with his hands palm up and open. A bright purple spot the size of a pinprick appeared between his hands and grew to the size of a small football. Its edges weren't as vivid purple as before; a more clear purple, like a forget-me-not in spring. He didn't have long. The orb throbbed and then floated up the road.

He sat in silence thinking about Jacob, Nancy, Mike and the boys. Why hadn't he told them about what had happened to the rest of the people in this town? He knew Nancy had one of the Vermin inside her – he could smell it on her – but instead of it splitting her head open on the way out, she had extracted it herself. How many bodies lay inside their homes, their heads cracked like an egg? With the size of the swarm, he guessed at least 5,000. In a town this size, that would leave 25,000 people hiding in their homes or who made it out in time. But where were they? Nancy didn't know about him and Dinah, but she would have to know, eventually. Just like she would have to find out the truth about what happened to her dad.

With his energy low, he didn't enter the orb from afar. He waited for it to return and become one with him again. Then he would search for what it had seen.

The Beast hadn't been for thousands of years. No one knew what it looked like; it was a scary story you told your children before bed. The images in his mind were from ancient legends and stories of warrior ancestors. Had there been anything before the Beast, he wondered. He could remember no stories from before the wars – no stories of peace. Was that because in peace there were no stories to tell? The idea was comforting. Stories, by nature, revolved around conflict. If there was no conflict there were no stories. Was that what peace was? The ending to a novel or even the beginning before the conflict began? He hoped so.

Movement from the window of the house whose courtyard he was in snapped him out of his reverie. A young girl stared out at him from the window. Her white skin glowed in the moonlight. Her hair was blue in the moonlight. The curtain she was holding fell silently. He smiled. Then the curtain pulled back again. Aatami waved at the little girl. She raised a hand

and waved back. There was no smile on her face. He pointed towards the front door. She shook her head. He put his hands together in a pleading pose. She seemed to contemplate this action. She raised a finger to him and closed the curtain.

Aatami crawled towards the front door over the cold wet patio slabs and was on the second step of three when the door opened just a crack.

"Can I come in?" he whispered.

"Who are you?"

"Mr Neil. And you?"

"Polly."

"That's a pretty name, Polly. Can I come in, please?"

"Mum and dad said I shouldn't let anyone in."

"Where are your mum and dad?"

"Mum took my little brother with her to the police station earlier, but she hasn't come back yet…"

"And your dad?"

"He went to work early."

"Has he come home?"

She shook her head.

"Polly, are you alone in there?"

Polly nodded. She had small blue eyes and freckles on her nose and cheeks.

"Your parents were sensible to say not to let anyone in, but it's dangerous out here, Polly. Please can you help me?"

The door opened a little farther and she stood to the side as he entered. "It's dark," he said, as she closed the door behind them.

"No electricity," she shrugged, "and mum said not to touch the matches, so I couldn't light a candle."

"I'm with a group of people, do you know what's been happening outside?"

She stiffened, her back stock straight and her arms by her sides. "Those things," she said.

"You've seen them?"

Polly nodded.

"How many?"

"About an hour ago, hundreds of them swarmed up the hill."

"Hundreds?"

"They were clambering over each other, they looked like a swarm of bugs."

"Have you seen any since?"

"Nope, no people either – just you."

"I'm with a group of people, Polly, friendly people. Three men, a girl a little older than you, and two little boys."

"Where are they?"

"They're waiting at the bottom of the road while I check it's clear."

"Is it?"

"Is it what?"

"Clear?"

"It seems to be."

"Will my parents and brother be coming home?"

"I don't know…"

"Where are you going?"

"We don't know yet, somewhere safe."

"How old is the girl?"

"Nancy? I'd say early twenties…"

"Is she pretty?"

"Um, I guess so."

"That's nice."

From outside, they heard a dog bark. Then the barks cut off and all they could hear were high-pitched yelps of pain, and then silence. Polly led Aaatami from the porch way into the living room. A thin sliver of silver moonlight from the window he'd first seen her in lit up the purple rug that covered exposed floorboards.

"Your home is beautiful."

"Thank you. Where do you live, Mr Neil?"

"Oh, I'm from Westford – the top end though, up towards the motorway."

"Must be noisy," she said.

"Well, we're not that close."

"Good."

"Are you going to bring your friends here?"

"Would that be okay with you?"

"I guess so."

"You're a very brave little girl, Polly."

"Thank you."

Aatami thought this strange little girl was either incredibly brave or a total dunce. Either way, her home provided an option to keep Nancy and the boys safe while they went to fight the Beast. If he spoke to Nancy first, he was sure she could charm this little girl with talk of… well, whatever little girls like to talk about. How many other little girls and boys were on their own waiting inside empty houses for their parents to come home? The easiest way to protect them all would be to end this insidious invasion before it spreads.

He sensed his orb approaching from the top of the road. "Polly, do you mind if I bring my friends here to meet you?"

"You must be quiet."

"I will, I promise."

"In which case no, I don't mind, it would be nice to have someone to talk to."

Aatami became one with his orb when it returned and felt his power drain. He kept low as he made his way down the hill towards the group while he took in everything his light had seen. Three separate swarms of Vermin, each with 200-plus creatures, stationed like sentries, stood: one at the top of the hill leading down to the college, one at the bottom of the hill leading to the college and the last on a through-road that ran opposite the college.

His light had made it to the entrance of the college. In the dark, he saw bodies hanging from the walls of the building and others impaled on the antennae on top. Stacks of bodies two metres high and three wide blocked the entrances. Women, men, children and animals. The college itself was large. A grey block-shaped building with a car park for 300 cars. It sat next to an equally wide building, though not as tall. This was the leisure centre. Like the college, lanced and skewered bodies were attached to the walls, like cow carcasses in a walk-in freezer.

He searched Mr Neil's memories and found a layout of both buildings. For a creature like the Beast, both buildings would be the perfect place to wait until it reached full power. Aatami stopped. He heard a scuttling sound at the bottom of the road, towards where the others hid. Falling back into the shadows of a nearby front courtyard, he watched as a swarm of Vermin turned the corner and came up the hill past the others and then him. They climbed over each other, their jaws filled with sharp teeth snapping at each other as their six legs moved fervently, almost independently of each other, along the tarmac. He let out a breath as they reached the top of the road.

Aatami stood for a few more minutes waiting to see if another swarm would come. When it didn't, he carried on towards the other group. As he approached, it was silent. The courtyard was empty.

"Psst..." came a sharp sound from the other side of the road. "Psst..." it came again.

In the dark he couldn't see anything. Then his vision cleared, and he saw the silhouette of two heads poking above a low stone wall. He checked both ways and listened. It was clear. Keeping low, Aatami ran across the road and hopped over the low stone wall into the courtyard. They were all there, and he thanked some faceless God they were okay, especially the boys and Nancy.

"We heard them approaching and one side of the courtyard we were in was open to the road; if one had taken a shortcut it would have come straight through us," explained Jacob.

"Well done," said Aatami. "It's good to see you all."

"What did you see?" asked Dinah.

"It's clear, up to the top of the road, anyway. After that there is a swarm at the head of the road leading to the college."

"Did you see anything else?"

"I met a little girl, she's alone in a house up there. She has offered to take us in." Bill's face hardened, but Aatami found he no longer cared.

"That's perfect," said Nancy. "Me and the boys can stay with her."

"That's the plan."

'One of OUR comrades is near, do you feel it?' Dinah spoke in his head, and he couldn't help notice the extra emphasis on 'our'.

'Yes, I felt it."

'This could work out well.'

He didn't understand her meaning. He turned and spoke to Nancy, "She's just up here on the left. Nancy, if you try to make her comfortable then the rest of us can get settled." Later he'd wonder, if he'd only paid a little more attention to Dinah's words, would things have worked out differently?

The others waited in the dark courtyard next door, while Aatami approached Polly's front door. He knocked gently, and it opened.

"You okay?" he asked.

She nodded. He stepped back from the door and saw a silhouette of one of the group poking out from behind the wall. He motioned for them to come.

One at a time, the group approached the houses and stepped past Polly into the entrance hall. Once they were all inside, Aatami closed the door and made introductions. His brow furrowed at the way Dinah looked at the little girl.

The house was cold and dark. He could only tell each apart from their silhouettes against the blue moonlight coming from the front bay window. Nancy and the boys sat on a soft sofa against the long wall, while Aatami, Jacob, Mike and Bill stood at the exposed brick fireplace. Polly stared in at them from the doorway.

"How did she survive?" asked Mike.

"By being quiet I'd guess – if she's still alive, there may be more in other houses," said Jacob hopefully.

"God, I hope so," replied Mike.

Dinah spoke to Aatami, "What did you see?"

"Three swarms, one at each end cutting off the college – I think that's the Hive and maybe the Beast is there?"

"Could be, but would the Hive and the Beast be at the same place?" asked Mike.

"Why not?" asked Dinah.

"Well, if I was invading a world, I wouldn't put all my eggs in one basket, if you understand the saying?"

Dinah went quiet for a moment and then looked at the group. "I understand, and you may be right, or you may not – either way, we attack."

"Okay, hold-up." Jacob raised his hands. "I understand you want to attack this thing, but they're my kids over there and I want to keep them safe. Trust me, I want to kill those things, but shouldn't we show a bit more patience? There are only two of you, a few weapons and two of us – can we win?"

'Two of us for now,' Aatami heard Dinah in his mind. Had she wanted him to hear, or had she let her guard down? One of their comrades was near. That she hadn't been wrong about, but getting them into a vessel would mean…

"Aatami, are you okay? What do you think?" Jacob asked.

"If we attack we would lose," he said and then turned to Dinah. "You know this, Dinah, we can't win with just us." The two boys were too little to be vessels, but Nancy, Jacob, Mike or even Polly could work. Could he sacrifice any of them? Would he? A day ago it wouldn't have even been a thought in his mind, but now…

"What do we do then? Should we search for one of your comrades? Do you know where they are? Can you find them?" asked Jacob.

"One's close, yes."

"And with a third of you, could we win?"

"We could put up more of a fight," said Aatami.

"Then let's split into groups and go find them."

"Nancy and the boys should stay here, Polly too…" said Jacob.

"No," said Dinah, "Nancy and the boys can stay, but we may need Polly. If our comrade is in one of her neighbours' houses, if they see this little girl they know on the doorstep, they will be more likely to let us in."

Aatami, understanding the logic, but still unsure, offered: "This is true, I shall take Polly and Jacob."

"No. If you are taking Jacob, as I see you had already planned, then I will have Mike who is old and fat – I will need the girl."

Mike choked on Dinah's words and turned to him when Jacob put an arm on his shoulder. "Not now." Aatami heard him whisper to his friend, whose cheeks had turned so red he could see them even in the dark.

"Then it is agreed, I shall take Jacob, while you take Mike and Polly; if she will go with you…"

"She will, I assure you."

"Where is your comrade, Aatami? Is he in one of the houses?" asked Jacob.

"He could be, but he's not a solid form. He's halfway between worlds and a ritual needs to be performed to bring him fully through."

"So, that's how you cross dimensions? A ritual?"

"It's more complicated than that, but in theory, yes. We break through the walls to your world and then we must find a vessel, without one, we are stuck in your dimension with no body."

"How do you choose a vessel?"

"Sometimes we have time to pick. If there's enough people around to choose from, other times it's the first creature we find."

"Creature? So it doesn't have to be a human?"

"Humans are specific to your world only, so we need to be able to take over all creatures."

"What about the Beast?"

"What about the Beast?"

"Could you take over him?"

"I couldn't, maybe someone strong enough and old enough could, perhaps. But no, I don't think so."

"And the Vermin? How did they arrive?"

"They smash through the walls in the dimension, usually inside what you call a meteorite."

They carried on through the deserted house in silence. Two doors up from Polly's house, they had crept into it through a back alleyway. Dinah, Mike and Polly were across the road in the houses on that side.

"Can I ask you something, Aatami?"

"Yes..."

"Do you like doing what you do?"

Aatami stopped and turned to Jacob. "I've never been asked that before?"

"Never?"

"Never. Where I come from, Jacob, we do what we have to do, not by choice, but by loyalty and through orders."

"So you don't get to decide? What about after you become a Citizen?"

"No one knows – once you are a Citizen, you never talk to non-Citizens again."

"How do you know there is anything after your missions then?"

"Faith, I guess."

"Faith? So you travel to other worlds, killing Vermin, taking over bodies all to become a Citizen – but you don't know what that means and you take it all on faith?"

"What else is there?" he asked. The sadness in his voice shocked Jacob and before he could stop himself, he pulled Aatami close and hugged him.

"What was that?" Aatami asked when they parted.

Jacob laughed. "Here on this world we call it a hug. We share them with friends and family to show them our love."

Aatami looked at his feet. "We should keep on searching…"

Jacob followed Aatami up the stairs. He felt as though Aatami already knew he wouldn't find his comrade in this house. That he was going through the motions in his search. But why?

"Aatami, what's going on? Why are we in this house, when I'm pretty sure you already know your comrade's not here."

"It's Dinah…"

"What about Dinah?"

"She's not right."

"Yeah, well sorry to tell you, bud, that's not exactly news to me…"

"No, I mean she's seriously not right. The Dinah I know is hard like stone, but she's careful, studious – this Dinah was ready to run into battle with no hope of winning."

"She's one of your kind, Aatami, I'll have to trust your judgement."

Aatami stopped walking and sat down on a soft bed in the room they were in. It creaked under his weight. Jacob stood with his arms crossed waiting for him to continue.

"I need to tell you something."

Jacob nodded.

"It's about the ritual…"

"Go on…"

"Well, I haven't told you everything."

"I'm shocked," Jacob said sarcastically.

"The ritual is dangerous, but it's the only way to take over a vessel. We do what we have to do for the sake of the universe, do you understand?"

"Why do I get the feeling I'm not going to like what you're about to say?"

"The ritual isn't dangerous to us – it's dangerous to *you*."

"Aatami, what do you mean?"

Aatami put his head in his hands.

"Aatami! What's going on?"

"Life is pure, innocent, and it's impossible to become a vessel if the body is innocent and pure…" He looked at Jacob. "To become a vessel, we get into your mind…"

A dog barked outside.

"How do you get into our mind? What do you do, Aatami?"

"We become like the Devil on your shoulder. We want you to become impure."

"How do you make us impure?"

"There's only one way to make someone impure, Jacob. Murder."

"Wait, what? I don't understand... what are you saying?"

"We make the vessel kill, Jacob."

"Kill who?"

"Not picky, whoever is convenient."

Jacob paced in front of the bed before spitting: "You're not our saviour, you're as bad as the Vermin." He turned to leave the room and stopped. He looked back towards Aatami.

"Dinah's with Polly and Mike."

Aatami nodded. Jacob ran out the room, along the landing and down the stairs, taking them two at a time. He forgot to be silent in the old house which creaked behind him.

CHAPTER 13 – POLLY

It didn't take much to convince Polly they needed her for this mission. This may have more been part of the influence Dinah already had over her than any sense of exuberance or adventure. If Polly had been in her right mind, she wouldn't have stepped out of her front door with a still-seething Mike and the strange man called Bill, who she also had overheard being called Dinah by some of the others. That was strange.

The houses on the opposite side of the road from hers were larger than the terraced ones she lived in. Most were detached with larger courtyards and mock Tudor fronts. Still, just because they had more money didn't make them any safer when the Vermin came calling.

She knew what people at school said about her behind her back – the name calling. They thought she was from a different planet. She'd always been a bit spaced-out, but it wasn't her fault she preferred looking up at the stars and her own company, more than after-school clubs or secretly drinking and smoking at the Rec. They were probably all dead now, she thought, and that made her sad. Whatever they said about her, they were at least something that was always there, something she thought would be permanent.

Where were her parents? Where was her little brother? She was sure she was in some state of shock, and as much as she wanted to feel something for the people that had gone, again, she was simply still here and they weren't. Her mind was blank. Was that normal?

To cross the road, they'd have to be out in the open for seconds. Would the 'Vermin' as this strange group called them, appear from the dark and feast on their guts?

Another voice had appeared in her mind, shortly after the group had entered her house. It was only a whisper at the moment, with no words she could hear or remember, but it was there all the same like the constant ticking in her house that she never heard until she consciously thought about it. She thought it was coming from one of the people she'd let into her house. But that was crazy, wasn't it?

She watched as Bill went first, keeping low as he ran silently across the road, followed by Mike. She waited to hear the scuttering sound of claws on asphalt, but none came. Something was drawing her to follow them, even though she wanted to go back to the house. The voice that had been a silent nagging feeling in the back of her mind spoke, *'Follow us, Polly, and you will get your parents and little brother back.'*

She turned around on the path, but no-one was there. At least one person in this group wasn't what they seemed, but the thought of seeing her mum and dad and baby brother made her follow. They understood her and always had time for her strange ways.

The black forms of Bill and Mike beckoned to her from across the road. She liked Mike, he seemed like a friendly uncle that always bought wonderful presents on special occasions. It wasn't Mike, she was sure, that was strange, but this Bill/Dinah person. But then she'd been through a lot and it was probably just the shock, but still…

'Your parents are waiting for you to save them, Polly. You do want to save them, don't you?'

She tripped over her feet as the voice spoke again. A high-pitched yelp came from her mouth and Mike darted forward and caught her before she fell. He held her in his arms and carried her the rest of the way. They crouched behind a low brick wall and held their breath as they waited for a swarm which never came.

Once they thought the road was safe, they turned to the imposing house behind them. There was a half-triangle mock-Tudor front with a square bay window jutting out to the left of them. A glossy black pillar came from the bottom of the triangle down to the floor, creating a covered porch area. The bottom half of the building was redmbrick, while the top half of the house was a wet sand colour. To the right of the house was a concrete driveway that led to the rear garden and a detached garage.

"This way," said Bill, and they followed him down the drive to the back of the property. Polly's eyes had acclimatised to the dark and the thin sliver of moon provided an eerie blue-white glow to everything. Without the artificial light of the streetlamps, she saw how beautiful and full of stars the night sky truly was.

"Keep up, Polly," Mike whispered from in front of her.

She moved forward again, following close to Mike who reached behind him and offered her his hand. She took it gladly. Bill reached over a wooden gate and undid the latch at the top. The gate opened inwards to the garden. They snuck through, closing the gate behind them. In the moonlight, the grass seemed to glow. The starry sky reflected perfectly in the still pond to the back of the garden. Pinpricks of white and the crescent moon were mirrored from above. It was beautiful, but she missed the sound of birds.

Bill tried the back patio doors, but they didn't move. He knocked on the window, but there was no movement in the house. Bill looked around for a rock and found one the size of Polly's hand.

"What are you doing?" Mike whispered. "You can't, they'll hear…"

Bill looked at the rock in his hand. A confused look crossed his face as if he'd never seen it before and had no recollection of picking it up. He put it back where he found it.

"Are you okay?" Mike asked.

"Yes, I… I… I just have a feeling about this house – we need to get in."

"We will."

He pulled Mike to the side, and Polly struggled to hear their whispers although she caught the words: Comrades, the Beast, and battle. When they turned back to the patio door, Polly turned away, pretending she hadn't been listening.

"How are we going to get in?" she asked.

"Polly, will you go and search under the plant pots over there, please? Sometimes, people leave their keys in safe places, don't they?"

Bill nodded next to him. She knew they wanted to be rid of her for a moment, and she didn't really care. Waiting to get into this house already bored her. Something was pulling at her to get in and go to the top floor like an invisible line. Polly turned and went to inspect the plant pots, not really bothered about how they would get in, just that they would.

As she lifted the third plant pot, she heard a click from behind her and the patio doors slid open.

"Oh…" said Bill, "I mustn't have pulled hard enough earlier."

Polly rolled her eyes and made her way inside the house, following Mike and Bill.

It was cold and dark inside. The patio doors led into a large dining room with wood flooring and shelves upon shelves with leather-bound books on the walls. In the middle of the room was a modern, glass dining table with four half-eaten bowls of cereal. A box of Rice Krispies lay on its side, scattered puffs of rice littered the tabletop and the floor. The milk was still open, and silver spoons sat in the bowls. If they'd ran so quickly, why were none of the doors left open? Polly wondered.

Now she was inside, part of her wanted to run up the stairs and into the loft area, while another part wanted to run back outside and to her own home. She knew there was a loft room upstairs. She could see it, even though she'd never been in this house before. It had two skylight windows, a desk and an enormous bed in the centre.

"What are we looking for?" Mike asked.

Bill thought about the question and finally answered: "You'll know when you find it"

Polly understood they were looking for someone, but why was Bill being so cryptic about it? Who were they looking for? Was it simply another survivor? She didn't think so.

"Well, there's three floors, so that would be a floor each, I sup–"

"I'll go to the top floor," Polly interrupted, "I mean, I know this house – I was good friends with the family who lived here. If someone's hiding, I'll be able to find them…" She wondered if Mike had picked up on her lie?

"I don't know about that, Polly. If you go to the top floor there's nowhere for you to go if something happens," said Mike.

"I'm quicker than both of you – if something happens I'll be able to get onto the roof or back down the stairs… piece of cake."

Bill smiled, but Mike still looked worried. "I guess that leaves the ground floor and the first floor?"

"I'll take the first floor," said Bill. "I'll be close by if anything happens." He looked down at Polly and smiled a shark-like smile.

"Looks like I'm staying down here then. Okay, so as long as nothing happens, we meet back here in 10 minutes', agreed?"

"Affirmative," Bill said in a robotic soldier-like voice.

"Affirmative," Polly mimicked.

Polly gave Mike a slight smile and a hug and then made her way up the stairs. She heard Mike whisper to Bill at the bottom. "You watch her, you hear me." Then she heard Bill's footsteps on the exposed wood stairs. They sounded ominous and full of danger. She sped up and ran across the landing to the second set of stairs.

The stairs corkscrewed around until she came out in the centre of the loft room she'd seen in her mind. It was exactly as she'd seen it. Through the skylight windows she could see the sky above, so full of wonder with its galaxies, stars, planets and moons. On the walls were heavy-metal band posters. She felt a presence, strong like electricity or ozone after a storm. It was something palpable, something she felt she could touch and taste and smell.

"Hello?"

There was no answer. Had she expected one? She felt faint. Dizzy. As if her mind was clearing and what was left was pure and simple nothingness. She sat on the bed in the centre of the room. Her feet just touching the floor. There were no hidey holes or cupboards she could see. Not even a wardrobe. The room was minimalistic. A bed, a metal desk with an assortment of arts supplies and a Stanley knife, with pencil shavings still attached, and the posters on the wall. That was all. Her right leg popped out in gooseflesh. She felt an icy touch on her leg, massaging and sensually touching her calf and moving its way up her thigh. A sensation she'd never felt before. In her stomach, she felt as if she'd eaten a cold ball of coal. Then as soon as the sensation had appeared, it left.

She stood from the bed and moved to the wall. Polly bent to look into the darkness under the bed. Nothing. Still. Silent. She let out a sigh and leaned against the wall. What was she doing here? Her shoulders went cold as something started pressing into her between them, making a circular pattern that pressed deep into her muscles and felt good. Really good. A chill ran through her, and she shuddered.

'Polly,' a voice inside her mind said. 'I want you. Do you want me?'

She answered breathlessly: "Yes."

'Give yourself to me. If you do, I will bring your parents and little brother back – is that what you want?'

"What do I have to do?"

'Lay back on the bed and let me in…'

Polly felt the icy massage stop. For a moment she stopped herself, but then the image of her parents and little brother flashed as real as a camera flash in her mind.

The bed was soft underneath her. Comfy and warm. The pillows were hard and moulded to her head – she usually slept on soft pillows. Something creaked, and she stiffened. A shadow, as dark as the deepest depths of the ocean, crawled out slowly from under the bed. It was long, and its limbs were gnarled and crooked. It took gasping breaths as it slid weakly along the floor. It raised itself to full height. Its shadow was so long it bent at an angle where the top of the wall met the ceiling. Long limbs hung limp by its sides. 'Polly,' she heard the voice say, as she lost control of her limbs. Her arms and legs stuck to the bed, held tight by an invisible force. The shadow approached, one of its gnarled tree-root like arms raised and pointing at her with an elongated twisted finger. She felt pressure at the end of the bed. The shadow was kneeling on it. The icy sensation came back up her right leg, only this time it felt wet and slimy. It hurt, each trace of liquid burning her skin. She wanted to cry out, to cry out to Mike, but her mouth moved wordlessly, silently. Something had stolen her voice. The shadow lurched forward and the gnarled arm punched down her throat. She felt the roots working their way inside her body, attaching to every nerve. And then she felt the shadow enter her. Vein-like-roots sent ice down every strip of flesh, every bone and tendon. Her body snapped forward as if she was having a heart attack and then she came down to lay flat and quiet on the bed. The shadow was gone.

Polly woke on the bed. She remembered everything. The icy sensation. The shadow. The loss of her voice. But she understood now: If she wanted her family back, she would have to let this shadow overtake her.

"What must I do?" she asked the dark.

The voice didn't answer. It was inside her now. It didn't need to speak with words when it could show her. It showed her what she needed to do. She wanted to block out the images as they entered her mind. 'One death for the lives of many, isn't that worth it, Polly?'

"Polly?" Mike called from below.

"Mike... I'm here. I'm okay, I'll be down in a minute."

She stared out the skylights, praying she'd see the moon and stars again one day...

Mike was at the front window, looking across the road to her house, where Nancy and the boys were tucked up safely. His shoulders slumped and he rubbed at his neck. Tears gathered in her eyes as she slowly approached him. In the room's corner, lurking in the shadows, she saw Bill. He nodded. She swore he was smiling. Out the window, past Mike, she saw Jacob run down the street. Mike turned, ready to run to help his friend, and as he did, Polly took the Stanley knife she'd found on the desk upstairs and drew it across Mike's exposed throat. The blade sliced through his skin like paper. His eyes opened wide, and he looked at her, surprised. Then blood spurted from the thin slice and covered her in his fiery blood. Mike slid to the floor, his arms grabbed hold of her shirt and then let go. He slumped to the ground where a pool of blood gathered below his resting head.

PART THREE

CHAPTER ONE – THE BEAST

The Beast walked where shadows dared not follow. He was the Son of Satan. Satan… It was one of the favourite names he'd heard his father called. It had a gravitas, almost holy and unholy at the same time.

He wouldn't make the same mistakes as his echo, the Leviathan, which drew him here. A group of weak humans wouldn't thwart him. He was stronger. The Exos had been sent as always, however his Vermin had taken care of them. He wasn't scared by an Exo, even two or three couldn't stop him.

He would unleash his father upon the universe. It was inevitable. This was the template world, the original that his father's father had created. Destruction and blood would bring a new age to the universe and he would be at the centre. The Commander in Chief of his father's legions.

CHAPTER TWO – JACOB

As he ran down the road, he saw Mike standing in the front window. Jacob shouted to him and he saw Mike turn. Then he saw him stop, a black shape moved with a flash, and then he watched Mike fall to his knees. Jacob called out again, not caring about the noise he was making or that the Vermin that would hear him.

A shadow stood over Mike in the window. The shadow was short. It was Polly. He knew Dinah had found her Comrade and the ritual was complete. Jacob ran down the side of the house and through the side gate into the garden. With only a glance at the reflected sky in the pond, he rounded the house and went through the patio doors and inside.

Polly and Dinah were gone. Mike lay on his front in front of the window. His arms at his side. A pool of blood still spewing from around his head. He hadn't put his arms up as he fell. He'd died quickly. The thought provided little comfort to Jacob. A sliver of moonlight shone through the rear window and alongside Mike, passing through one of his hands, making it look as though he was holding a thin silver dagger.

Jacob fell to his knees alongside his neighbour. He rolled him over. Mike's eyes were glassy and stared past Jacob into dead space. His mouth was frozen in an 'O' of shock. A thin black line traced across his neck under the still seeping blood. Then he heard the scuttling, claws-on-tarmac sound from the open patio doors. At first, he didn't move, but as the sound got closer, he turned, and on his knees, crawled to the back patio door and slid it shut, pulling the curtains closed. He sat with his back against the wall and thought about Sam and Jack and Nancy across the road. Where was Aatami? How could he let this happen to them? They had saved his life.

CHAPTER THREE – NANCY

Nancy had heard Jacob shouting from the sitting room in Polly's house. Both the boys were dozing on the sofa, one on each side of her. She stood, careful to avoid waking the boys, pulled an inch of curtain back and looked out the window. She saw Jacob run down the side of the house opposite and then nothing. Nancy stayed at the window watching. Movement from up the hill caught the corner of her eye. The Vermin were back. She pulled the curtains and turned towards the boys. Her heart rate increased and she felt cold and dizzy. Nancy stood with her back to the window watching the boys, unable to move for what felt like hours.

Sam stirred across from her. She'd been lost in her own thoughts, worried about Jacob. Had he made it into the house before the Vermin? Nancy bit down on her lip, nearly drawing blood. What if he hadn't? The road outside was silent now. No scuttling sounds, no shouts. Should she go find him? But what about the boys?

Something creaked on the first floor. Nancy tilted her head. It creaked again, directly above her. Could they have got into the house?

It was an older house than hers. Maybe it was just the natural sounds of it settling for the evening? The creak came again, louder this time and in a succession. Not just a single sound. She strode across the sitting room in two long bounds and shut the door that led to the hallway, followed by the other which led to the kitchen. Then she crouched in front of Sam and shook his knee. He looked up in the dark. "Daddy?"

"Not daddy, Sam, it's Nancy. Daddy's waiting for us in another house. We need to go in a minute though, okay?"

The little boy yawned and sat. He looked at Jack and pointed. "Jack still sleepy."

"That's okay. I'm going to pick Jack up without waking him, which means you'll have to hold my hand as we walk, okay?"

146

"Okay," he said breezily, suddenly wide awake.

Sam got off the sofa and paced around the dark sitting room. Nancy got in position next to Jack and scooped him up to her chest. He let out a little wail as she stood, but then was silent again. She reached for Sam's hand and he took it. "Ready?" she asked. "We might have to run, okay?"

Sam's smile faded, and he said: "I'm scared."

"Don't be scared. Daddy is out there – we're just going to find him."

Nancy grabbed the door handle as she heard the creaks again from above. They were becoming louder and more excitable. She took a deep breath, and after checking Jack was stable, she opened the door to the hallway and tiptoed through. The front door was closed, but not locked. The handle turned in her hand and she felt the cool autumn air on her face. She pulled Jack's hood from his coat to cover his face. Next to her, Sam did the same. They walked out into the night. Nancy knew if they ran, Jack would wake up and Sam would get tired. Their best chance was to keep to the shadows and move quietly.

They exited Polly's courtyard, and keeping close to the low walls of the other courtyards, they made their way up the hill. It meant leaving Jacob, but if something happened to him inside that house, or to Mike, Bill or Polly, she knew he'd want her to take the boys away. She realised where she was for the first time. She was five minutes from her flat.

A road ran to the left, which led to the top of the Rec, and another to the right, which led to the sports fields of the college and the private school. Where would be safe? She could take them back to her flat and barricade them in until this was all over. She had some food in the cupboards and running water. They could wait it out in relative comfort, as opposed to breaking into another house with no idea of what was on the other side of the door. She could see one problem though. Hadn't Mr. Neil said the Vermin had three swarms guarding the roads leading to the college? Should she really think about going closer to the Hive?

She remembered a memory from long ago, sitting in her father's study. He was reading a book about warfare strategy or something and he looked up at her – she was no older than 10 – and his face turned serious, frown lines appearing on his forehead. *"If anyone ever tries to grab you, Sweetie, and Lord, I pray it doesn't happen, you hide, okay? But when you hide, hide somewhere close by – don't waste your time running. The bad person will always chase you, or think you've left the area. They wouldn't expect you to hide close by, understand?"* She hadn't understood at the time, but she did now. They would go to her flat and wait things out. Jacob would know where to find them when the time came.

There was a cut-through to the park near her flat which she hoped wouldn't be guarded by the Vermin, but she would have to get past the large swarm at the top of the hill first. She could hear the scuttling and the snapping of jaws as they approached in the shadows. They were 100 yards away, but she could see the creatures climbing over each other in a writhing, spiked sea of black in the moonlight.

To go around would mean heading back towards the Rec. Keeping to the top of it and then coming back through from the other side. However, that would mean walking next to open-countryside. The thought terrified her. She thought it might have been because of the wide-open space in the dark. Sam knelt next to her and Jack was, thankfully, still asleep. They had to go past the swarm. It was as simple as that.

"Sam," she started, "you need to be as silent as a sleeping bunny, okay? We're going to go past these naughty creatures and to my home."

Sam nodded seriously at her.

"Keep hold of my hand and don't let go for any reason."

As she started to move, she saw the gigantic house opposite them, on the corner of the top of the road to the college. She thought they could sneak through the garden and head through it, coming out on the other side, so they didn't have to pass the swarm and could come out halfway down the road. Nancy paused as she thought about it. The house stood imposing in the dark, with tall modern windows overlooking the landscaped gardens.

"This way," she said, making up her mind and crossing the road in a jog. Tall ferns stood on both sides of the open metal gates that led to the brick driveway. These ferns bordered the entire plot of the property. Once they had entered the gardens, Nancy kept close to the ferns following them around the diameter of the garden towards the back, where she hoped a gap would allow her to exit onto the main road to the college.

"Psst…" came a noise from the house. "Over here."

Nancy stopped and pulled Sam close, then looked towards the dark building. She saw a figure in a window on the first floor.

"Hey, lady, not that way. You don't want to go that way. Come to the front and I'll let you in."

"Petey, what are you doing? Who are you talking to?" came another voice.

"There's a woman out there, Luke, with two little kids. I saw them with my Night Vision goggles."

Nancy watched as another black figure appeared at the window.

"Shit, you're right, she must be crazy."

"I can hear you," Nancy hissed back.

"Whoops, sorry – listen, lady, you really don't want to go that way, Petey was right. Come to the front and we'll let you in – we have food and water."

At the thought of food and water, Nancy's stomach gurgled. If she was this hungry, how must Sam and Jack be feeling? Plus, they sounded like teenagers – what could they do?

"Okay, I'm coming." Nancy pulled Sam towards the way they'd come, cutting across the grass this time. She rounded the corner of the house, passed under the large porchway with white wisteria growing up the brickwork, and standing at the front door, waiting, were two teenage boys and two teenage girls. One of the teenage boys was short with glasses, the other had shaggy brown hair and a good-looking face. One girl had strawberry blonde hair, while the other looked a lot like the good-looking boy.

The boy without glasses reached his hand towards Nancy. "Hi, I'm Luke. This is Petey, Ruby – my girlfriend – and Lisa, my sister. Pleased to meet ya."

The house wasn't theirs. They had been on their way to the college when one of the first attacks happened. It was a preview day ready for the following year when the two girls would start. Luke was walking Ruby, and Petey had tagged along with nothing better to do. As they entered the car park, they'd seen a crowd of teenagers ripped apart in front of them. They seemed oddly calm about the situation, thought Nancy, putting it down to shock.

After watching a boy called Stevie, who they knew from school, get his throat ripped out, they turned from the college and ran up the hill towards the Rec and the town centre. However, as they got to the top of the road, they heard more screams and the now familiar sound of scuttling claws on tarmac. Luke ducked under a fern bush, followed by the others. Petey had tripped and bumped into all of them as they crouched and they fell through the bush into the garden.

As had happened to her, a voice called down from the top window offering to let them in. It was a stern-looking man in his early fifties. He opened the grand, white double front doors, and the teenagers ran inside. His eyes opened wide and his mouth opened ready to speak, but Luke got there first.

"Something's attacking the college."

"What?"

"Rat-like creatures – they're all over the college, biting and eating people."

"Don't be ridiculous, boy," he said to Petey.

"It's true," Lisa said.

"Okay, well we'll see won't we." The man grabbed an expensive Barbour jacket from a hook and opened the front door.

"You're going down there?"

"If I can trust you lot not to steal anything, I am."

"Scouts' honour," Luke said.

They never saw the man again. The power went out shortly after, leaving them stuck in the gigantic house with little to entertain themselves and with no knowledge of what was going on outside. The swarm that sat less than 20 yards from the property had them pinned down.

"We heard some gunfire a few hours ago, but besides that, we haven't seen or heard anyone besides those things..."

"Vermin," Nancy said.

"Vermin?"

"That's what we call them."

Petey tilted his head then said. "As good a name as any I suppose. You know it kinda reminds me of this old novel about rats..."

"James Herbert," Nancy answered. "Classic novel."

Lisa shook her head. "Whatever... listen, Nancy, do you know what's going on out there?"

"We were in Locke's hospital, but we had to make a run for it."

"We?" asked Petey.

"This is Sam and Jack. Their dad, Jacob, is still out there as is his neighbour, Mike, and two other men and a little girl. We got separated."

"How's the town look?" asked Ruby.

Nancy shook her head. "Not good."

"Shit... I thought we'd left fucking weird behind us," said Luke grumpily.

Nancy flashed her eyebrows, but the kid didn't say anymore. Jack was still asleep, cuddled into her. "Do you have anywhere I can put this little one? He's out for good, I think."

"Sure, there's a downstairs bedroom just down the corridor," said Lisa.

"Thanks." Nancy turned to Sam. "Wait here buddy. These are friends, okay?" Sam looked at the older kids suspiciously, then Petey stepped forward.

"Do you like Lego, Sam? It is Sam, isn't it?"

"Lego?" asked Sam.

"I saw a huge set of Lego in the kitchen. Do you want to come and look with me?"

Lisa stepped forward and put her hand out to Sam. "I do. Will you show me what you can build, Sam?"

Nancy looked at this group of teenagers and sensed something special, something heart-achingly good about them and felt herself well up. "Thank you for taking us in, I don't know what we would have done otherwise."

"Anytime," Luke said. "Now let's check out the Lego."

Nancy lay Jack down on a bed in the room next to the kitchen and left the door open. She noticed for the first time that she could see inside the house, then noticed the candles lit on the sides in the two rooms. "Do you have anything to drink?"

"In the fridge," said Petey.

She opened the American-style fridge and saw beer, wine and soft drinks. Her hand hovered over a bottle of beer, but then reached past and grabbed a can of Coke. She turned to ask if Sam wanted anything, when she saw he was already happily enjoying a carton of orange juice and munching on a packet of cheese and onion crisps. The sensation of safety within this group of teenagers came stronger than before and she went back to the room where Jack was snoring and she put her head in her hands and wept.

CHAPTER FOUR – AATAMI

Aatami got off the bed. Jacob was long gone. He stood alone in the dark with his thoughts. Had he done the right thing? Maybe they could have defeated the Beast without a third Comrade. Voices came up the stairs; Dinah's and Polly's – or Adlai's, as was the name of his Comrade who was now in Polly's body.

"Aatami, it is done. Adlai is with us now."

"Comrade," started Adlai, "it will be good to see you again, and together, we can stop this. Come down…"

Aatami stopped at the top of the stairs. Images of Mike, dead in the house across the road, flashed through his mind. He stumbled and had to reach and hold on to the stair rail. "What have I done?" he whispered.

"Aatami, are you ready?" Dinah called again.

He gathered himself as well as he could, with strange feelings causing his stomach to lurch and roll. He made his way down the stairs. At the bottom, in the dark, Dinah and Adlai – in Polly's blood-soaked body – waited for him. They smiled humourlessly at him. Black-looking blood covered Polly's face, and in the dark, her teeth and eyes shone white like a hyena.

Adlai approached him and embraced him as was their custom. He put both arms around Aatami's shoulders and neck and looked deep into his eyes, Aatami leaned forward so he could rest his forehead on his. Aatami felt the sticky blood on his forehead. Mike's blood. Blood that was on his hands as much as Adlai's.

"It's good to see you, Adlai."

"You too, Comrade. It's been too long," he responded, before adding. "Isn't this your last mission? Hell of a last mission!"

Adlai, like Dinah, was a career soldier. Aatami suddenly felt very much felt like the odd one out. Any security he'd previously felt when surrounded by his comrades had left him. Aatami now felt uneasy in these two's company.

"It is, Adlai. My last mission before I become a Citizen."

"That must be exciting for you…"

"I'm not thinking about it until we have finished with the Beast. Dinah has updated you on the situation, I take it."

"She has. Who would have thought it? This shitty world with its puny inhabitants would be the template world…" Adlai laughed in wonder.

Aatami didn't laugh. He wanted to save the world, but at what cost to his own soul. Could he look at his wife and children the same way, knowing now what he had done. Not just on this world, but all the others too.

"It is a wonder," Aatami said

"Dinah said you were injured, Comrade. Shall we fix you now – before we move onto the Beast?"

Dinah and Adlai moved closer together. Aatami watched them close their eyes and move their hands in front of themselves, palms up. Dinah's green orb appeared first, followed by a red glowing orb in Adlai's hands. The orbs swirled around each other, sometimes floating through each other creating a deep earthy brown colour. They throbbed as one and then Aatami felt them enter him. A warmth grew throughout his body. His strength returned and his shoulder felt hottest of all. Then the warmth was gone. He rotated his shoulder, happy that the dull pain was gone too. He felt refreshed, as if he'd had an entire day's sleep after two nights with none. His mind was awake, and the guilt ran deeper now he could feel clearer.

He hadn't spent long enough thinking about other options. He'd simply gone along with Dinah's plan without even offering an alternative. The humans were stronger than he'd ever given them credit for, and he felt they could have been of use in the ultimate battle. But now, Jacob had gone, Mike was dead, Nancy and the boys were hiding. He'd lost them all. He'd betrayed them.

"Aatami, soldier-up? You don't look ready for a fight?" said Dinah.

"I am ready, I was just thinking about my family."

"Aatami, focus. Remember their faces when the final battle arrives."

Dinah turned and picked up the duffel bag. She had all the primitive weapons, except for one pistol which Jacob had taken with him. Primitive, but as Dinah knew well enough, effective against the Vermin. They could hold back their real power for the final fight.

"Okay, Comrades, the last fight is upon us. The one we knew would come one day, but no-one believed it would be today, not for us. The Beast is upon this world, surrounded by his Vermin and who knows what else… If he summons his father, he will destroy this world and all other worlds. It is up to us to stop him. No-one else is coming. I am ready to die, are you?"

Aatami nodded, he may not have believed in the way they had gone about it, but he was still ready to fight. Dinah was right, if they didn't win, the entire universe would be at risk. Adlai put an arm around both Dinah and Aatami's shoulder. "We will fight till the last drop, and we will win, my Comrades."

They left the house together and side-by-side walked up the hill towards the top of the road that led to the college. A cloud passed over the moon, setting them in total darkness for a moment, before passing. To their right, an enormous house caught Aatami's attention. Nancy and the boys are in there, he thought. He looked at Dinah and Adlai, but neither of them had taken any notice of the house. Their eyes were forward and locked on the mass of writhing Vermin ahead.

The thought of taking out the Vermin was comforting. It could be his way to atone for his sins. Killing Vermin was something that was second nature to him, something he didn't need to think about. As they approached, Aatami split off to the left, Adlai to the right and Dinah in the centre. They didn't need to worry about being silent on their approach. Now there were three of them, the Vermin were easy prey. Still, they wanted to save their powers. Aatami and Dinah took a knee as Adlai ducked next to a wall only 20 feet from the swarm. In his hand he held one of the grenades. He pulled the pin and let go of the lever as he rolled it along the tarmac into the swarm. The sound made the Vermin's movements more intense. They climbed and clawed at each other, unsure of what was going on.

The night erupted with a flash of yellow that was so bright, Aatami had to turn away. He felt warm air and something grazed his cheek. In the open, the boom was enormous. When he turned back to the swarm, he saw limbs still moving, jaws still snapping and claws still scraping – only they weren't attached to bodies. A small fire burnt in the middle from the explosive, but the fragmentation grenade had done its job. A handful of Vermin had survived the blast and Dinah took care of those mid-run with one of the pistols. A Rorschach dark stain spread from the centre of where the swarm had been by about two metres.

Aatami stood watching as Dinah and Adlai moved closer. Dinah passed Adlai the pistol as she pulled out the shotgun. He followed a few steps behind. They stopped and he caught up with them at the top of the hill. He took one look back at the house on the corner and saw shadows move in the windows.

Houses spread down both sides of the road, more modern than the ones from where they'd come from. Halfway down the long road, Aatami saw the antenna on the top of the college. A shadow moved up the hill towards them. Another swarm of Vermin. If what he had seen earlier had been correct, there were two more before they had a clear run at the college – there might even be more, he thought.

"Break formation," Dinah ordered.

Aatami broke right, Adlai left and Dinah moved back to the head of the road. They waited in the shadows as the sounds of the approaching Vermin reached their ears. If Aatami had looked up again, he would have seen five figures staring down open-mouthed at him from the large house now and then turning away suddenly. Above the roar of the fire, there was another sound. The crash of something hard against wood.

CHAPTER FIVE – JACOB

Jacob sat holding Mike's head in his lap. Drying tears cleaned a way through his dirty face. No dogs barked outside. His mind was empty – blank. He didn't know how long he'd sat on the floor next to his dead neighbour. He needed to get back to Nancy and the boys. Then he planned to find Dinah, followed by Aatami. He clenched his fists. They'd left them behind, 'done them over,' as his ex-wife would say. Who were they to take control of this fight? This was his world, his friends that were dead. He would find th....

The sky outside the window lit up yellow, followed a second later by a crash that shook the house. He stood and went to the window which still vibrated. The explosion had come from the top of the hill towards where Aatami had said the first swarm was. He looked towards Polly's house opposite. He could see no movement, and they had left one of the curtains open.

Jacob ran out the back patio doors and up the driveway and across the road to Polly's house. He tried the front door. It was unlocked. As he entered the dreary house, he frowned. They had told Nancy to lock herself in.

"Nancy?"

He heard a creak from upstairs. He poked his head around the door into the sitting room. Nancy and the boys were gone. A creak came again, followed by another. There was no blood, which gave him hope. He stepped back into the porch way and saw a shadow pounce from the top of the stairs. The yellow eyes seemed to hover in slow-motion as they careered through the air towards him. He fell backwards out the door, tripped over the doorstep and landed on his butt with a hiss. Jacob jumped up and slammed the door just as the Vermin clattered into it.

He turned towards the road, nearly tripping over his own feet. He looked down the hill towards town and then up the hill to where the fire burned. Hopefully they had cleared a path for him. He sprinted up the road and then remembered this was where they had first picked up Nancy. He stopped running and lent over, trying to catch his breath. She lived up here. She'd even mentioned the address in an earlier conversation, he was sure of it. Had she taken the boys to hers?

At the top of the hill, to his right, he saw a large house looming over the entrance to the college road. Something had smashed through the white double front doors and there was a flicker of orange light inside. He looked up and saw it would give him a suitable vantage point over the college road. He ran through the gates and into the house. The smell of fire, not from an explosion, but from candles, wafted into his nostrils. He touched the wick of one; the wax was wet and warm.

He followed the porch into a large kitchen-breakfast room. A couple of candles were still lit. He saw empty packets of cheese and onion crisps on the floor as well as a half-finished Lego model. Beyond the Lego model, towards the patio doors and past the dining table was a pool of blood and one of the Vermin picking at the bones of a fresh kill. Not an adult body. The disfigured head was too small. And, it was wearing Sam's coat...

CHAPTER SIX – NANCY

The explosion was close. Just the other side of the ferns. It woke Jack, who screamed. As well as the sound of the explosion, Nancy also heard objects hitting the outside of the house. One of the frag grenades, she thought. That would explain the objects hitting the house. Was it Jacob?

"Wait here," she said to the group of children and teenagers on the floor of the kitchen. Jack she passed to Lisa, who took hold of him like a natural.

Nancy ran up the stairs, stopping as they split in two, with one set leading left and the other right.

"Left," a voice shouted from downstairs. "Left will take you to the window overlooking the road." Nancy guessed it was Petey, the boy with the glasses.

She followed the advice and ended up in a dark bedroom with a four-poster wooden bed and patio doors leading to a Juliette balcony. She flicked the netted curtains away and stared out into the night.

A fire burned below. Around it lay the bodies, some complete, most not, of a swarm of Vermin. They'd taken out an entire swarm. She saw three ominous figures. Mr Neil and Bill she'd expected to see, but she didn't expect to see a blood-drenched Polly shooting Vermin with a pistol like she was an expert marksman. Nancy noticed all three worked in sync together, moving with the same movements, the same purposefulness. Bill had never been sporty in all the years she'd known him, but now he too moved around like he'd done five tours with the Marines. The figures separated into a V formation, with Mr Neil right below her. He was moving pretty well for a guy close to death a few hours ago. None of this makes sense.

A scream from downstairs broke her concentration, followed by the crunch of something hitting the front door.

This time she took the stairs three at a time and skidded at the bottom into the kitchen. The teenagers pointed past her towards the front door.

She saw the shadow of something large through the opaque windows on either side of the front door.

"What the fu–"

"Let me finish for you. What the actual fuck!" Petey said. The creature outside was as wide as a cow was long. "That's not the Vermin, that's a single thing out there."

"Luke?" Nancy started. "Are the back doors unlocked?"

"I think so, yes."

"Good, we're going to have to make a run for it, okay?"

"A run for it? Where the fuck too?" asked Lisa, who covered her mouth and looked towards Sam and Jack.

"My flat – it's just down the road."

"Clarify, 'just down the road,' please?" asked Petey.

"Opposite the colle…"

"Woah, lady, let me stop you right there. Those things are all over the college."

"Okay, so any other ideas?"

"Bluecoats," Ruby blurted out. "Bluecoats Primary School. They have a bus parked there – we could use it to drive out of here."

Nancy tried to picture the primary school. It wasn't far, a 10 minute walk and the roads were definitely quieter now. They might be able to drive out of this mess.

The creature at the door struck again, and this time they all heard the wood shudder and splinter in its frame. Fuck, that thing must be 10 feet tall as well as six feet wide. What the hell was this new monstrosity and how could they hope to get out without it chasing them down?

"Any ideas how to stop that thing from breaking through and following us?" asked Nancy.

Luke looked at her as if he was trying to think of something. Then his eyes opened wide and he jumped up off the floor. He ran to the side of the kitchen and opened a door Nancy hadn't seen. It was a walk-in freezer.

"Petey, come and give me a hand."

Petey went into the freezer and together they pulled out a …

"Haha, dead piggy," said Sam laughing.

"This should do the job, don't you think?" asked Luke. Behind him he dragged an entire pig. Its trotters dragging along the cream tiles.

"Do the job? I don't get how that's going to help."

"Simple, we dress him up in a coat and a hat and sit him at the table, that thing will think it's one of us and attack it instead. It might not buy us much time, but it'll buy us some…"

Nancy blew out her cheeks. "Better plan than I have, I guess," she said. "Sam, come over here, buddy."

She turned Sam around and pulled his coat off. "Lisa, over there," she pointed towards a rack of coats. "Grab one of those, please. It'll be a bit big Sam, but it'll do."

"Why don't we put this coat on the pig?" Lisa asked.

"Because this one has Sam's scent all over it. I just figure it might be more tempting to that thing outside."

Lisa shrugged and then nodded. Nancy passed Sam's coat to Luke, and he and Petey dressed the pig like Sam. They added a hat and pulled wool gloves over the trotters. They all stood in a row behind the dressed-up pig admiring their fast handywork.

Luke smirked and nudged Petey. "Remind you of anyone?" He winked and they both laughed. The door crashed behind them and they heard a harsh bray-like growl.

"Time to move…" Luke said.

Ruby and Lisa slid the sliding patio doors open just enough for the largest of them to fit through, and once they were all outside, closed them again.

"Go, now," said Nancy, pointing towards the edge of the garden and the ferns. "Do you remember where you fell through?"

Luke nodded and they ran across the grass. Lisa held Sam's hand this time while Nancy carried Jack. From behind them, they heard the crash as the door gave way. They didn't stop to look back. Luke went first through the gap in the fence, followed by Nancy and Jack, Lisa and Sam and finally Petey and Ruby. They stood in the shadows next to the fern trees and looked down the road.

They saw the three figures, one on each path on the side of the road and one in the middle. They were walking towards a swarm of Vermin.

"Friends of yours?" Petey asked.

"I really don't know what they are."

"Who cares? They look like wild west gunslingers, and in my books that makes them good guys."

Nancy saw one of the figures stop and turn around. She was too far away to tell for sure, but she was sure it was Mr Neil and he'd seen them. "Go, go, go – that way," she said.

CHAPTER SEVEN – AATAMI

They were alive. And there were more of them. He sensed something strange from the four figures that stood beside Nancy, Sam and Jack, but he couldn't delve any deeper without letting Dinah know he'd seen them. The other swarm was fast approaching. They'd assumed their tried and tested formation, with Adlai on the right, him on the left and Dinah bringing up the centre. After this swarm, there would be just one left. He hoped.

He'd sensed something else, something bigger than the Vermin, moments before he saw Nancy and her group. Was that why they'd left the safety of the property? It hadn't come from the college, it had come from the town centre, from behind th....

He saw it as it came crashing through the ferns on his left. Just a hulking shape at first. It turned and looked at him. Its face was an elongated white skull; not human like, but closer to that of an antelope. The white bone glowed in the moonlight. Two metre long and inch-thick spiraling horns came from the forehead and stretched into the air, coming to a point at the ends. Around its body, Aatami saw huge locusts and long and thin grasshoppers buzzing. It had a thick-set body similar to that of a man, only twice as large with shoulders six feet across, as if a man had been crossed with a bull.

It stared at Aatami with dead eye sockets. Aatami stared back. He couldn't let it stalk Nancy and the group she was with. If he let it go, it would catch them and rip them apart. Aatami picked up a rock from the verge and checked whether Dinah or Adlai was watching. They weren't. He tossed the rock hard and it hit the creature in its thick chest. It didn't move and stayed silent, except for a low grunt. Vapour came from the jagged gaps in the skull and its eyes glowed bright red suddenly.

"Dinah," Aatami said. "Is that the Beast?"

Dinah turned to him, her mouth in a snarl, angry that he'd taken away her concentration from the Vermin. Aatami pointed towards the monster. Dinah followed his finger and saw it. They were trapped between the oncoming swarm of Vermin and this creature.

"No, that's not the Beast," she hissed. "Adlai, you good to take care of the swarm?"

Adlai frowned at her, then saw the hulking form at the top of the hill. He nodded.

"Remember, no science, use the human weapons. You'll need all your strength."

"Aatami, pass me the last grenade," said Adlai.

Aatami removed the grenade from his pocket and threw it to Adlai who caught it with one hand. Adlai took Dinah's place in the centre of the road, while she came and joined him on the path leading to the creature.

"I don't think the shotgun will be much use," said Aatami.

Dinah looked at the shotgun she held in one hand. "I think you're probably right."

"Any ideas?"

From behind them came an explosion as Adlai tossed the grenade into the swarm. Fragments of shrapnel flew at Dinah and Aatami who ducked. The grenade took out most of the swarm and Adlai finished off the rest with his pistol.

The bright explosion lit up the creature's skull. Locusts and bugs crawled in and out of the eye and nose sockets. Still it stood, watching them.

"What's it doing?" asked Aatami.

"Waiting…"

Gunshots rang out like popcorn in a microwave and then slowed as Adlai finished his extermination.

"Are we clear?" Dinah shouted.

"Affirmative," Adlai's voice came back.

"Let's go. We can't fight this thing and still have power to take on the Beast."

They had given Nancy a few minutes' head start, thought Aatami. Hopefully that's enough.

The creature moved. It lowered its head and with a grunt which expelled more mist into the air, stalked across the road, back after its initial prey.

"That's odd," said Aatami. "I was expecting to have to run from it."

"It's got the scent of something else. Take it as a good sign, Aatami. Now, onwards to the last battle."

CHAPTER EIGHT – JACOB

Another explosion rocked the street outside, but Jacob barely noticed. The Vermin had turned on him when he entered and without ceremony he shot it between its glowing eyes. Sam's body lay next to the dead Vermin. He sobbed openly and unashamedly, falling to his knees, his heart ripped in two. He'd failed. His vision blurred and he fell forward, hitting his chin on the floor, which caused his teeth to snap together with his tongue between them. Blood filled his mouth, but he didn't bother picking himself up. He lay on the floor, one arm reaching towards his son's body. Red spittle and snot fell onto the tiles. All his energy drained.

There was no face, just a mangled mess of pink flesh, red blood and white skull. The hood was partly pulled over the back of the head. He was wearing blue gloves. Sam hadn't been wearing blue gloves. It was on the to-do list for the weekend ready for the winter – buy the boys' new hats and gloves. Now he looked, the hands in those gloves looked mis-shaped, even though there was no sign that the Vermin had got past eating the face. A flash of hope passed through him. His heart thudded in his chest. Jacob pushed himself up and moved closer to the body. He hadn't seen it earlier, but no legs came from the bottom of the body. Not human legs anyway. He ripped a glove off one hand and sat back, open-mouthed. It was a pig's trotter. He cried out as he shuffled back away from the body. His skin was wet with sweat and the smell of the candles was suddenly stronger. They were alive. They'd been in this house, but something had come crashing through the door.

Jacob looked around the kitchen. He picked a bottle of water from the side and downed it in one go. His stomach gurgled and rolled. They must have gone out the back door when whatever it was came through the front door. He tried the door and it was unlocked. He slid it open and felt the cool breeze on his skin. Two fires now glowed through the fern trees on the road on the other side.

Something had created a large gap in the ferns. He looked back through the patio doors at the mangled pig in his son's coat and then turned and made his way to the gap in the trees.

Besides the flickering fires at the top, and halfway down the college road, it was quiet. Shredded, dead bodies of Vermin littered the road and paths. The frag grenades had ripped apart some, while they had shot others. He held his pistol out in front of him, in case any had survived.

If Aatami had rejoined Dinah and Polly, then they would be on their way to the college. Would Nancy follow them thinking that was safe? He hoped not. Why had they kept everything secret from her? If she knew, she would know that Mr Neil, Bill and Polly were no longer themselves and couldn't be trusted, but she didn't know because of him.

They could have gone another way to get to hers, he thought. She definitely lived around here. If she avoided this road, she would have to go up and across the top and then come back down towards hers the back way. He stood in the dark of the ferns, looking back and forth between the college and the top of the road.

After a moment's hesitation, he turned and walked past both fires to the top of the hill again. At the top of the road he turned right. He looked at his watch, it was past eight now, but felt more like midnight. He followed the road, keeping his eyes peeled for any sign of Nancy and the boys. From now on, he wouldn't leave them again – any of them, including Nancy. Houses, more modern than Polly's, lined both streets and a closed garage with a forecourt of banged-up cars stood dark at the end of the road

Jacob turned right, back towards the college, but coming in from an adjacent road not knowing that Nancy and the boys had been at the same junction less than 10 minutes earlier and had turned left towards Bluecoats school.

As had the skull-faced creature that stalked them.

CHAPTER NINE – NANCY

They jogged together, Nancy carrying Jack and Sam on Luke's not small shoulders. The houses on either side had turned into small terraced properties from the turn of the century, with stone archways over the doors and alleyways leading to rear gardens. At the head of the road was a crossroads. Left led back to the Rec, while straight on went to a cul-de-sac of council houses. They went right towards the *'Slow. School Children'* signs.

There was an open piece of grassland with a pathway leading through a small wooded area before they came to the school. The gates were shut as expected. Opposite the school stood a deserted building. It looked like a large house, but had a commercial car park and a large crucifix cut-out window to the side of the stonework that faced the road. A white sign stood outside the church that said *'Christ Church.'* It wasn't the crucifix window or the sign that held her eye, but the black minibus parked behind it.

She turned and saw the others looking at it too.

"That'll do," said Luke.

"Anyone have any problems with breaking into a church?" asked Petey. "We need to find the keys."

They looked at each other and shook their heads.

"Didn't think so. So who has the honour?"

"After what happened at the Priory and the warehouse, I think it's your turn Petey," said Lisa.

Petey rolled his eyes. "Fine. Who's coming with me?"

Luke and Ruby shrugged their shoulders. Nancy looked at the two young boys and shrugged too.

Lisa stepped forward. "Looks like it's me and you again… come on."

They jogged across the road, while Nancy, Luke, Ruby and the boys faded into the trees next to the wall of the school.

The entrance to the church was at the side of the building. A wheelchair ramp led to the main door. Petey tried it, not expecting it to be easy, and wasn't surprised when it was locked. Lisa tutted: "What did you expect?"

They climbed over the metal railings of the wheelchair ramp and searched for another way in. They found a fire door at the back of the building, but it wouldn't budge. Windows ran along the top of the grey brick just under the roof; too high for them to break and climb in or out. They walked back to the front of the building. Petey gave a brief wave towards the trees where the others were hiding and then followed Lisa to the front of the building. There was one addition to the church on this side: A floor-to-ceiling feature window. They stared up at it, Petey with his hand cupping his chin and Lisa with her hands on her hips.

"It'll make one hell of a crash if we smash it," Petey said.

Lisa nodded. "Do we have another choice?"

"Not that I've seen."

"In and out, okay? I'll smash it. You run in, grab the keys and meet me out here – then we jump in the minibus and get moving. Deal?"

"Deal," Petey said. "We need them over here now." They turned towards the others and beckoned them over. They came at a trot.

"Right," Lisa started, speaking to the entire group. "I'm going to smash this window – it will be loud, so you need to be ready. Petey will run in and grab the keys and then all on the bus and off we go."

"Okay," said Nancy. "Come on guys, let's wait near the bus."

As Nancy led the others to the back of the bus, away from where any shattered glass would fall, Lisa looked around for a rock in the verges of the car park. Petey jogged on the spot next to the window.

"Found one," Lisa said. "You ready?"

Petey nodded his head enthusiastically while clenching his hands into fists.

"Now…"

The window smashed. It was loud in the silence and the echoes of falling pieces of glass seemed to go on forever. Before all the glass had fallen, Petey was already through the narrow gap and inside the church.

A high-pitched wail came from behind the mini-bus. Lisa looked at the group and saw Sam on Luke's shoulders scrambling to get down in hysterics. He fell to the floor and ran to Nancy. She knelt next to him and put an arm around him.

"What's the matter?"

"I saw a monster."

"Where?"

Sam pointed down the road, back the way they'd come. Expecting to see a swarm of Vermin, her heart turned to ice when she saw the hulking figure striding towards them. It was still 100 yards away, but she could see two spiralling horns sticking up in the air like a devil. It was impossibly wide and tall.

"Luke, go help Petey – we need those keys!"

Without hesitating, Luke ran past the minibus towards Lisa and the broken window. Ruby helped Nancy calm the boys and Lisa joined her a second later, but not before she'd glanced down the road and seen the monster moving purposefully towards them.

Inside, Luke called out to Petey "We need those keys ASAP, Petey. Have you found them?"

"Not yet, I've checked the kitchen so far."

"The kitchen? Petey, for a smart person, you really are dumb sometimes."

Luke looked into the dark room. It wasn't like a church, more like a village hall with old carpets and children's drawings on the walls. He saw the entrance for the kitchen and next to it a closed door. He ran past Petey and tried the door, praying it would open. It did. He stood in a bare office with a desk with a chair behind it and two other plastic chairs in front of it. Luke ran to the desk and started hunting through the drawers.

"Petey," he shouted. "Come help me."

Petey ran through the doorway, looked around the room and smiled. On the wall to his right was a coat rack and next to that a metal key box. He ran to it and pulled it off the wall.

"Luke, I've got it. I can see it inside."

"Great, let's go."

They ran through the church and out the smashed window, their shoes crunching on the shattered glass. Petey looked up and saw the creature only 50 yards away. It had no face, just a white skull and glowing red eyes. The shape of the thing looked fuzzy, and Petey realised it wasn't his eyes. Cockroaches, grasshoppers and locusts were jumping from and all over the monster.

"What the fu…"

"Not now, Petey," said Luke, grabbing hold of his best friend and leading him to the minibus. Nancy and the others were crouched behind it. Sam was sniffling and Jack was crying in Ruby's arms.

"We've got them."

Petey showed them the key box he held in his hands. He fumbled at the latches and his face fell. "It's locked. The fucking box that holds the fucking keys is locked."

"Who cares?" said Lisa, snatching the key box from Mike and slamming it onto the ground. It made a metallic thud, but didn't open. She stamped on it. It didn't open. Luke picked it up. He inspected the lock, and then slammed it against the floor on its edge. The keys inside jangled. Again he hit it against the ground. The thin metal latch that was holding it shut poked out the side a little.

"Hit it again!"

Luke smashed the box against the floor once, twice, and on the third time the key box rattled open. Luke picked up the keys with a matching leather keyring and pushed the button. The lights on the mini-bus flashed twice. Luke ran to the door and slid it open.

"Get in."

Lisa and Ruby climbed in first, and Nancy passed Sam and Jack to them. They took them to the back of the bus and sat down. Then Petey and Luke jumped in. Nancy slammed the door behind them and ran to the driver's side. She could smell the monster now. A sulphur-like moth-ball smell. It was on the school side of the road, next to where they had been hiding. She could hear its deep breaths and see the mist that came from the black hole where its mouth was.

The door opened, and she climbed in, just as a dozen locusts and grasshoppers hit the driver's side window.

"KEYS!"

Luke passed the keys through to her. She fumbled with them and then put them in the ignition. The girl's screams joined the wails of Sam and Jack as the thing started to cross the road.

"Fucking GO…" said Lisa.

"I'm trying…"

The engine ticked over and then came to life. Nancy released the handbrake and revved the engine. They shot forward, and she turned just in time to miss the wall and go out the open gate. The skull-faced monster turned and watched the minibus as it sped down the road towards the Rec.

CHAPTER 10 – AATAMI

Aatami, Dinah and Adlai approached the college gates. A blue double-decker bus sat empty in the bus lane. The green metal gates were open. A handful of cars were scattered around the large concrete car park. Past these, Aatami saw a pile of bodies at least one-storey high blocking the main entrance of each of the three buildings.

The building in the centre looked the oldest. It was the tallest too, with spindly antennae on the top, silhouetted against the crescent moon. The building to the right was triangular and more modern, with reflective-glass windows, and the newest building had an art déco feel to it with an overhanging roof and floor-to-ceiling windows.

The third swarm hadn't appeared. Adlai and Dinah studied the layout of the college.

"Where do you think the Beast will be?" asked Adlai.

Dinah was silent for a moment, and then said: "He'll need certain things for his ritual. If he's planning on bringing Satan back, he'll need access to the four elements: Earth, air, water and fire."

"What else do you know about the ritual?"

"Only what I studied a long time ago, which isn't a lot," Dinah admitted. "This was one passage I memorized from the ancient books, *'Satan is born of fire from the earth. We need air for fire to burn and water to stop the fire from burning too strong, and to solidify Satan as a being,'* I understand the words, but not in this context… I just don't know."

"Where is Satan?"

"In a cage in Hell."

"How do you get to the cage?"

Dinah shrugged. "I don't know, and if we kill the Beast, the last being that does will take that information to its grave." She stared across the college. "As long as we kill the Beast, it doesn't matter."

They didn't hide as they approached. They walked out in the open through the car park, side-by-side. Adlai threw the pistol to the ground. It would be of no further use. Dinah dropped the shotgun. No dogs barked, no birds tweeted and no cats prowled. The air was still, the breeze gone.

A thin figure appeared on top of the pile of corpses. He was cloaked in shadow, so they couldn't see his features. His neck was thin and long, his perfectly oval head looked as if it should be lolling side-to-side like a metronome. The arms were stringy, stretching down past his knees. He raised them, showing elongated twig-like fingers which he snapped with a crack that echoed in the silence. A dark-leather leash appeared in each hand. At the end of the leashes, invisible monstrosities snapped their jaws. Aatami saw cowboy-like lasso's over a metre in diameter, pulling to get away from their Master.

The figure started down the pile of corpses, using heads and torsos as steps. As he walked, the shadow slunk up his body, slowly showing gangly legs in black too-short suit trousers that showed his white ankles. On his feet he wore brown leather espadrilles. As the shadow rose, it then exposed his torso. He wore a black velvet tuxedo jacket, with a white rose in the button, which was open showing his bare white skin underneath. Next, his thin neck was white with purple ligature marks swirling around like a coiled snake. Finally, his face appeared. Pasty white skin shone like the moon, eyes with dark yellow-green bags underneath bulged. Sharp cheekbones and smooth skin gave the face a snake-like quality. A fat tongue licked at thin black lips and then smiled.

"Why hello, you beautiful, sexy people. Who wants to fuck?" He thrusted his hips forward. "I know I do – I want to fuck all your pretty little throats."

The three Exos stood in silence.

"What's the matter? Cat got your tongues? Maybe you're just waiting to see it?" His bulging eyes flashed bright and he fiddled with the zipper on his trousers. "Yes, that's what it is, you came here to see my monstro…"

Dinah threw a ball of green light at the figure. One of the invisible beasts jumped in front of its master and the ball of light vanished.

"Now, now… What no foreplay?" He did a ticking motion with his elongated index finger. Then he put the tip of the finger into his mouth and sucked it, all the while staring at Adlai, Dinah and Aatami. "Mmmm… tastes good. Isn't that why you came? To taste me? You can, you know, I look forward to it. But maybe I want to taste you too."

"The only thing you will taste, Beast, is the edge of my sword," said Adlai, and closed his eyes. A moment later a red glowing long-sword appeared in his hands.

"Too hasty again, my sexy little one… I like a little bit of edging before the real thing." With another click of his gangly fingers, a swarm of Vermin, larger than the previous two, came over the top of the pile or corpses. Hundreds of them hustled and tousled over the carcasses of dead bodies, coming in a non-stop stream of snapping jaws and black stripes.

As the Vermin swarmed over and around his feet, and Adlai, Dinah and Aatami stepped backwards, the Beast undid his zipper and pulled out his thin, veiny cock and waved it at them, then with a laugh, turned and climbed back up the pile of corpses and disappeared into the shadows. Still more Vermin came.

"We don't have time for this," said Dinah. "Adlai, you handle the Vermin, make a way through for me and Aatami. We can't let him perform the ritual."

With the hand not holding the sword, Adlai turned it palm up and a red glowing orb grew and throbbed. He let it grow till it was the size of a car tyre. All the while the light from his sword decreased, and he said through Polly's gritted teeth: "Ready?"

Aatami and Dinah nodded. The orb raised from his hand and floated through the air, about six feet off the ground towards the centre of the swarm. It hovered for a moment, throbbed, and then dropped. When it hit the ground a blinding pink light flashed silently in the dark, lighting the sky.

"Go!" shouted Dinah, and she and Aatami ran through the frozen swarm of Vermin and up and over the pile of corpses after the Beast.

CHAPTER 11 – JACOB

A blinding pink light lit the sky which came from towards the college. Jacob raised a hand to his face and squinted into it. No sound accompanied the explosion. He was only one road over from the college. Jacob had been walking the roads, hoping he'd see a street sign that triggered the memory of Nancy's address.

He'd seen no Vermin so far and was pretty sure the final battle was at hand. Jacob no longer cared; he just wanted to find his boys and Nancy and get the hell out of Dodge.

He was at a roundabout and the light from the explosion showed him two white-barked trees stretching up to the skies with spider web-like branches. There were three exits, the first would take him away from the college to the outskirts of town and cul-de-sacs of houses, the second would take him to the main road, and the third back to the college.

A blonde-haired woman appeared from the first turning. She looked about 40 years-old and was wearing a pair of jeans and a hoodie. The woman ran up to Jacob and stopped in front of him only a metre away.

"Who am I?" she cried.

"What?"

"Who am I?"

"Sorry Miss, but if you don't know who you are, I don't stand a chance."

"Miss? Shit, fuck, cock-it … you said Miss, didn't you?"

Jacob nodded and took a step backwards. The woman started pacing back and forth on the road in front of him, mumbling to herself, "It's happening again… why the fuck is it happening again… we stopped it… we killed the Leviathan… shit, shit shit."

Jacob stepped towards her. "Did you say Leviathan?"

The woman eyed Jacob. "Why? Does that mean something to you?

Where is everyone?"

"You don't know?"

"Know what?"

"There was an attack."

"What sort of attack?"

"Something fell from the sky and then these creatures started attacking people. A lot of people are dead."

"Fell from the sky… I remember that, how many days ago was that?"

"It's Monday night," replied Jacob. "The thing fell on Sunday afternoon."

"I only woke up 20 minutes ago…" the woman stared at the light in the sky. "What's that light?"

"I don't know…"

"So if that thing fell from the sky, does that mean these rat-like things are… aliens? That's fucking crazy, and I know crazy."

"I was there, when that thing fell from the sky. I've seen those creatures up close."

"And?"

"Just don't get close to them. If you see one, run."

"I hear you loud and clear on that brother."

Jacob frowned. "What's your name?"

"Luca – sorry… Lucy."

"Right," Jacob replied with an eyebrow raised. "Lucy, I'm Jacob, you can stay with me if you want and I will explain more, but I need to find my two boys and Nancy – she's kinda my girlfriend… I think."

"Kinda your girlfriend, right, totally understand." Lucy slammed him on the shoulder with a smile. "Where to then, Jacob?"

Jacob's shoulders slumped. "I don't know."

"How old are your kids?"

"Four and two."

"Young, then. I'll help you find them and then we can get out of here – if you'll help me find some friends after we've found your family?"

"Deal, of course. Thank you, Lucy."

"No worries, dude, we'll sort it."

Jacob didn't know what it was, maybe it was the hit on the shoulder, or the use of the word 'dude,' but he liked this woman even if she reminded him of a very laddy lad.

CHAPTER 12 – NANCY

Nancy turned in the driver's seat to ask if everyone was okay, when the pink light lit up the sky.

"Pretty lights," said Sam from the back seat. Everyone else was staring at the sky out the minibuses windows.

"What is it?" asked Ruby.

"I don't know," replied Luke, taking her hand.

"Jacob," said Nancy.

"Sam and Jack's dad? How do you know?" asked Petey.

"I don't, but I sense it… we can't leave him behind. We need to find him." She hit the brakes and reversed the car down the road, back the way they'd come. The skull-faced monster wasn't in her rear-view mirror and hadn't been for the two minutes they'd been driving. She put the car into forward and turned left, back onto the road with the deserted garage. She went past the garage and followed the road around. The kids were silent in the back seats.

"Keep your eyes open, guys and girls."

They came to a T-junction. One road would lead them back to the college road, and the other to the road that ran adjacent – towards her flat. If they were going to make it out of this town, they'd need supplies and maybe, just maybe, Jacob would come looking for them there. She remembered telling him the address, she just hoped he'd remembered. They could spare an hour before they set off. She took the next turn and came down the cul-de-sac that led to her flat.

She looked in the mirror. "This is my home. We're going to go in, grab some supplies and wait for an hour to see if Sam and Jack's dad comes, okay?"

"Daddy," said Sam.

"That's right, Sam, daddy's on his way and we're going to wait for him."

She searched her pockets and found her keys. "When I say go, you run into the house."

Nancy stepped out the minibus and went down the steps that led to her front door. She put the key into the lock and opened it. Then she went back to the minibus, slid open the door and said: "Go!"

Luke passed Jack to Nancy and then lifted Sam down. Lisa took Sam's hand when she jumped out and together they ran down the stairs and into Nancy's flat.

Nancy found two holdalls in her bedroom, and passed them to Lisa and Ruby, who went through the cupboards in the kitchen filling them with food and drink and pill bottles. Jack and Sam settled on her sofa. Both looked dog-tired with red eyes, and couldn't stop yawning.

"When's daddy going to be here?" Sam asked.

"Soon, Sam, soon," she replied.

Nancy sat on the floor, legs crossed, watching the two beautiful boys and praying that Jacob would find them soon. She also prayed for her father, wherever he was.

Once Lisa and Ruby had packed the holdalls, they joined them in the living room. Luke and Petey stared out her back garden towards the college and the pink-light which was now starting to fade. It had only been 10 minutes, but with every minute that passed, so did any hope Nancy had of Jacob finding them.

Luke took Ruby to a corner and whispered to her: "Is there anything you can do? Do you still have any magic juice from the rock or the tree left in you?"

"I don't know, it's been a long time, Luke. What do you think?"

"We have to try, I can't stand the idea of those kids leaving their daddy behind, you?"

Ruby glanced at the sad, tired little boys on the sofa. "No."

"Nancy," Luke started. "Can we use your bedroom?"

Nancy's eyebrows raised.

"Not like that... Ruby gets headaches and needs a lay down."

"Of course," she said. "It's just through there," Nancy pointed down the hall.

Lisa and Petey nodded at them as they went into the bedroom and shut the door behind them. They sat opposite each other, cross-legged on the king-size bed. The room smelled of body odour and stale vomit. They blocked the smell out, and both pulled out a stone from their pockets. Luke put his in his mouth and Ruby did the same and then they kissed.

At first, nothing happened, and then they both felt electricity coming from their fingertips. They thought about Jacob, using Sam and Jack as a catalyst. an out-of-body sensation replaced the darkness in their minds. They had become one and floated together out the front door of Nancy's house. They went high into the sky, so they could look down at the surrounding roads. To their right they saw a mass of frozen Vermin and a man with a glowing red sword. They sensed it wasn't Jacob. Movement caught their eye and they zoomed down onto two people. A man and a woman walking down the road opposite this one.

That's Jacob,' they said as one.

'How do we get him here?'

'Fly into him?'

'What?'

'Try it, let's fly into him.'

They fell from the sky at a dizzying rate and hovered less than a metre in front of the man and woman as they walked.

'Ready?'

'Ready.'

As one, they stopped moving and let Jacob walk into them.

CHAPTER 13 – AATAMI

Aatami and Dinah raced through the college grounds. More mounds of bodies were littered in front and to the sides of the buildings. There must have been over a thousand corpses rotting. The ground was slick with blood like a battlefield. They'd lost the Beast, but there was only one way to run. They followed. Aatami's inside warrior had taken over, and now they were here they had to finish it. Next to him Dinah ran with a sick smile on her face.

They rounded a corner and at the far end, they finally saw him. He was walking, but he still moved faster than they ran. He was heading past the college building towards the attached leisure centre and the sports fields behind.

They pushed on, moving faster, trying to catch up. They left tarmac and entered the boggy field. Directly behind the leisure centre was a hole the size of a detached bungalow. They stopped running and approached in a crouch, trying to keep low to avoid being seen in the fading pink-light. The Beast had vanished.

Aatami leaned over the hole and peered down into darkness. "How far do you think that goes?"

"All the way to Hell," Dinah replied. "He's been busy with the help of the Vermin."

The edges of the hole had been smoothed away all the way round. Blood seeped in places and poured in others, down into the dark.

Aatami looked at Dinah.

"Part of the ritual – blood, of course. Blood is the Fire of life."

"And Earth?"

"Look around, Aatami, we're surrounded by earth?"

"So, what happens next?"

The Beast appeared on the other side of the hole. "You like it? I love a big hole me… a nice moist hole to put it into." He jerked his hips again.

"Beast," Dinah said.

"I love it when you talk dirty," he licked his thin lips. "Come over here so I can screw the fight out of you. You can't stop me, so you might as well enjoy it."

A roar, deep and rolling, rumbled out of the earth from the hole.

"Yeah, yeah, yeah… so fucking impatient my Father," the Beast said, and shrugged his thin shoulders. "But what can you do?" He smiled and clicked his fingers. This time a white flame spouted from the tip of his middle finger. He lowered his other fingers and showed Aatami and Dinah his flaming middle finger. Then he laughed, before biting into the base of his finger, gnawing through the flesh, muscle and bone. He pulled it from his hand using his teeth and still smiling, spat it into the hole. "You might want to take a step back," he said, with bloodied lips and vanished.

Aatami grabbed Dinah, who had moved to chase after the Beast, and pulled her back from the hole, just before a jet of yellow flame shot up into the sky. It burned loud and hot as he and Dinah lay on the ground watching open-mouthed.

"Get off of me," she said, getting to her feet.

Dinah watched the fire with her arms at her side. "There's only one more part of the ritual… Water. We can't let the Beast put any water into this hole."

Aatami stood. He saw the Beast rise behind the flame towards the back of the enormous windows of the leisure centre. Inside he saw a swimming pool. "The pool," he shouted to Dinah over the noise of the fire. "The pool! He's going to flood the pool."

Dinah looked through the fire and understood. They had no more chances. "Aatami," she started. "We need to combine our power and stop him."

Aatami moved next to Dinah and they joined hands. A light flickered in front of them. Aatami's blue and Dinah's green light combined to create a cyan colour like the Mediterranean sea. The orb grew, throbbing with power. It was the size of a tyre, then a bike and finally it floated an inch off the ground, a perfect circle of throbbing cyan the size of a car.

'Unleash your sword, Aatami,' he heard Dinah's voice in his mind. He concentrated and a blue sword appeared in his hand. He looked across and saw Dinah with a green one, larger than his, in hers. *'Attack as soon as the orb blows – don't hesitate.'*

Together they stood, holding hands with a glowing sword in their spare hands. The sound of the fire was background noise now. They fixed their eyes on the Beast, who was doing something at the back of the leisure centre. He looked towards them as they let go of the orb. It flung across the hole, as if catapulted, and through the flame when it exploded where the Beast stood. Dinah and Aatami sprinted around the hole towards the Beast, who was stuck in place. His bulging eyes moved in their sockets, but something rooted the rest of him to the ground. Dinah raised her sword and brought it down. The Beast toppled himself over at the last moment, and the sword merely lopped off a chunk of his right shoulder. Now laying on the ground, the Beast looked up as they stood over him. Fire danced in his eyes. But there was no fear.

Aatami stabbed the Beast in the chest, feeling the hot blade slice through the rib cage. Still the Beast looked at him without fear. Dinah roared and brought her sword down in an arc towards the Beast's still-smiling face. It stopped an inch from the neck and then her forearm snapped back 90 degrees. The sword disappeared as if it was never really there. Aatami turned and saw the leash of the invisible creature and followed it till he saw the lasso. It was biting and tearing at Dinah as she flailed in its huge jaws. It had her by the waist in its massive jaws and he could see invisible teeth perforate her skin. Blood poured down her body and out her mouth. She looked at him and shouted: "Never surrender."

Thoughts of self-sacrifice flooded Aatami's mind and he knew what she was about to do.

"NO! DINAH STOP!"

But it was too late. She exploded the power inside her. A power that was strong when it was used mentally, but when it imploded, was like a concentrated nuclear explosion. He turned to run as blinding green lights broke through her skin. Everything the beams hit disintegrated, including the Beast and the windows to the swimming pool. The side of the pool disintegrated, sending a deluge of chlorine-smelling water cascading out the window and into the hole. Aatami ran across the field, as he heard the sizzle of the fire followed by a tremor through the earth that sent him toppling over the ground.

Looking back, he saw the last of the fire extinguish and an immense cloud of steam rise out of the hole. In the thick steam, shadows danced and then a laugh echoed from deep within the earth. Aatami stood and sprinted away from the college. He ran past the piles of bodies and through the still-frozen Vermin. Adlai was nowhere to be seen.

CHAPTER 14 – JACOB

Jacob stopped walking and turned around on the path. Lucy stopped and looked at him.

"You okay?"

Jacob looked at Lucy and said: "I think so, I just had a really strange feeling…"

A flame shot out from behind the houses and towards the college, which rose miles into the sky. Jacob watched the flame flicker in Lucy's eyes and then turned around himself.

"Was that your feeling?" Lucy asked, still staring open-mouthed at the flame.

"I don't know, I don't think so… it felt more like I was being guided."

"Jacob, don't ask me why, but I would recommend following your instincts on this one. Where does the feeling want you to go?"

Jacob looked back the way they had come and then started walking. "This way."

Lucy followed behind as Jacob led the way. He turned right at the first turning and then stood stupidly staring at a street sign. "This is it."

"This is what?"

"This is Nancy's road."

"That's great. Do you remember the number?"

Jacob closed his eyes. The flame roared into the sky to the side of them now. His eyes shot open. "Seventeen… it's number 17."

Lucy ran to the closest house. "This one is 56, and the one next to it is 54 – we need to be on the other side of the road." She pointed. "That way."

They ran side-by-side, staring at house numbers as they went. "25, 23, 21," Lucy said breathlessly. A black minibus was parked at an awkward angle in front of them. "Seventeen, Jacob… it's here."

Without catching his breath, Jacob ran down the stairs and to the front door. He knocked, not caring how loud he was. He heard voices from inside and then Nancy opened the door. She looked at him. Orange flames jumped in his eyes. She wrapped her arms around his neck. He kissed her on her cheek and then she released him. He walked past her, tenderly touching her face and walked into the living room. Four teenage kids, two boys and two girls were sitting cross-legged on the floor, and on the sofa he saw Sam and Jack asleep cuddled up into each other. Sam opened his eyes: "Daddy?"

"Daddy's here, baby, daddy's here." Tears ran down his face and he took the space in two strides and picked Sam up in his arms, kissing him on both cheeks and holding him in his arms. He rested his cheek against Sam's and breathed him in. "I'm never leaving you again, okay?"

After five minutes of very confusing conversation, where Luke and Petey gave Jacob and Nancy the rundown on their past adventure, and Jacob gave everyone the rundown on the current situation, they decided it was best to stick with their current plan and get out of Dodge.

"I keep thinking," Lisa started. "It can't be coincidence we're back together again."

"I don't think it is," said Lucas. "And if what Jacob says is true, then this is a lot bigger than the Priory and the Vermin."

"So where are we going to go?" asked Jacob.

The teenagers and Lucas looked at each other. "Grandad's," they said as one and laughed.

"How far is it?"

"Ten minutes' drive – you've dealt with these Vermin more than us, can we make that?"

"Yes, I think so," said Jacob. He looked at the group in front of him. "This time, from now on, we all stay together."

They left the flat and climbed into the minibus. The fire in the sky was gone. There was plenty of space for all of them and the two bags. Nancy and Lucas/Lucy sat in the front seat. Jacob sat with Jack asleep on his lap and his other arm around a dozing Sam.

"Right, we're off," Nancy said and started the engine.

They got to the end of the road, Nancy took a left and they were at the roundabout where Jacob met Lucas/Lucy. Something large thudded into the side of the minibus and screams echoed into the night. Jacob turned and saw a flash of a white face and two horns, spiralling into the sky. It was huge, as wide as he was tall and higher than the minibus. The minibus stalled. Nancy turned the keys and the engine ticked over. She accelerated, but they didn't move.

"It's holding the back," a voice screamed. Bodies lurched forward towards the front of the minibus, away from the double doors at the back. Jacob stood and carried Sam and Jack to the front and passed them through the gap to Nancy and Lucas.

"Get ready to drive," he said. Jacob leaned through the gap and kissed both boys on their foreheads. "Daddy will be right back, okay?" And then he took Nancy's face between his hands. "Thank you for looking after my boys." He kissed her firmly on the mouth. When he pulled away, she looked into his eyes. "I will, I promise."

Jacob took a deep breath and grabbed two kitchen knives from one of the holdalls taken from Nancys. "Open the doors."

Nancy's hand lingered over the lever, but she couldn't pull it. Lucas put his hand over hers, and together they pulled. The doors opened with a mechanical whoosh and Jacob stepped out into the night. Jacob walked around the side of the van, keeping his distance. The creature swung for him, but didn't let go of the minibus. Oversized locusts and crickets jumped and buzzed in Jacob's face, but he didn't flinch. He screamed in the monster's face. His eyes wide and his mouth furious. His cheeks were flushed as he screamed an animal-like scream at the monster. "Fuck you, fuck you, fuck you... Aaarrrggghhh!!!"

The skull-faced monster let go of the minibus. Jacob shouted "Go!" as it approached him. He held out the two knives but knew he wouldn't last longer than another 10 seconds.

"Jacob!" he heard a voice shout. He turned and saw Aatami running towards him. "Jacob, go... run... get out of here, I've got this one."

Jacob stood frozen to the spot as the monster approached. Aatami reached him just as a bear-like arm arced down. Aatami reached inside of himself and a glowing blue sword appeared and sliced through the arm. The monster screamed and cockroaches flew like spittle from its mouth.

"Jacob, I'm sorry..."

The monster loomed over them both. "Jacob, run... I understand now because of you. Your family needs you and if I can do one thing it is to give you to them..." Aatami put his head against Jacob's forehead. "Run, Brother, run, get out of here..." he pushed Jacob towards the minibus and screamed: "I'm sorry... Run!"

Jacob ran to the minibus. When he got to the open doors at the side, he turned and watched as the monster attacked. Aatami dodged the attacks and dealt some of his own blows with his sword, but then the light from the sword faded. Aatami turned to Jacob and smiled. He mouthed: "Go" one last time, as a plague of locusts attacked his face, giving the monster the chance to pick him up. Jacob got on the bus and ran to the back window. Nancy put her foot down on the accelerator. The last thing Jacob saw was the monster bring down Aatami's body onto its monstrous knee, snapping his back. He saw the body go limp and the sword vanish.

They drove through the deserted town, looking out the windows. They saw no Vermin. As they turned onto the country road towards grandad's house, the lights on the side of the road switched back on.

EPILOGUE

He awoke. It was cold. Where was he? When was he? He opened the curtains and looked out into a pale blue sky. If he was awake, then so must be Satan. He walked bare-chested through the dark bedroom and out onto the wooden veranda that overlooked the lake. It was frozen at the sides.

The greatest trick Satan had ever pulled was making people think he wasn't real, and he'd done it again…

The End

Author Notes

Vermin was easier to write than The Priory. I don't know whether that was because it was my second novel, or because all the links came easier than The Priory. If you couldn't tell, it was inspired by James Herbert's The Rats trilogy, however, with my own spin on it and a different story. (If you haven't read any James Herbert I recommend you go find any of his novels – he is British Horror royalty!) The editing was easier too, and I have my good friend Andrew Ormiston to thank for the final editing job he has done on it. Likewise, Katrina Scott is a fantastic designer who has created the epic covers and the promo material!

As mentioned earlier, Vermin although finished in February, was edited throughout March and April 2020, which as history will tell was Lockdown time in the UK. Writing was one of my releases during this period. It has been a rough time, especially without seeing my sons as much as I usually do… I hope when this is all over, we will have found a way to be kinder to people and to not take anything for granted! Positivity is life's biggest force and I have a thousand-and-one people to thank for helping me stay positive no matter what.

Now, whilst on lockdown I have found editing easy and therapeutic, however, writing from scratch has been a bit harder. The third and final part of the trilogy has been rattling around in my head for some time, but finding the motivation to get writing has been a struggle. However, as I write this I am now thirty-thousand words in and the story has taken shape. It's an epic the story, much larger than The Priory and Vermin on scale, which I believe is the way third parts of anything should be – bigger, better, and way more bonkers! I hope you are looking forward to it as much as I'm enjoying writing it. It has more Westford, more danger and more excitement.

About the Author

Jonathan Wheatley is a professional copywriter and editor by trade and a novelist by night. Influenced by the likes of Dan Simmons, James Herbert, H. P. Lovecraft and Stephen King, his novels are a mixture of contemporary horror and historical fact. A treasure trove of general knowledge and a dedicated movie, book and TV buff, his books are filled with easter eggs to entertainment culture and the history of his local town, Stamford.

Born and raised in Stamford, Lincolnshire; when he finally puts down his pen and paper and stops reading, he is a dedicated dad to his two sons, Sonny and Harlan. Jonathan wants to introduce writing and reading to a new generation and promote and encourage young and new writers.

The Priory is his first full-length novel, after previously publishing short stories and a serial novel on Wattpad and he is currently studying for a degree in Creative Writing and Literature with the Open University. Vermin is the sequel and the third part, The Knights of Westford will be released at Halloween.

Printed in Great Britain
by Amazon